Raves for Selma Eichler and the Desiree Shapiro Mysteries

"A highly entertaining series."   —Carolyn Hart

"Desiree is a doll—fat, fun, late to everything."
—*Mysterious Women*

Murder Can Depress Your Dachshund

"Great dialogue and interesting characters along with a mystery that makes you work for the solution."
—Reviewing the Evidence

Murder Can Run Your Stockings

"The murder is seamlessly plotted, and the characters are colorfully written."   —*Romantic Times*

Murder Can Mess Up Your Mascara

"Tantalizing. . . . Old-school New York charm and even a touch of romance make this book worth gobbling up."
—*Publishers Weekly*

Murder Can Botch Up Your Birthday

"A highly engrossing read that shouldn't be missed."
—*Rendezvous*

Murder Can Rain On Your Shower

"An exciting private investigator tale that is fun to read . . . delightful."   —*Midwest Book Review*

Murder Can Cool Off Your Affair

"A laugh-out-loud riot. I love Desiree's sense of humor."
—*Mystery News*

continued . . .

Murder Can Upset Your Mother

"Eichler scores again. . . . [A] delicious cozy."
—*Publishers Weekly*

Murder Can Spoil Your Appetite

"Desiree Shapiro is a shining creation."
—*Romantic Times*

Murder Can Singe Your Old Flame

"Witty dialogue . . . hilarious characters."
—*Publishers Weekly*

Murder Can Spook Your Cat

"Queen-sized entertainment!"   —Barbara D'Amato

Murder Can Wreck Your Reunion

"Witty repartee, lots of possible suspects, and even an intriguing subplot will keep you turning the pages to find out who done it—and why."
—*Baldwin City Ledger* (KS)

Murder Can Stunt Your Growth

"Poignant and satisfying . . . just plain fun to read."
—*I Love a Mystery*

Murder Can Ruin Your Looks

"Dez is a delightful character with a quirky, distinctive voice, and I'd love to go to dinner with her."
—*Sue Feder's Magical Mystery Tour*

Murder Can Kill Your Social Life

"Humor, food, and just plain good writing."
—Tamar Myers

Other books in the Desiree Shapiro mystery series
in the order in which they were originally published

MURDER CAN CRASH YOUR PARTY

A Desiree Shapiro Mystery

Selma Eichler

AN OBSIDIAN MYSTERY

OBSIDIAN

Published by New American Library, a division of
Penguin Group (USA) Inc., 375 Hudson Street,
New York, New York 10014, USA
Penguin Group (Canada), 90 Eglinton Avenue East, Suite 700, Toronto,
Ontario M4P 2Y3, Canada (a division of Pearson Penguin Canada Inc.)
Penguin Books Ltd., 80 Strand, London WC2R 0RL, England
Penguin Ireland, 25 St. Stephen's Green, Dublin 2,
Ireland (a division of Penguin Books Ltd.)
Penguin Group (Australia), 250 Camberwell Road, Camberwell, Victoria 3124,
Australia (a division of Pearson Australia Group Pty. Ltd.)
Penguin Books India Pvt. Ltd., 11 Community Centre, Panchsheel Park,
New Delhi - 110 017, India
Penguin Group (NZ), 67 Apollo Drive, Rosedale, North Shore 0632,
New Zealand (a division of Pearson New Zealand Ltd.)
Penguin Books (South Africa) (Pty.) Ltd., 24 Sturdee Avenue,
Rosebank, Johannesburg 2196, South Africa

Penguin Books Ltd., Registered Offices:
80 Strand, London WC2R 0RL, England

First published by Obsidian, an imprint of New American Library,
a division of Penguin Group (USA) Inc.

First Printing, May 2008
10 9 8 7 6 5 4 3 2 1

To my husband, Lloyd,
for his unwavering support through fifteen Desirees

ACKNOWLEDGMENTS

Many thanks to my friends:

Irma Baker, whose idea it was to send Desiree off to a mystery conference in the first place;

Barbara Comfort—who provided the route for Desiree's drive to Connecticut; and

Dolores Getcher for helping me see to it that "poor Rob" had a proper memorial service.

I am also grateful, as always, to my editor, Ellen Edwards, for the insightful comments that helped me iron out the kinks in the story line.

Chapter 1

It was the strangest case I've ever had. Or—and I can say this without a single reservation—ever will have. And I guess it really had its inception back in April. . . .

I was sitting in my office, my head buried in the lunch menu from a local coffee shop. Why, I can't tell you. I mean, I could have recited that menu by heart. Anyhow, I'd just narrowed my choices to a pizza burger or a ham sandwich when the intercom buzzed.

"Some woman's on the line; she wants to speak to you," my secretary, Jackie, announced. She sounded put-upon. The thing is, Jackie's actually only my one-third secretary—I share her services with the two very nice lawyers who rent me this cigar box I call an office. So it was quite possible she was up to her ears in work just then. Either that, or the phone call had caused a thirty-second delay in her plans. She was determined, she'd confided to me that morning, to dash out of here at the stroke of noon in order to get to the Lord & Taylor lingerie sale "before all the good stuff's gobbled up."

"What's her name?" I asked, quite reasonably.

"I didn't have a chance to find out."

"I don't suppose she—"

"Gotta run, Dez," Jackie said firmly—just before clicking off. I checked my watch: twelve-oh-five. The Lord & Taylor lingerie sale. Definitely.

Seconds later I was talking to a woman who opened with a hesitant, "You don't know me, but . . ."

It turned out that her name was Kathy Grasso. "I'm phoning to ask you . . . that is, to invite you to be the, uh, guest speaker at the Arresting Women's conference this July. We really hope you—"

"Arresting Women?"

"Yes, it's a convention of women mystery writers and their fans."

Well, how do you like that! With a name like Arresting Women, I figured it was some kind of female police officers' gathering!

"It's being held on Saturday and Sunday, July twelfth and thirteenth, in Green View Lake, Connecticut, which isn't far from New Haven," Kathy recited.

"And you want me to *speak* at this conference?"

Now, you might have the idea that for someone whose profession can, on occasion, leave her open to genuine physical danger, talking to an audience like that would be a piece of cake. But you'd be wrong. The very thought shook me to the roots of my glorious hennaed hair.

"We'd be *so* pleased if you would."

"Tell me, how did you get my name?"

Evidently, Kathy wasn't expecting that question. (Although I can't understand why not.) "We . . . um . . . we've heard a lot about you—you're really pretty famous."

"I'm *what*?"

"Famous. That is, among individuals who know anything about . . . you know, about your line of work," she finished lamely.

"Apparently, no one in your group is familiar with the name Bo Dietl," I remarked.

"Who?"

"A private investigator who actually *is* famous."

"This person is a man?"

"That's right."

"Uh, the thing is, most of our writers have female sleuths—either amateur or professional—so we felt it would be more beneficial for them to . . . to hear from a woman investigator, you know? Of course," Kathy put in quickly, "it has to be an individual who's well respected in her field."

I couldn't suppress a smile. She sounded so earnest, so *forthright*. But I didn't believe a word she said.

Listen, do you know how many members of the feminine gender are listed under "Investigators" in the Manhattan yellow pages? Two, the last time I looked—including me. (And I doubt there's even *that* big a choice in any other city.) The way I figure, there was an excellent possibility that after my only competition declined to participate, Kathy went to the telephone directory—and there I was. Or could be she found us both in the directory, and a coin toss decided her on which of us to try first.

But it didn't hurt to be polite. "I thank you for the invitation, Kathy, only I'm really not comfortable—"

It was as if I hadn't spoken. "Naturally, we expect to compensate you for your time—well, somewhat, at least. Unfortunately, we can't afford the sort of rate that I'm sure you earn on your cases, but we *can* manage a small fee. And, of course, we'll take care of your travel expenses and one night's lodging.

"By the way, we've been holding our yearly conferences at the Green View Lake Inn for a few years now, and everyone just loves the place. The inn itself is so-o pretty, sort of like a country manor. I understand that some of the pieces in the lobby there are genuine antiques. It has a fireplace, too—the lobby, I mean—a *beautiful* fireplace."

A beautiful fireplace. How's that for a selling point when you're talking about the middle of July?

"The guests' rooms are a nice size and really comfortable," Kathy chattered on.

"Sounds lovely," I slipped in when she paused for breath, "but—"

"Oh, it is. Quite a few of our attendees stay on until Monday. You might decide to do the same. We're not in a position to pay for that second night, I'm sorry to say," she added hastily, "but maybe you'll like it there so much you'll want to do it on your own. Did I mention that the Green View Lake Inn is actually *situated* on a lake? So if the weather's nice you can go swimming or rowing or even fishing, if you like."

I *didn't* like. Swimming was absolutely unthinkable. I won't tell you how much weight I carry around on my five-foot-two frame—not even if you pull out all of my fingernails—but I love to cook, and I love to eat. Plus, my idea of exercise is walking from the refrigerator to the kitchen table carrying a dish of Häagen-Dazs. So you're not about to catch me wearing a bathing suit— not in this lifetime. (For which you can consider yourself fortunate.) As for the fishing part, just the thought of sticking a slimy, squiggly little worm on a hook makes me want to gag. And while I have no real prejudice against rowing, I can't say I have any great desire to pick up an oar, either.

Still, the old inn was beginning to sound inviting. And it suddenly occurred to me that it might be nice to get away— even if only overnight. Maybe if I had a little wine before that talk . . . "Uh, how long would I have to speak? That is," I tagged on hurriedly, "if I decide to do this?"

"Only forty minutes—and you'd be surprised at how fast the time goes." Then, with an anemic little giggle: "It really *does* fly. Oh, and after your talk, you take a few questions from the audience—and that's it. By the way, ours is a very small conference—we don't get more than seventy-five, eighty people, tops—and that's in an exceptionally good year. And not everyone will be attending your session, either. We'll schedule another program for that same hour—you know, to keep you from being overwhelmed."

"I can't even figure out what I'd say," I protested— but weakly now.

"Just talk about whatever you think would, you know, interest the audience."

"That's another sticking point. I have no *idea* what would interest them."

"Okay, let's see. You could tell them what made you decide to become a private investigator in the first place, and I'm sure they'd also enjoy hearing about some of your cases. I know I would."

"Are you a mystery writer yourself?"

Kathy sighed. "No, just a fan, I'm afraid. But maybe

someday . . ." she murmured wistfully. "Oh, I almost forgot. We'll be sending out flyers about the event, and a couple of the local newspapers have promised to, you know, give us a nice write-up. Also, we'll be getting a mention in a few of the newsletters put out by writers' groups. Naturally, the name of our guest speaker—*your* name, I'm hoping—will be prominently featured in all of this. A little publicity can't hurt, can it?" She lost no time throwing in, "Not that you need it—not somebody with *your* reputation."

That's what she thinks! (Or, more likely, what she wants me to think she thinks.) "I don't know. I have real reservations about doing this. What if I suddenly draw a blank?"

"Oh, you won't," the woman assured me blithely. "It's not as if you'd have to *memorize* anything. Practically all of our speakers have notes with them."

I turned things over in my mind. Suppose I got the scary part over with at the beginning of the conference . . . "I was wondering, Kathy, would it be possible for me to give my talk fairly early on Saturday? The earlier the better."

"I don't see why not. In fact, I'll make sure of it."

Well, under those circumstances, I figured I could actually wind up enjoying myself at this thing. At the very least, it would be a change of scenery. I might even gain some perspective with regard to that frustrating, angst-producing love life of mine. And it wasn't as if going out of town for a couple of days would have any impact on my career. I mean, ask me when I last saw a bunch of prospective clients queuing up outside my door, clamoring for my services. Never, that's when.

So in the end I said yes.

As soon as Jackie returned from her descent on Lord & Taylor, she stopped in my office to display her impressive haul. After which I told her about the convention.

She refused to accept my version of how I happened to be contacted. Gathering up her possessions now, she shook her short blondish brown hair. "Listen, they phoned you because you're a damn good PI."

I blew her a kiss.

"I mean it," she called out as she headed for the door. "You're the best! And it looks like the word's finally getting around."

Is it any wonder I love that woman?

Oh, and by the way, in the highly unlikely event you're wondering what I finally settled on for lunch that day, it was the pizza burger.

Chapter 2

Initially, during the three-plus months before the mystery writers' conference, my workload was really, *really* light. But then things picked up a bit—briefly, anyhow. And although none of these new cases were what you'd call major, there was enough activity to cover a decent portion of the bills. I'd just have to forgo all that caviar and Dom Pérignon (no problem; I'd been forgoing them since birth) and persuade myself to stay out of Bloomingdale's for a while (which wasn't as easy as it sounds).

At any rate, as the conference drew closer and closer, I found myself looking forward to it almost eagerly. The fact that my career was in free fall again wasn't the overriding reason, either—any more than it was what had prompted me to accept that invitation in the first place. Uh-uh. Both these things could be attributed to what was currently a whole lot more troubling: the precarious state of my love life.

Don't misunderstand me. I wasn't under the delusion that at Green View Lake I'd miraculously gain the insight to come to grips with the problem I was facing. But at least I'd be forced to focus on something else for a day or two.

So while my mouth went dry and my hands still shook a little at the mere thought of speaking to a roomful of people, I considered this a small price to pay for that opportunity.

July twelfth was a near-perfect summer day. And although the weather mavens had forecast that the temperature would climb well into the eighties, when I started out at just past ten a.m., the thermometer hadn't risen much above seventy yet.

I have to confess that my nerves had been so jangled earlier, at breakfast, that I couldn't even manage my usual Entenmann's corn muffin. (Listen, I was lucky I could swallow the Cheerios.) But as soon as I got onto I-95, aka the Connecticut Turnpike, I switched on the radio. After that, I was no longer in any danger of coming apart.

I mean, I simply wouldn't permit tonight's little speech—or anything else that had been giving me agita—to set up camp in my head. And it was just about impossible for unwanted thoughts to intrude as Elvis and I harmonized on "Hound Dog." Ditto when I gave Rod Stewart a hand with "If I Had You." And, of course, the same was true during my duet with Judy (I'm hoping you don't have to ask, "Judy who?") on "Over the Rainbow." Even on the occasions I wasn't familiar with the lyrics, as, for example, when Britney Spears, Christina Aguilera and—are you ready?—Busta Rhymes were singing their little hearts out, I bopped right along anyway. My fellow drivers on I-95 could consider themselves in luck. I was able to keep the windows rolled up that day since, for once, the air conditioner in my ancient Chevy was actually working.

The one downside to the trip: It was l-o-o-n-g. Apparently, I missed my exit (something I have a real talent for doing), and the "hour-and-a-half, hour-and-three-quarters, tops" drive I'd been led to expect was extended to nearly three.

I was standing in line at the registration desk when an attractive, dark-haired young woman descended on me. "It's our . . . our VIP!" she squealed. "I am *so* happy to meet you, Desiree!" And with this, she enveloped me in a bone-crushing hug. I noticed the name tag—KATHY GRASSO—as soon as I was able to extricate myself from her clutches. (How is it that so many smiling, seemingly friendly ladies greet you with an embrace that's practically lethal?)

"You look exactly like the photo you sent us," she gushed. "With that gorgeous red hair, though, it's, you know, an awful shame that our program book isn't in color." Forget a broken bone or two; I *liked* this person! She checked her watch now. "I was, uh, hoping I could help you get settled in, Desiree, but I'm supposed to be at a meeting in five minutes. I'd better get going, too. The thing is, uh"—her voice dropped precipitously here—"I have to tinkle first." She started to hurry away, then stopped and whirled around. "Oh, we hope you'll join us at the head table for dinner this evening."

"Thank you. I'd like that."

"The Blue Room, seven o'clock," she called out over her shoulder.

As soon as Kathy left, I glanced around the lobby. I conceded that my new very dearest friend's assessment of the fireplace had been right: This *was* a thing of beauty. It was set in the center of a handsome, wood-paneled wall, an integral part of the architectural design being a large frame about a foot or so above the opening. In the middle of this was a small, framed painting of two almost ethereal-looking women seated in a lush garden.

I didn't find anything else in the room particularly attractive, though. Certainly nothing here was worthy of the designation "antique." All I saw was a lot of beat-up old furniture. The large Oriental rug was faded and close to threadbare. The badly scarred wooden table standing on top of it may have been quite handsome in its day, but it was obvious that day—whenever it was— had long since passed. And the same could definitely be said about the four wooden chairs surrounding the table.

Anyhow, I was eventually assigned a room on the second floor. It was simply furnished, but fairly large and super-clean. There was a desk, a couple of comfortable chairs, and a brass bed with a mattress so thick that at first I was wondering how I'd manage to climb up there. I eventually came to learn that the mattress was lower than it looked—or else I was higher than I realized. The one disappointment was the view. It didn't exist—not from this room, anyway. (Unless, that is, you happen to

have a thing for parking lots.) Now, with a name like
the Green View Lake Inn, I'd expected to get at least a
glimpse of water. True, I didn't care to be either in that
lake or on it, but this didn't mean I wasn't interested in
looking at it! So much for that VIP status Kathy had
assigned to me.

I quickly (for me) unpacked, then took a nice, long
nap (well over two hours' worth, in fact). After that, I
sat at the desk and got down to business, practicing my
spiel out loud again and again. Finally, I broke away to
get ready for dinner.

There were ten of us at the table, including a writer
who'd been on one of the two four-o'clock panels that
day—this being the time slot I'd coveted—which, due to
what Kathy referred to as "unforeseen circumstances,"
had at some point become unavailable to me. So there
I sat, a smile pasted on my face, attempting to be conge-
nial while the pressure of that talk continued to hover
over me.

Fortunately, it wasn't long before the waiter came
around for our beverage orders. And—also fortunately—
half a glass of Merlot later, I'd begun to unwind a little.
(In my case, this is about all that's required to take the
edge off things.) Anyhow, now I was able to enjoy what
turned out to be pleasant company, along with a really
excellent meal. (Listen, how does this sound to you: Cae-
sar salad, Cornish game hen with cherry sauce and wild
rice, and chocolate fudge cake à la mode?)

Following dinner, I went back upstairs to go over my
notes one final time. Then, after foisting a brief pep talk
on myself, I freshened my makeup, checked out my gray
silk suit in the full-length mirror, and headed for the
elevator.

When I walked into the Colonial Room, I gulped. It
was still early—almost fifteen minutes early—and a number of people were already seated there. *Why can't they
all attend that panel down the hall—"Finding the Humor
in Murder"?* I wailed. But silently, of course.

Kathy was already busy adjusting the mike at the lectern to a height appropriate for a short person. "Hi, Desiree," she called out when I approached. "Looks like you'll be getting a nice turnout, a *very* nice turnout." Then, noting the expression on my face: "Uh, but it's still much too early to tell."

By the time I was scheduled to begin speaking, however, there were actually people *standing* in the rear. But, like the trooper I am, I flicked my tongue over my lower lip, and, haltingly, I began. . . .

"Hi, everyone, my name is Desiree Shapiro, and I'm a licensed private investigator with an office in Manhattan. You already knew that from the program book, though, right?" This brought a few smiles and even a welcome little titter.

"Um, I'm really not too sure what you'd be interested in hearing about. Maybe some of you are curious as to whatever possessed me to become a private investigator in the first place." A girl two rows back—any female under thirty is a girl to me—was nodding enthusiastically now.

"Well, when I was too young to know any better," I said, "I thought it would be a nifty career for a woman—really exciting. Then, once I got my license—and I probably shouldn't admit this—I could hardly wait for people to ask me what I did for a living. You'd be surprised at the kind of impact it made when I said I was a PI. It still does, actually, but this was especially true in those days."

"Just when *were* those days?" some loudmouth in the back of the room yelled out.

I answered with a straight face: "Around the time Roosevelt was inaugurated. Naturally, I'm talking about *Theodore* Roosevelt." Here, the audience response was not only laughter, but a smattering of applause. After a quick glance at my notes, I went on to say that when I started out—and for a long while afterward—I wasn't involved in the sort of cases that were apt to precipitate a physical attack. "I handled mostly divorce and insurance matters, along with missing persons, child custody disputes—that kind of thing. Um, the truth is, I was about a thousand percent more likely to get a scratch from a paper clip than I was to wind up with a bullet wound. But then came the day I was persuaded to look into the murder of an old woman. And homicides have been a part of what I do ever since. As you might expect, that's led to a few instances where things have gotten a little . . . um, hairy." And now, with some help from my trusty notes, I gave a brief synopsis of a couple of the investigations I'd conducted that had nearly cost me my life.

I wrapped up my presentation by explaining that I try not to think about the risks involved in my profession. "Besides," I pointed out, "we expose ourselves to risk every time we get behind the wheel of a car or put on a pair of skis or even cross the street. None of which are likely to bring the tremendous satisfaction that every so often comes with this job of mine: the satisfaction of bringing a killer to justice."

An enthusiastic round of applause followed. And then I took questions from the audience on everything from what usually enables me to identify the perpetrator ("mainly lies and inconsistencies") to how long it takes me to solve a crime ("too long—no matter how quickly I manage to do it").

Finally, Kathy rose from her seat in the front row, pointed to her watch, and thanked me—which produced a lot more clapping.

Well, after months of anxiety, it was over. At last I could breathe a sigh of relief.

And I did.

Chapter 3

I was up at nine a.m. on Sunday, which on a weekend is practically the equivalent of daybreak for me. But I had to make up my mind this morning whether to extend my visit here.

The thing is, since I'd left the city, my super-aggravating personal life hadn't so much as entered my thoughts. True, most of this could no doubt be attributed to all that anxiety involved in my public speaking debut. Still, I couldn't disregard the possibility that simply getting away had also been a factor. And it occurred to me that maybe—just maybe—if I stayed over another day, my luck would continue to hold. Anyhow, I planned to come to a decision at breakfast.

I opted to eat outdoors at the Patio Café, where I requested a table facing the water. I mean, I figured it was about time I got a look at the "Lake" part of the Green View Lake Inn. And while I don't suppose this particular lake was any great shakes as far as lakes go, I found the sight of it sort of relaxing, soothing even.

I'd just had some orange juice and was eagerly awaiting my eggs Benedict when a pleasant, slightly high-pitched male voice said, "May we join you?"

I lifted my head to find a slim, boyish-looking individual smiling down at me. (It was a nice, friendly smile, too.) I estimated him to be somewhere in his thirties. At his side was a tall, striking woman, who was maybe just a tad theatrical-looking. Her carefully made up face was shielded from the sun by a wide-brimmed straw hat decorated with flowers that matched the flowers on her flowing cotton print dress. And although her features were partially hidden by the hat, I noted that she had a straight nose and nice, full lips. Plus, her hair—what little of it was visible—was a very becoming silver. But while I figured the woman to be older than the man, I couldn't so much as take a stab at the age difference. I mean, the lady's skin appeared to be taut and virtually unlined. However, whether this was due to her having inherited an enviable bunch of genes or whether she'd been the recipient of some expert snipping and stitching was anybody's guess.

At any rate, I was a little taken aback by the couple's request, since there were a number of empty tables available. Naturally, though, I responded that of course they were welcome to join me.

"This is Belle Simone," the man informed me once the two of them were seated. Belle glanced at me and nodded perfunctorily. "Uh, Belle isn't up to carrying on a conversation until she's had her morning coffee," he explained, looking somewhat embarrassed. "Oh, by the way, I'm Gary Donleavy, Belle's secretary, companion, and also very good friend—I hope." He tittered when he said this last part.

Before I could introduce myself, our waitress materialized at Gary's elbow, pencil poised. He ordered breakfast for himself and the mute Belle. Then, as the woman began to walk away, he added hurriedly, "We'd like the coffee now, though, please."

"Uh, I'm Desiree Shapiro," I announced, finally having the chance. This established, Gary and I shook hands. Belle merely nodded.

"We know who you are," Gary responded. "Belle and I attended your presentation yesterday evening. We enjoyed it immensely, too." Belle nodded again, this time favoring me with a little smile, as well. (Although I can't swear it wasn't gas.)

I murmured a thank-you.

"With a profession like yours, you have to be a pretty brave woman," Gary commented.

I laughed—actually, it was more like a guffaw. " 'Brave' is hardly an adjective that applies to me. The truth is, I'm chicken. I never expose myself to danger—not if I can help it, anyway. You know how in the movies these female PIs—decked out in their stiletto heels, no less—are always running after the bad guys? Well, when there's danger involved, you can bet I'll be running, too—only in the opposite direction. What's more, I don't own any stiletto heels. Not a single pair."

Gary howled at this (I didn't think it was *that* funny), while Belle produced another tepid smile.

It was at this point that my breakfast, along with my companions' coffees, was set on the table.

Gary turned to me. "Eat!" he commanded. "Listen, if my waistline hadn't expanded *two inches* this year, I'd have ordered the eggs Benedict myself. And, trust me, I wouldn't have waited for someone else to get served before digging into those scrumptious things."

I smiled gratefully at him. "Thank you. Uh, would you like a bite or two before I get started?"

"And risk adding another eighth of an inch to my middle? Heavens, no!"

I'd managed to get in a forkful when he asked, "Do you plan on staying over tonight?"

"I'm not sure yet. What about you?"

"No, as soon as we've finished eating, we'll settle the bill and head back to Manhattan."

"Ah, a fellow New Yorker," I commented. "Incidentally, are the two of you mystery writers—or readers?" I glanced from one to the other, immediately following which a second forkful of eggs Benedict was en route to my mouth.

Surprisingly, it was Belle—apparently fueled by the coffee—who responded in a low, resonant voice that was a perfect complement to her appearance. "Gary is definitely a reader. And while I don't have as much free time as my friend here does"—she flashed him a playful grin—"I guess you could place me in the reader category, too, even though I'm a published author. And many times over, I might add—but in another genre." She shrugged. "Still, I take it that you've never heard of me."

"Umm . . . I'm . . . uh . . . sure that's because I don't

do much reading—outside of mysteries, that is. What sort of books do you write?"

"Romances. Very *popular* romances. As a matter of fact, my novels have been making the *New York Times* best-seller lists for years. But as you can tell, I'm not the sort to brag," she declared, attempting to suppress a smile.

"That's quite an achievement!" And now it occurred to me. "But if you're not an avid mystery fan—and I gather you're not—what brought you to Green View Lake this weekend?"

"You did, sweetie."

"*Me?*" I practically screeched the word. "I don't understand."

"I wouldn't expect you to, so I'll explain. About a month ago, as I was in the process of completing my first mystery, I received an Arresting Women flyer in the mail. I was about to toss it into the wastebasket when I noticed a heading that interested me. It seems that a private investigator—an *experienced* private investigator—was to be the guest speaker at their convention."

"And you wanted to talk to me because one of the characters in your new novel is a female PI. Is that it, Belle?"

"Nope. I wanted to reassure myself that the homicide in my book can actually be solved. And who better to confirm this for me than a professional detective like Desiree Shapiro?"

"I'd be very happy to read your book. But the fact is, I don't do all that well when it comes to figuring out a crime that exists only on paper. Luckily, I'm more successful in real life, probably because I'm able to question the suspects."

"I promise that you'll be provided with valid clues. These, by the way, haven't been included in the text as yet, simply because I'm still trying to decide where to insert them. But they should enable you to uncover the identity of the killer. Presuming, of course," she added lightly, "that you're clever enough to figure them out. I warn you, though, the clues are complex. You see, I wanted to write something a lot more intricate than the average whodunit. But anyhow, if you *do* succeed in deciphering my little puzzler, I'm prepared to pay you the tidy sum of $24,940."

I laid down my fork. *Did she say $24,940?* Then, as soon as I'd regained the power of speech: "Why would you want to do something like that?"

Belle smiled fleetingly. "My reasons, Desiree, are my own. Anyhow," she went on, "you'll be receiving the manuscript in a day or two, along with a copy of the agreement you'll have to sign. That is, if you decide to accept my proposition." The words had barely left her lips when she demanded impatiently, "So?"

Well, I ask you, what PI wouldn't jump at an opportunity like this one? And to a PI who once took on a client who planned to cover the fee with her babysitting money (which, of course, I'd had no intention of accepting), it was like a gift from the gods.

"So?" Belle repeated. "Yes or no, which is it?"

"Yes," I answered.

I mean, wouldn't you?

Chapter 4

After that astonishing breakfast, I certainly didn't want to spend another day in Connecticut. I couldn't wait to go home and share my incredible, my *unbelievable* news. At a few minutes past one, after saying good-bye to Kathy Grasso (and subjecting myself to another near-fatal hug in the process), I got into my car and headed back to Manhattan.

Almost immediately, I began spending the money I didn't have yet.

First off, I'd treat myself to new carpeting—the stuff presently covering my floors was an embarrassment. I'd replace the sofa, too. Definitely. The way I saw it, the only faded and lumpy thing that belonged in my living room was me. And come to think of it, the club chairs weren't in such hot shape, either.

Minutes later, however, I had a change of heart. What I needed most was a new car. "Sorry," I said aloud, patting the seat cushion next to me, "but it's about time you retired, old girl." I wondered idly how much a BMW sold for. *Too much,* I supplied at once. *All right. So how about—* I stopped short. Never mind that I hadn't received that windfall yet. The thing is, I couldn't be sure it would happen at all.

I mean, suppose I wasn't able to solve the murder. *Nah!* I refused to entertain even the possibility of failure.

Okay, then, what if the proposition wasn't for real? Listen, this could be some sort of hoax. How did I know the woman I'd broken bread with this morning was a best-selling author? Or, for that matter, whether her name was actually Belle Simone? Now that I thought about it, I'd never even heard of a successful writer by that name. I reminded myself that there must be hundreds of successful writers I hadn't heard of. Well, it should be easy enough to establish whether or not my prospective client was who she'd represented herself to be. And I'd look into it first thing tomorrow.

But hold it a minute. Let's say I was able to verify the lady's identity. This was still no guarantee the proposition was bona fide. After all, simply having a flourishing career doesn't prove you're operating on all four burners. On the other hand, though, if she *was* a popular romance author, there was at least a decent chance this thing was on the level. At any rate, I wasn't about to hold off until I'd checked her out before informing Nick of my (very likely) good fortune. Never mind that he was the reason I'd just run away from home—more or less—to begin with.

The traffic on I-95 had been heavy (and, yes, I also missed my exit again), so I didn't make it back to East Eighty-second Street until close to five.

The first thing I noticed when I walked into my apartment was that my answering machine was winking at me. There was a message from Nick.

"Hi, Dez. I hope everything went well with your speech and that you enjoyed the conference. I'll be heading down the shore to my sister's place in a few minutes—she's throwing an engagement party for my niece. I should probably be too embarrassed to admit this, but I had the date all screwed up; I was under the impression the thing was *next* Sunday. Fortunately, I was talking to my mom this morning, and she straightened me out. It's tonight!

"Anyhow, most likely I'll stay over and drive to work from there in the morning. I'll call you later if I can sneak away for a couple of minutes. If not, I'll give you a ring tomorrow." A pause, then softly: "I miss you, Dez."

My knees turned to jelly. "I miss you, too, Nick," I whispered to the machine. I was practically in tears now. I'd been so pumped up about sharing my big news with Nick that I was suddenly very depressed. In fact—and this is a rarity for me—I even lost my appetite! Fortunately, it returned shortly thereafter, and I was able to do justice to the eggplant parmigiana that had been biding its time in the freezer.

Is she or isn't she?

It was a thought that sprang to mind the instant I opened my eyes Monday morning.

Now, being a hotshot PI, I was familiar with numerous methods—some of them pretty esoteric—for confirming an individual's identity. But I took a much more prosaic route.

Before heading for work, I made a pit stop at a Borders bookstore not far from my office. They had three Belle Simone paperbacks (reprinted from the hardcover editions) in stock. The first one I picked up—*Dark Passions,* it was called—had a photograph of the author on the inside back cover. And yes, *that* Belle Simone and *my* Belle Simone were, praise the powers that be, one and the same.

"So? How'd it go?" Jackie demanded the instant I walked through the door.

"Pretty well, actually."

I was all set to tell her about Belle's proposition when she said hurriedly, "I want to hear *everything*—only it'll have to wait until later. First, I've got to finish typing this brief for Elliot." (Elliot Gilbert is one half of the two lawyers who, as I mentioned earlier, rent me my office space. Incidentally, his partner is Pat Sullivan, hence the firm's legendary theatrical name of you-can-guess-what.)

I was already walking away when Jackie called after me, "Oh a messenger was here a few minutes ago with a package for you. I put it in your office."

For one of the very few times in my life, I actually began running (well, speed walking, anyhow). And by the time I reached my cubbyhole, which was only a short distance away, my palms were so slippery I had trouble turning the doorknob.

Anyhow, sitting in the middle of the desk was a gray envelope, a very *lightweight* gray envelope. I ripped it open; inside was a manila folder. And inside *this* was what appeared to be a manuscript, on top of which were two copies of a brief agreement, already signed by Belle and witnessed by Gary Donleavy. The terms of the agreement were simple:

I was to sign and date both copies and return one of them to Belle by registered mail. Immediately upon its receipt, I'd be supplied with the first of three clues necessary to the solution of the mystery. The second clue would be provided to me only after I'd deciphered the first. And I'd have the third—and final—clue after solving the second.

I was given three months to submit my findings to Belle. Then, within two weeks of successfully identifying the murderer, I'd receive a cashier's check for the sweet little sum of $24,940 dollars. And if I goofed? Hopefully, I'd at least learn who dunnit.

At any rate, there was no longer any doubt about it: Belle Simone was in earnest.

I focused on the manuscript itself now, which was surprisingly thin—more the size of a novella than a novel. (I later saw that there were just eighty-two pages.) *Good!* I'd been afraid I might have to deal with something the size of *War and Peace*. I noted that the title page was missing, very likely because Belle hadn't decided on a title yet. But in its place was a note:

Desiree,

I'm sending you an abbreviated version of the actual novel, since I feel that, this way, it will be simpler for you to concentrate on the mystery itself. Rest assured that nothing relevant to its solution has been withheld.

Good luck,
Belle

It was very tempting to sit there and start reading, but I was anxious to make this thing official. Even so, I had to practically coerce myself into getting my bottom out of that chair and out into the hall, where I grabbed a passing law clerk to witness my signature. (There was a space for that purpose on the agreement.) As soon as he did the honors, I left for the post office with the executed document.

My luck, the air-conditioning at the post office was on the blink, and it took more than fifteen minutes for me to conclude my business there. I mean, the lines in that place extended practically into New Jersey! Now, after an ordeal like that, I'd normally have treated myself to a nice lunch. But not today. Today, I'd just have something at my desk.

Jackie was still typing away when I came back toting a little nourishment bag from Burger King. She stopped and waved a couple of message slips at me. Before allowing me to take possession, however, she did the same infuriating thing she usually does: She recited the contents!

"Nick called. He'll phone you at home." She glanced at the second paper. "About ten minutes after he called, Ellen checked in." (Jackie was referring to the other very special person in my life: the wonderful niece I acquired when I married my now-deceased husband, Ed Shapiro.) "She said she was in meetings all morning, and she has appointments with vendors this afternoon." (Ellen's a buyer at Macy's.) "But she can't wait to hear all about your convention. *She'll* talk to you tonight, too." And with this, Jackie handed over the message slips.

"Thanks, Jackie," I muttered. Then, crumpling the now redundant little papers in my hand, I hurried to my cubbyhole—and Belle's manuscript.

Chapter 5

Rob Harwood wasn't handsome, the introduction began. He wasn't even particularly good-looking. He hadn't been blessed with high cheekbones. Or a classic Roman nose. Or a smile so dazzling, one's eyes had to be shielded from its glare. As to his own eyes, they were brown. Not a *liquid* brown. Or even a *warm* brown. Just a plain, run-of-the-mill brown. He wasn't very tall, either—not more than five-eight, at most. And he wasn't particularly muscular. What's more, a substantial portion of his once-thick dark hair had years ago separated from his scalp. Rob Harwood was no longer young, you see. You might even say that he was on the cloudy side of middle age. Then what was it about him that, even now, so many attractive—even beautiful—women found so compelling?

Certainly his looks didn't appear to be much of a factor. It is also unlikely that his bank account was the draw. Granted, he was a successful Realtor. But there were many wealthier men whose beds were cold at night.

No doubt some of Rob's appeal could be attributed to his vitality. He didn't walk into a room; he *strode* into it. He was an excellent tennis player, an avid skier, and he still managed to jog three miles a day. He laughed easily and often. This zest for living, this enthusiasm of his was almost contagious. He had a special way of listening, too—eyes half-closed, head tilted to the side, and an understanding nod when called for. But if the man had a single dominating feature, it was his voice—deep and soft and as stirring as a caress.

Oh, yes. There was one thing more: From all accounts, he was an incredible lover, both tender and passionate, who inspired the fervent devotion of countless women, along with the envy of any number of men.

Then, suddenly, it ended.

One summer evening, many years ago, Rob was celebrating his sixtieth birthday with family and friends at a lavish party in his own home—when someone slipped something into his champagne.

And for Rob Harwood, the party was over.

I had a few bites of my cheeseburger, scarfed down some fries, and was all set to start part one: "The Surprise Party, August 1983," when Jackie walked in. She plopped down on the chair on the other side of my desk, which was the only vacant seat in this teeny office of mine. "Tell me about your weekend," she demanded.

I gave her a quick rundown. Then I got to the part about Belle Simone's wild proposition.

At this, Jackie's eyes almost doubled in size. "It doesn't sound kosher to me," she said when I'd finished. "I don't care if she *is* a hotshot author. She's also some kind of nut if she's going to give you all that money just for sitting on your keister and solving this mystery she wrote. What reason did she give, anyhow?"

"She didn't. She said that her reasons were her own."

"Well, you should have had Elliot or Pat take a look at that contract before you sent it off. It's one of the perks of being in an office with lawyers—nice ones, anyhow."

"Why bother either of them? I really have nothing to lose here, Jackie. The very worst that can happen is that I'll read Belle's book and legitimately identify the perp without getting the money promised to me. Of course, I'm not saying I won't be angry if the woman reneges— I'll probably be furious. But the document she sent was pretty straightforward, so I don't really see that happening. Besides, I look at it this way: I read mysteries all the time, and suddenly there's a possibility—a very *good* possibility, I like to think—that I'll be paid a bundle of money for doing what I've always done for free. Also, the monetary gain aside, I like the challenge; this thing really intrigues me. So I'm willing to take my chances."

"I bet you'll solve it," my loyal secretary and very good friend responded firmly.

"Thanks. Now get out of here. I have some important reading to do."

Part one opened with:

Doubtless, Rob Harwood took great pride in the fact that his lack of height was no obstacle to his acquiring the sort of female companions he found it necessary to look up to—in the literal sense of the words. So it was not unexpected that, like virtually every other woman in his life—past and present—the woman he chose for a wife would be tall and willowy. It was also fairly predictable that, although close to forty by this time, Tess Harwood would still turn heads wherever she went.

Today is Rob's sixtieth birthday. And to celebrate this milestone, Tess is throwing a surprise party for him at the couple's Manhattan penthouse. A dozen friends and relatives are gathered in the enormous living room this evening, two white-jacketed waiters moving among them. One of the waiters is proffering vintage champagne, the other such tempting little delicacies as pâté de foie gras, caviar, *feuilleté* of chanterelles and wild berries, and filet mignon with béarnaise sauce on toast points. There is no doubt that both the champagne and hors d'oeuvres are well received; they repeatedly disappear the moment they're served. Of course, this was not unanticipated, since tonight the Harwood kitchen is in the hands of the most highly touted—and expensive—catering firm in New York.

By now, the majority of the guests have been at the apartment for close to an hour. And the hostess begins to glance surreptitiously at her watch: 6:20, it reads, then 6:25, then 6:29. Rob had assured her he'd be home by six to shower and change before the pair ostensibly went out for an intimate little birthday dinner. It isn't like him to be late, Tess frets, particularly since she'd stressed that their reservation was for seven fifteen.

Finally, at six thirty-three, the doorman buzzes the apartment twice to signal that the guest of honor is on his way upstairs.

The lights in the living room are hurriedly extinguished. The crowd turns instantly, almost eerily silent. Soon, there is the sound of a key turning in the lock, following which Rob enters the foyer. He is slightly disheveled and appears to be perturbed. "I'm home!" he calls out. No answer. He walks into the darkened living room and switches on the lights.

It is the signal for twelve people to respond with an almost ear-shattering, "Surprise!"

"Oh, for God's sake," a stunned Rob murmurs.

Tess hurries over and hugs him. "Happy birthday, dear," she says softly, as she leans over to kiss his cheek. "I was beginning to worry."

"Some drunken idiot rammed into the car, and—" But the couple is now surrounded by well-wishers.

As soon as he is able to, Rob pulls his wife aside. "Thanks, honey," he whispers, touched. "This is great. How did you manage it without my knowing?"

She laughs. "It wasn't easy." With this, she plucks a flute of champagne from the tray of a passing waiter and hands it to her husband. "How about some caviar?" she asks. "There's pâté de foie gras, too, and—"

"In a few minutes," he interrupts. "I'd better get cleaned up first; I feel really grungy." He places the untouched drink on the end table behind him, then hurries away.

Tess is soon approached by two of the guests, and the three of them stand there and chat. At one point, Tess notices that a waiter is about to remove the unattended champagne from the end table. "That's my husband's, and I've sworn to guard it with my life," she tells the man, smiling.

Rob comes downstairs within fifteen minutes, dressed in a lightweight, beautifully cut tan gabardine suit and a brown, tan, and yellow striped tie. He takes a brief stroll around the room, shaking hands, bussing cheeks, and exchanging a few quick words with his guests. Then he joins the group surrounding his wife, which has expanded a bit by this time. "I'll get your champagne," Tess volunteers, taking the four or five steps to the end table behind them. Seconds afterward, she hands her husband the drink, smiling lovingly at him as their fingers touch.

Rob downs it quickly. "I could use another one of these," he remarks to Tess, tapping his glass and looking around for a waiter. "I don't think the jerk did too much damage, though." Then, noting his wife's expression, he laughs. "I'm talking about the accident with the car."

"Thank God you weren't injured; that's the important thing," she tells him. "Rob was in an automobile accident today," she explains to the others.

"Nothing serious," the birthday boy chimes in, proceeding to relate the details of the minor mishap. A few minutes later, he whispers to Tess, "I could go for about a dozen of those hors d'oeuvres right now, too. I'm starved." Then, only partially in jest: "When do you think we'll be eating, anyway—midnight?"

It is at this precise moment that the dining room doors open. Dinner is about to be served.

Some of those gathered around the table that night maintained that he'd enjoyed both the humor and praise of the good friend who stood up to make the toast. Others insisted that even before the waiters had finished pouring the champagne, he was flushed and—in retrospect—appeared to have trouble breathing.

But one thing no one could dispute: Very soon after twelve glasses were lifted to his "very good health," Rob Harwood was dead.

Chapter 6

I'd had some paperwork to finish up, which kept me busy for a couple of hours. Just now, though, I took out the manuscript again and was giving serious consideration to going on to part two when Jackie poked her head in my office. "For crying out loud! You still at it?" she inquired in her normal sugar-sweet tone.

"Why? What time is it?"

"Almost six."

"I don't believe it!"

"Wanna bet?"

Automatically, I checked my watch: five minutes to six. "I had no idea it was this late. I guess I'll pack up and go home. Why are *you* still here?"

"I'm meeting a cousin of mine for dinner. In fact, I'd better get moving. See you in the morning," she said, her head disappearing from the doorway.

"Enjoy your dinner!" I called after her. I was about to transfer the manuscript to my attaché case when Jackie's head was back.

"Give yourself a break and relax tonight. You've had a hectic few days. That mystery of yours'll hold until tomorrow, you know."

"You're right. I'll just watch a little TV and go to bed early."

She looked at the manila folder in my hand and then at the open attaché case. "Liar!" she accused as the head vanished again.

Since I wasn't particularly hungry that evening, I made what my niece, Ellen, refers to as one of my refrigerator omelets, so named because it consists of just about everything in the refrigerator that isn't soggy, moldy, or hard as a rock. To be honest, though, tonight the red pepper was pretty wrinkly, and I wondered whether the ham was maybe just the tiniest bit slimy. But considering that I didn't have a whole lot to choose from, in the end I decided they both passed muster.

Following what might very generously be termed my entrée, I had a cup of coffee, accompanied by a good-size portion of Häagen-Dazs macadamia brittle, which I admit is an addiction of mine. You know what, though? The Häagen-Dazs almost succeeded in earning that pathetic supper a passing grade.

Now, I'd been looking at the clock as I ate—in spite of giving myself strict orders not to. The phone finally rang at just before eight. *Nick!* I thought to myself excitedly. It was my niece, Ellen.

Naturally, she wanted to know how my speech went. I said that I thought it had been fairly well received. The president—and sole member—of the Desiree Shapiro fan club bristled. "*Fairly* well received? You never give yourself enough credit, Aunt Dez. I'll bet people—*plenty* of people—loved it."

I couldn't help smiling. Ellen is *so* loyal—and *so* predictable. "Maybe. But listen, something strange happened while I was there. A woman—she's an author, by the way—offered to pay me $24,940 if I could solve this mystery she's written."

"You're kidding, right?"

"Wrong."

"How did she come up with an amount like that, anyway?"

"Beats me."

"She must be some kind of wacko."

"I tend to doubt that. In fact, you may have heard of her. Belle Simone? She writes romance novels."

"It doesn't sound familiar, but then, I never read romances. Anyhow, I hope you said yes."

"You do?"

"Certainly I do. You know how much I worry about

your being in such a dangerous profession. In this instance, though, you'd be going after a killer who only exists on paper, which is a *big* relief. I'm assuming, of course, that the woman's not some dangerous lunatic. So? What did you tell her?"

"I said I'd do it."

"I'm *really* glad. Oh, I almost forgot the second reason I called. Mike and I are hoping you can come over for dinner next week. We're both off on the same night, for a change." (Mike, Ellen's terrific, recently acquired husband, is a resident at St. Gregory's hospital.) "Is a week from Thursday okay?"

"It's perfect," I told her.

"Good. I'd better hang up now; I've got another call. Talk to you soon."

I'd already made up my mind to forgo the reading tonight, so I turned on the TV. I was still flipping through the channels when I heard from Nick.

He opened with, "How'd everything go this weekend?"

"Not bad at all," I said. "At least I didn't flub it—the talk, I mean."

"I didn't expect you to. Were you very nervous?"

"I was a wreck all day. But then I had a little wine with dinner. And you know me: You don't have to do much more than wave the cork under my nose. So a few sips of Merlot and things weren't quite so scary anymore."

"Good. I was positive, though, that you'd do just fine."

"How was the engagement party?"

"Very nice. Tara—my niece—has herself a great guy there, too. And she deserves it; she's pretty great herself."

"Um, something really wild happened at the conference on Sunday morning." I proceeded to fill him in on what had transpired over my eggs Benedict. His response? Silence—a good three or four seconds of it.

"Nick?" I finally ventured.

"I'm here; I just have no idea what to say. The whole thing's so . . . well, bizarre!"

"I know it is."

"Are you certain this lady's who she claims to be?"

"Yep. I checked her out today. She's Belle Simone, the author, all right."

"Even if she is," he mused, "it's extremely odd that she'd want to part with that kind of money to induce you to solve some mystery she's written."

"I admit it's *slightly* above the normal fee for my services. The truth is, I might have considered taking the job for, say, a thousand or two less."

"No kidding," Nick muttered. "Seriously, though, why $24,940? That's a pretty weird figure, don't you think? Why not make it a straight twenty-five thousand?"

"I have no idea. When I asked her why she was willing to shell out all that money, she refused to say. All she told me was that she was anxious to reassure herself that the mystery *could* be solved. And she felt that a professional detective would be the person most likely able to verify this."

"And you say she'll even be providing you with clues to this mystery of hers?"

"That's right."

"Hmm."

"What?"

"This thing gets curiouser and curiouser. I only hope the woman's legitimate and that this isn't some little game she's playing."

"That makes two of us."

"I'll bet," Nick responded, chuckling. Then: "By the way, about Saturday night . . ."

I knew it! My heart plunged straight down to my toes. Nick and I had made a dinner date for Saturday, but evidently his itinerary had changed. (Surprise, surprise!) I waited impatiently for him to inform me that something had come up and that he'd be spending the entire weekend with Derek—he's Nick's just-turned-ten-years-old son.

"Look, Tiffany"—she's Nick's ex-wife—"is taking Derek to Fire Island on Friday," he explained, "and they'll be staying until Tuesday. This being the case, I'm available on Sunday, too—which is when Derek and I had made plans to have supper together. Uh, what about you? Are you free Sunday?"

I hadn't realized I'd been holding my breath until I let it out. "You're in luck. As it happens, I just freed up. Marcello ate tainted caviar last night, and he had to cancel our date for next Sunday." Marcello is my make-believe admirer.

Playing along with my little joke, Nick clucked his tongue in faux sympathy. "Poor, *poor* Marcello," he murmured. "But tell me, how would you feel about driving over to New Jersey? I ran into an old friend the other day, and he was raving about some little restaurant that just opened up outside Princeton—in Wheeler. He also used the word 'charming' to describe a bed-and-breakfast that's five minutes from the restaurant."

"Sounds wonderful."

"Doesn't it? I'll make the reservations. Is dinner at eight o'clock all right with you?"

"It's fine."

"Uh, Dez?"

"Yes?"

I can't wait to see you."

"Ditto," I murmured.

Now, anyone overhearing this exchange might have been under the impression that at this point everything between Nick and me was practically idyllic. WRONG! I mean, while I happened to be absolutely gaga about him, Nick was the reason I'd wanted to get away for a couple of days in the first place. And unhappily, nothing had changed.

But to give you some background . . .

Many years ago, I was married to—and completely mad about—a very special man named Ed Shapiro. I had every expectation of spending the rest of my days with Ed, but then he choked on a chicken bone and died. I realize that sounds like a joke, but believe me, there was nothing comical about it. Anyhow, after a long while, I started dating—usually with less than positive results. In fact, a couple of times the outcome was a genuine disaster. Then, over a year ago, Nick Grainger moved into my building. Also, my life.

Things didn't get off the ground all that quickly. Being a fairly recently divorced father, Nick wasn't exactly open to a romantic entanglement.

Me? I was smitten almost as soon as I got a look at him. Physically, the guy's perfection—at least, from what my friends insist is my rather warped point of view. They claim it's my nurturing nature that had me responding so positively to his short, lean (okay, skinny) physique. And I suppose Nick *does* look as if he could use some tender, loving care. Still, how about the fact that I was also crazy about his receding hairline and that slightly bucktoothed grin of his? Maybe you can explain what those things have to do with this purported nurturing nature of mine!

At any rate, in spite of his initial reluctance, Nick and I eventually began seeing each other. And I found him to be intelligent, generous, thoughtful—all sorts of nice things. Hey, he actually sent me flowers for no reason at all. And I'm certain he'd have done that even if he didn't own a florist shop.

So what more could I want? you might ask. It isn't that I wanted *more*; what I longed for was *less*. Everything would have been ideal if only Derek were out of the picture. (No, I didn't want the kid dead. But I definitely wouldn't have objected to his being on another planet.) I know, I know, my attitude with regard to Derek must have you thinking I'm an A-one bitch. But that's because you've never been the target of his machinations. I'll fill you in later on the rotten, underhanded, *Machiavellian* stuff that darling child's pulled on me.

Enough about my little nemesis, though. I made up my mind that for the next four days, I wouldn't even think about Derek. I'd restrict my focus to Nick himself and the fact that we'd soon be spending an entire weekend together—or at least a decent part of one.

It would be the first time we did, too. And—while I wouldn't acknowledge this even to myself—on some level I feared that it could also be the last.

Chapter 7

I couldn't seem to get myself together on Tuesday, so it was after ten thirty by the time I arrived at the office. Even before I opened the door, I steeled myself for one of Jackie's lectures, these being doled out whenever I fail to notify her I'll be coming in late that morning. (The "late" varying with her mood du jour, but usually starting right around now—give or take a few minutes.) Normally, she reminds me that in light of my line of work, she should be kept posted with regard to any change in my arrival plans. My failure to do this, Jackie has no compunction about laying on me, causes her to imagine all sorts of dastardly acts that might have been inflicted on my person since yesterday. Apparently, though, this morning she'd been too busy handling the phones to begin checking the local hospitals yet.

She had just finished dealing with one call when another one came in. As soon as she saw me, she frantically waved a message slip in my direction. For a moment there, I figured she expected me to wait until she was free so she could read it to me. And that following this, I'd be on the receiving end of a delayed talking-to. But instead, she handed over the slip. (Grudgingly, I thought.)

Gary Donleavy had phoned at nine. Belle, the message said, wanted to know if I could "do lunch" that day. Suddenly I felt as if my knees were about to give way. If I wasn't mistaken, my eccentric client would soon be providing me with the first clue to her mystery—and in person, too!

I hurried to my cubbyhole and, without even taking the time to sit down, reached for the telephone.

"Belle Simone's residence," Gary's voice informed me.

"Hi, Gary, it's Desiree."

"Oh, great! So, are you available for lunch today? Belle's treat."

"I am, thank you—I mean, her. When and where?"

"How is twelve thirty?"

"That's fine."

"Belle wonders if you'd mind very much coming up-town, to the West Seventies. We're on West Seventy-third, and she was hoping to avoid spending any time going to and from. She has *so* many things to tend to this week."

"That's no problem." *Listen, for the kind of money this woman was paying me, I should mind?* I immediately corrected the thought to "the kind of money this woman *might* be paying me sometime in the future."

"Belle wanted me to ask how you feel about Eskimo food."

Now, I was probably being very unfair to Eskimo cuisine, but the first word to spring to mind then was "blubber," which did nothing positive for my appetite. "I wasn't even aware that there was an Eskimo restaurant in the city," I responded evasively.

"Neither was I until this one opened up a couple of months ago, only a block from Belle's place. Uh, suppose I tell her that while you were agreeable to having Eskimo, you didn't appear to be too thrilled at the prospect, so I let you off the hook."

"Don't do that. I should at least try it. Maybe I'll be pleasantly surprised."

"Trust me, you won't be. Listen, I'd consider it a really big favor if you would let me do as I suggested."

I didn't answer at once. In light of my contract with Belle, I certainly didn't want to say or do anything that might displease her. But on the other hand, Gary sounded almost desperate. Besides, I felt I could have a rich, full life without ever sampling Eskimo food.

"We-ll okay," I finally agreed.

"Thanks a bunch, Dez. Oh, may I call you Dez?"

"Of, c—"

"I haven't worked up the nerve to level with Belle yet. She loves the restaurant, and she keeps dragging me over there for lunch. But the truth is, I *loathe* that stuff, only I don't want to hurt her feelings. Anyway, are you okay with Chinese? There's a very nice place on Seventy-sixth and Broadway—Ping Toy, it's called."

"Sounds good to me."

He gave me the address. "Thanks, Dez. I owe you."

When I walked into the restaurant—which, although fairly large, had a nice, homey quality about it—Belle and Gary were already sitting side by side in a booth, sipping what I took to be piña coladas.

I remember thinking that, if anything, Belle was even more attractive than when we'd met this past weekend. Once again, she was wearing a pretty floral dress. And once again, she was perfectly made up. But now that she was hatless, I was able to fully appreciate the silver hair, which fell in soft waves to her chin, framing the lovely oval face. For the first time, too, I could really see her eyes, which were an almost startling shade of green.

"What would you like to drink?" she asked as soon as I sat down opposite them.

"The same, thank you," I said, indicating their cocktails. "That is, if those are piña coladas."

"They are." She turned to Gary, who signaled the waiter. And almost immediately, the drink was set in front of me.

"I thought it might be nice to have our lunch first," Belle suggested. "Then, when we've finished, I'll provide you with the first clue to the mystery. Okay with you?"

"It's fine."

Before long, we were eating our way through what seemed like tons of spareribs and spring rolls and scallion pancakes and pot stickers. After this, we shared the main dishes: lemon chicken, shrimp with black bean sauce, and beef with tomatoes and onions. We were having tea and fortune cookies (by some miracle we actually found room for cookies!) when I commented on how much I'd enjoyed the lunch.

Belle was obviously pleased. "It *was* good, wasn't it? As it turned out, it's fortunate you have that aversion to Eskimo food."

Somehow I managed to eke out a kind of half smile. After which I turned to Gary and fixed him with a malevolent glare. He was already beet red and was presently doing his best to avoid meeting my gaze.

"Well, let's get down to business, kids," Belle said, sparing her secretary from any more of the death rays I was sending in his direction. "Why don't we let Desiree have her first clue, Gary."

He opened his briefcase, removed a folder, and handed it to me—still avoiding my eyes. Inside the folder was a single sheet of paper with these words typed midway down the page: "To solve this mystery, you must first recognize the key. And to accomplish this, it's essential that you think the way the French do."

"Oh," I said.

"Don't look so worried. I have every confidence that, at some point, this will become clear to you," Belle said encouragingly.

"I hope you're right," I responded. But, I'm afraid, without a whole lot of conviction.

When I left Belle and her spineless liar of a secretary, my head was spinning.

Think the way the French do? What the hell did *that* mean?

Chapter 8

In the taxi on the way back downtown, I gave myself a little pep talk. Belle could be right. This thinking-the-way-the-French-do thing might very well make sense to me once I was further into the story line.

Still, I wasn't quite ready to begin testing that theory, so I had the cabbie drop me off at a Duane Reade near the office. I managed to spend a good forty minutes there, replenishing such absolute essentials as mascara, lip gloss, nail polish, eyelash curler, eyebrow pencil, talcum powder, Pretty Hands and Feet, and Oreo cookies. Then I headed for work, all set now to deal with part two: "The Investigation Begins," chapter one.

Heading the investigation into Rob Harwood's death was homicide detective Gabriel Wilson: intelligent, resourceful, hardworking, committed, and just the least bit paunchy. He'd been promoted to sergeant only weeks earlier, and this would be the first murder case (if, indeed, Ron Harwood's death *should* turn out to be murder) where he'd more or less be making the important decisions. But while Gabe was excited by the prospect, upon learning the facts of the crime (again, if there even *was* a crime), he anticipated that it could very well be like baptism by fire.

"I have a new assignment," he'd informed his wife during dinner on that first day.

"Anything interesting?"

"I guess you could say that. There's a good possibility the deceased was poisoned."

"It's not definite, though?"

"Well, the cop who accompanied the EMS to the man's home last night was suspicious enough to warrant calling in a homicide detective and the medical examiner."

"Who was the homicide detective?"

"Jack Gray. But he's leaving on vacation tomorrow, so I inherited the case. Jack took care of the preliminary work last night. He brought in the forensic team, had photos taken of what's very likely a crime scene, and talked briefly with all the people who were at the apartment when this Harwood fellow died. He went through his notes with me this afternoon. And then the two of us visited the apartment together."

"Back up a sec," Lily instructed. "Did you say *all* the people who were present? How many are we talking about, anyway?"

"Seventeen."

"Are you serious?"

Gabe nodded. "The man had just turned sixty; he died at his own surprise birthday party."

"He musta been surprised, all right," fourteen-year-old Gabriel Wilson, Jr. piped up.

"That's not funny, Gabie; somebody's *dead,*" Lily admonished, frowning.

Gabe went on as if this exchange hadn't occurred. "There were a dozen guests, including the deceased's wife and stepdaughter. There were also five people from the caterer's—Catering by Celeste, the outfit's called. Anyhow, the staff consisted of two waiters—one serving the drinks, the other passing around the canapés—and three to help in the kitchen. None of the crew would admit to having met Harwood previously, and Jack is inclined to believe this is true. *I'm* inclined to believe he's right. But naturally, I'll have a talk with them myself and take it from there. At any rate, they did their jobs well—too well, from my point of view."

"What makes you say that?"

"Unfortunately, the glasses used during the cocktail hour had already been washed before emergency services arrived. Which means that if there was poison involved here, the vehicle for the stuff may very well be too pristine now to tell us anything."

"I guess it's early to have any idea of a possible motive yet," Lily murmured.

"I wouldn't say that. One of the EMS people overheard a woman guest comment to her husband—or whoever he was—'I suppose it was only a matter of time before Rob played around with the wrong man's wife.' Those weren't the exact words, but that's the gist of it. Then the fellow she was talking to grunted something that Tom—the EMS guy—didn't catch. The only problem is, Tom had his back to the couple at the time, and he has no idea which ones they were."

"Sounds like this Harwood might be dead courtesy of a jealous husband," Lily remarked.

Gabe shrugged. "Or maybe not. If he did play around, it's just as likely he was offed by one of the ladies he loved and left."

"I suppose that's true. And poison's supposed to be a woman's weapon, anyhow, isn't it?"

"So they say. Still, I'd like a buck for every man who's flavored a meal with a little arsenic. But listen, Rob Harwood may have been killed for another reason entirely. At any rate, time will tell—I hope."

And so began Gabe Wilson's involvement in what he would always regard as the most baffling case in a long and otherwise very productive career.

Before I had a chance to read any further, the phone buzzed. "You've *got* to come out front right now and see what's here for you!" Jackie commanded excitedly.

"Uh, I'll be there in a few minutes, Jackie. I want to do a little more reading first."

"It's almost five, you know. Time to give it a rest."

"You're kidding! I had no idea it was that late!"

"You didn't get back here until close to four," she reminded me.

"True. Anyhow, I'll read fast."

"Suit yourself. It's a gorgeous bouquet, though."

"A *bouquet*? And it's for me?"

"That's what the tag says."

Nick! I exclaimed to myself. Not that there was any reason for his sending me flowers now. *But, I mean, if not Nick—who?*

I was up front as quickly as my short, stubby legs could get me there. And sure enough, sitting on the counter next to Jackie's desk was a very lovely floral arrangement.

"Your boyfriend's something else, you know that? What's the occasion, anyway?"

I shrugged. "There isn't any."

"I have a suggestion, Dez."

"Which is?"

"Read the damn card!"

And I did.

The message said, "Please, *please* forgive me, Dez. I swear to you that nothing like that will ever happen again." It was signed, "A very repentant Gary."

"Well?" Jackie demanded impatiently. "What does the card say?"

"That it wasn't Nick who sent these. They're from Gary, Belle's secretary. He was apologizing for something silly that occurred at lunch."

"It must have been *damn* silly to warrant that kind of an apology. What happened?"

"It wasn't anything important, honestly."

Jackie's phone rang before she had the opportunity to conduct a really thorough interrogation, so I made my exit.

Back at my desk now, I decided to call Gary. I was still furious with him, but the flowers had no doubt set him back a bundle.

I told him how beautiful they were, after which he began a profuse apology. "I acted like a coward, Dez, also—excuse the expression—a real schmuck. I was afraid that just saying you didn't seem to be too keen on Eskimo food wouldn't do it for Belle. She'd probably have insisted that was because you'd never eaten it at *this* restaurant. And frankly, I couldn't *bear* the thought of another meal there, so—"

"Let's just forget it, okay?"

"That's very kind of you, Dez. And I want you to know I'm going to tell Belle the truth: that *you* never objected to going there—*I* did. I fully intended to fess up this evening—I swear!—but Belle had just made a dinner date. Maybe tomorrow." He amended this a split second later. "No. Definitely tomorrow. And you can also be absolutely certain that I will never put you in this kind of a position again. Do you believe me?"

"I think I do."

"Friends?" Gary asked timidly.

"Friends." Actually, I couldn't swear to it, but I'd try. I mean, there was something very sweet, very appealing about Gary. (Only keep in mind that I *am* a Scorpio.)

And then, very quietly: "Um, Dez? I hope you solve the mystery."

"*Now* you're talkin'," I said.

Chapter 9

Since I'd done such an admirable job of stuffing myself at lunch, I wasn't all that hungry when I got home from the office. So I had a light supper (after all, a person still has to eat *something,* doesn't she?), then settled down on the sofa with my mystery.

Chapter two of part two—the chapter I'd been about to start before the arrival of Gary's peace offering—dealt with the interrogation that Sunday of the five-person crew from Catering by Celeste. (The quintet, incidentally, did not include Celeste herself—real name Gladys Fink—who, on the evening of Rob's surprise party had been feeding the folks at a little get-together hosted by a member of the United States Senate.) Anyhow, to summarize . . .

Gabe confided to Ray Carson—the good-looking twenty-eight-year-old detective who'd been assigned to the case with him—his reason for beginning the questioning with the catering team. He was so intimidated by the size of the suspect list, he admitted, that he was determined to reduce it. And these people, who were the least likely to have had any personal involvement with the deceased, appeared to be his best hope.

The two policemen were given a small office at the catering facility in which to conduct their inquiries. They talked to one person at a time, beginning with those who'd worked in the kitchen that night. In this group were two stocky, middle-aged women and a young, blond Czechoslovakian man.

Both women, in turn, emphatically denied witnessing

anything of a suspicious nature that evening. And both insisted that none of the guests had gone into the dining room by way of the kitchen. Not a single guest had so much as set foot in the kitchen prior to the tragedy, the officers were assured—and this was also true of Mrs. Harwood herself. Furthermore, both women informed them that the catering crew kept going back and forth between the kitchen and dining room, setting things up for dinner—often, in fact, leaving open the door that separated the two rooms. So even if someone had entered the dining room from the living room, the detectives realized, it was doubtful this individual would have gone unnoticed. One of the ladies—Mildred—obviously concerned that she and her partner, Claire, might be suspects—volunteered that neither of them had ever laid eyes on "that poor fellow" before seeing him slumped over the dining room table, "dead as a mackerel." In fact, they'd never heard the *name* Rob Harwood—not until they were told they'd be preparing the food for his birthday dinner.

Communicating with the third member of the kitchen staff was considerably more difficult. Petr—who couldn't have been much over twenty years old—had immigrated to the United States less than a year earlier, and his English was limited. He did, however, manage to get across that his duties with the catering firm were confined to the more menial tasks. "I do—what you call it?— garbage work," he said with a grin. Asked what he meant by this, he explained that he washed the dishes, scrubbed the pots, cleaned up the kitchen, took out the garbage, "and like that." Petr confirmed, in just about every detail, the statements of Claire and Mildred.

After this, the detectives spoke to the waiters, one of whom Gabe put in his fifties, while the other he took to be in his early thirties.

Arnold, the older waiter, answered the questions much as the others had. He, too, saw nothing, heard nothing, knew nothing.

The responses of the younger waiter, Sean, were close to identical. Then, as he began to walk out of the room—

his hand was already on the doorknob—he turned and, with a sheepish smile, retraced his steps.

Sean confessed that he hadn't been a hundred percent truthful in his answers before—although he doubted that his information would be at all helpful. Still, he felt he should probably have mentioned this one little thing, regardless.

As soon as he returned home from that job, he phoned his fiancée to tell her what had occurred. Well, *she* was familiar with the name Rob Harwood, all right. Only a couple of weeks earlier, her best friend had complained that some old geezer by that name had come on to her when his wife was only a few feet away—and this was at a funeral, too!

The chapter concluded with:

In spite of cautioning himself against jumping to con-clusions, Gabe left the catering hall that morning all but convinced that Rob Harwood had been murdered. It followed that he was equally confident as to the motive for the crime.

And that day, five names were deleted from the sus-pect list.

Chapter 10

My eyes were almost at half-mast by the time I finished the chapter, so I closed the folder and returned it to my attaché case, where it lay ready to be shuttled back to the office in the morning.

Later, in bed, I told myself it was fortunate I wasn't involved in any other cases at the moment. It meant I could devote all my energy to solving this one. But I didn't actually believe me. Even if I did come through, who knew when that would be? And how was I supposed to pay my bills between now and whenever?

That night, I dreamed that I never did solve Belle's little puzzler. And the word spread. No one wanted to hire me when they learned I'd failed to identify Rob Harwood's murderer. Elvin Blaustein even put in an appearance in my dream. Elvin was a former client of mine, dating back to the days when the chances of my getting killed on the job were about on a par with my being chosen Miss America. Anyhow, he went around telling everyone that because I was such a lousy PI, someone he loved ended up dead. And I guess, in a way, this was true enough. Except that this "someone" was a *thing*: Elvin's pet boa constrictor. The creature—if I remember correctly, the name was Stretch—had crawled into the radiator and found his (her?) way into the building's heating system. By the time I located poor Stretch, it had gone on to its reward,

At any rate, as a result of my failure to attract any new clients, I wound up having to give up my apartment. Following which, I moved into a shelter for abused women. (I know; technically, I don't qualify. But this was a dream, remember?) I'd barely unpacked the pathetic cardboard box I had to use for a suitcase when a fellow abused woman falsely accused me of pinching her purple lipstick (which hardly goes with my glorious hennaed hair). Then, she promptly kicked me in the stomach.

I woke up thoroughly depressed—and with a terrible stomachache, besides.

I still hadn't managed to shake the mood when I got to the office. "Hi, sunshine," Jackie called out, my scowl evidently prompting the greeting.

"Hi, yourself."

"What's with you? You look like you're ready to chew nails."

"I didn't sleep too well, that's all. Any messages?"

"Yes, as a matter of fact." She picked up a pink memo slip, which she read to me while I gritted my teeth. "Pat Wiz . . . Wiz . . . you know, your friend who's had all those husbands. Anyhow, she wants you to get back to her as soon as possible." And now, Jackie graciously handed over the slip.

Less than five minutes later, I dialed the number Pat had left. "Hi, Pat. It's me."

"Oh, Dez, I've been waiting to hear from you."

"Is everything okay?"

"Sure, why?"

"Well, this *is* your home number."

"Oh, yeah, that's right. No wonder you're such a hot-shot PI," she said, chuckling. "I'm playing hooky today."

"You also left word for me to call you as soon as possible," I reminded her, "so I thought maybe there was something urgent on your mind."

"Oh, *that*. It's just that I'll be leaving the house in a little while. Burton and I are going out and celebrating tonight. (Burton is Pat's fourth and—judging from the way things look—forever husband.)

I was racking my brain trying to think of a birthday or other special occasion of Pat's and/or Burton's that fell on today's date when Pat cleared things up for me. "Burton recently received a very nice raise, and come evening, my dear, we shall be dining at a *très* fancy restaurant. So this morning I'm having my hair done and getting a manicure, *and* I'm also treating myself to a pedicure. By the way, Dez, I plan on dragging you with me the next time I go for a pedicure. They make a woman feel *deliciously* pampered.

"But anyhow, the reason I wanted to talk to you is that this cousin of Burton's is concerned that the man she intends to marry in a few months has been lying to her—she'll tell you all about it. Her name's Irene McNamara, and by the way, she's no chippie. She's fifty-four years old, and this will be her second marriage—that is, if it ever comes off. I told her you're the best private investigator in New York, and she's very anxious to have you look into things. Oh, incidentally, Irene's late husband left her *very* comfortable financially, so if you should choose to hike up your fee a little, she won't feel a thing."

Directly after this, Pat provided me with Irene's number. Then I told her to congratulate Burton for me, wished them both a great time, and we hung up.

The conversation had no sooner ended than I got in touch with Irene McNamara. She sounded relieved when I gave her my name. "Oh, Ms. Shapiro, I'm so glad to hear from you."

"It's Desiree, Ms. McNamara."

"No, no. Please. Call me Irene."

"All right. I understand, Irene, that you believe your fiancé's been lying to you. What do you suspect him of lying *about*?"

"Well, when we began seeing each other, Clive let me know almost at once that although he's past fifty, he's still a bachelor. However, several days ago, we had a marvelous lunch at the very lovely hotel where we're planning to hold our wedding in October. And when we returned to my apartment, I asked him if he was still pleased with our choice. Actually, I was merely making conversation. At any rate, Clive said something like, 'It sure beats Vegas.' I would have regarded this as an innocuous little joke, except that suddenly his face turned very red. And then he quickly threw in that a friend of his had been married in Las Vegas, and this friend told him how horrendous the ceremony had been. And after *that,* Clive apparently felt it necessary to add that he himself had never even been there. He went on about the thing just a little too long, you see. I suppose I should have prefaced this by mentioning that he'd had quite a bit to drink that afternoon. And I've come to believe that because of the liquor, he let his guard down a bit."

"And you want to know if Clive's ever been married?"

"Yes. I've been going over and over that incident in my mind, and I've come to accept that if he lied about that, there's no telling how many other things he's lied to me about. So, Desiree, will you help me find out the truth?"

"I promise you I'll do my best."

I asked Irene what she knew about the man.

"Not much. The one thing I can state with certainty is that he's a salesman at Tanya's."

"Tanya's?"

"It's a pricey women's shoe store on the Upper East Side. That's where we met," she elaborated, following the information with an embarrassed little titter. "As to anything else, I can only tell you what he told me: That his full name is Clive Harvey, that he's fifty-two years old, and that he came here from Chicago six months ago."

Irene asked about my fee then. And I don't have to mention—do I?—that I ignored Pat's pronouncement.

Except for a brief lunch break at my desk, I spent the rest of the day gathering information on the man the two of us—Irene and I—were inclined to regard as her duplicitous fiancé. And it turned out that the two of us were right.

Now, when you've been in this business as long as I have, you're bound to acquire a bunch of sources, and I made use of any number of them that day. After so many phone calls that my index finger was numb, I learned that about the only thing Irene's intended had been straight with her about was his name. (And thank God for that, since it facilitated my gathering some of the other facts about the man.) Anyhow, he wasn't fifty-two at all; he was forty-five. (I speculated that he must have tagged on a few years to make himself more age-appropriate for the wealthy widow.) He wasn't from Chicago, either; he was from Cleveland. He'd been married in Las Vegas, just as Irene suspected. *Plus,* he'd also tied the knot in a couple of other cities. What's more, as far as I could determine, lover boy hadn't bothered divorcing even one of his wives!

It was close to five when I phoned Irene with the news.

"Thank you, Desiree; I appreciate your handling this so quickly. Send me your bill, will you?" And then, in a thin, tremulous voice: "I'd better hang up now. I have a wedding to cancel."

Chapter 11

I left the office that day without having so much as glanced at the manuscript. Before going up to the apartment, I stopped at my local D'Agostino's and replenished my supply of everything from onions to ice cream to toilet paper.

About twenty minutes after I got home, the purchases were delivered, and I fixed myself a salad. Then I went to the freezer for what was left of a month-old lasagna and zapped it in my microwave. (I'm probably the last person in my building to buy one of those things—maybe the last person in the entire country! But now that I have one, I can't figure out how I managed to live without it.) Following the lasagna, I had two cups of coffee to help me stay awake and some macadamia brittle to keep the coffee company. Then I cleared away the dishes, took out Belle's manuscript, and—determined not to get too comfortable tonight—sat down at the kitchen table, opening to chapter three of part two.

Compared to dealing with the widow (possibly *grief-stricken* widow), interrogating the catering crew could be regarded as a piece of cake. Gabe Wilson would have taken an oath on this even before he met with Tess Harwood later that afternoon. And being a genuinely sensitive man, he recoiled at the prospect.

Ray Carson, also a sensitive man, shared his partner's reluctance. "Geez, I hate this," he mumbled in the elevator on their way up to the apartment of Tess's sister, where Tess and her daughter were temporarily staying.

The woman who came to the door was tall and slender, with a thick mane of curly chestnut hair and a wide, dimpled smile. She was dressed in a pair of tan slacks and a formfitting dark brown sweater. Gabe estimated that she was about forty—a very attractive forty.

"Uh, Mrs. Harwood?" he asked, flashing his badge.

"No, I'm her sister—Catherine Feller. Come in, please."

The detectives introduced themselves, and Catherine led the way into a large, lavishly appointed living room. Seated on one of the three sofas here, wearing a simple (although, no doubt, expensive) black dress, was another good-looking woman. A fact that even the absence of makeup, the red-rimmed, vacant eyes, and the tight set of the mouth couldn't quite conceal. Gabe judged her to be two or three years younger than her sibling.

"Have a seat, officers," Catherine directed, indicating the two pale green cut-velvet chairs opposite the sofa. "I suppose you'll want to talk to Tess alone. But can I get you something before I excuse myself? Some coffee perhaps?"

"Nothing for me, thank you," Gabe responded.

"I'm fine, too, ma'am," the younger officer said, quickly adding, "But thank you."

Catherine left the room ("flounced out of the room" would be a more accurate description). And, turning to Tess now, Gabe murmured," We're very, very sorry for your loss, Mrs. Harwood."

The widow nodded. "Thank you, Detective . . . ?"

"It's Wilson—Sergeant Wilson. And this is my partner, Detective Carson."

She nodded again. "How can I help you?"

"We'd like to ask you a few questions; we'll be as brief as possible."

"All right. Go ahead," Tess responded, the words punctuated with a sigh.

"Did you notice anything suspicious, anything even the least bit out of the ordinary, on the night of the party?" Gabe inquired.

The woman appeared bewildered. "No, nothing. I don't understand what's happening. The police appear to suspect . . . to suspect that my husband was murdered. Why *murdered*? Couldn't Rob simply have died of a heart attack or . . . or something?"

"The cause of death hasn't been definitely established yet, Mrs. Harwood; we'll have to wait for the results of the autopsy to know that. In the meantime, though, we'll be talking to everyone who was at the party Friday evening while the details are still fresh in their minds. This is just in the event there *was* foul play."

"That autopsy report—when do you expect it to come in?"

"In two, three weeks, possibly longer."

Another, deeper sigh. "All right. Ask me whatever you like."

"Did your husband have anything to eat or drink before dinner that night?"

"He didn't eat anything, but—"

"You're certain of this?"

"Yes."

"And to drink?"

"A glass of champagne."

"Only one?"

"That's right."

"The champagne—was it left unattended at any time?"

"Unattended?"

"Did Mr. Harwood put down the glass somewhere and walk off for a while, or maybe have his back to it at some point?"

Tess's eyes opened wide. "Yes, actually, he did," she answered softly. "I handed him the champagne soon after he arrived at the party, but he went upstairs to change and left it on the end table."

"How much of the champagne had he had by then?"

"None. He didn't even taste it until he returned."

"Did you see anyone near the glass while he was upstairs?"

"No. A group of us were standing only a few feet away, but most of the time we were busy gabbing, and I didn't really pay much attention."

"So you didn't notice anyone *at all* near the table."

Tess shook her head. Then, perhaps a split second afterward: "Wait. There *was* the waiter. He was all set to remove Rob's glass, but I said for him to leave it, that it was my husband's drink, and he'd be returning at any moment." Suddenly Tess's hand flew to her mouth. "My God! If I hadn't stopped the man from taking away that glass, Rob might be alive today!"

"Listen," Gabe said kindly, "as yet we haven't even established that Mr. Harwood's death was a homicide. Besides, if it *should* turn out his champagne was tampered with, it's every bit as likely that this occurred *after* the waiter walked off." Then hurriedly changing the subject: "Uh, that group you were talking to, do you recall who was in it?"

Tess's forehead pleated up. "Well," she murmured, absently fingering her wavy auburn hair, "at first there were just three of us: me, my very dear friend Ellie White, and Ellie's husband, Phil. A short time later, we were joined by my sister, Catherine; my daughter, Anne; and let's see . . ." After two or three seconds, Tess smiled apologetically. "I'm afraid I can't recall who else, not at the moment, at any rate. Besides, if anybody did poison my husband's drink, isn't it just as plausible that it was an individual who *wasn't* standing near that table? After all, couldn't someone have dropped whatever it was into the glass while passing by?"

"Believe me, we're not overlooking that possibility," Gabe assured her.

"There's something else I'd like you to explain. Assuming again that Rob was poisoned, why are you so convinced this occurred during the champagne hour? Rob may have sipped some water at the dining table. Why couldn't that have been contaminated?"

Realizing now that he had given Ray almost no chance to participate in the questioning, Gabe looked at his partner and nodded almost imperceptibly.

Ray took the cue. "I wouldn't say we're *convinced,* but that *is* much less likely, ma'am. The fact is, whatever your husband was drinking at dinner would have been sitting on the table, directly in front of him."

"I realize that," Tess responded impatiently. "But couldn't someone have sneaked into the dining room a little *before* dinner and put something in his water glass? There were place cards to indicate where everyone would be seated, you know."

"Well, we can't swear this didn't happen, but it's not too probable. I understand the double doors separating the living room and dining room were shut until the meal was about to be served. So it would have been pretty tough for anyone to both enter and leave the dining room without being observed. And to make this an even riskier proposition, the caterers tell us they kept walking back and forth between the kitchen and the dining room, setting up. Also, the only other access to the dining room is through the kitchen, correct?" He didn't wait for confirmation. "But the catering crew swears no one at the party came into that kitchen until after the tragedy. Still, we're not about to dismiss any scenario that's at all feasible. Anything your husband might have drunk from that night—that hasn't been washed, of course—is being tested for traces of poison."

I see," Tess murmured. And now she sat there motionless—except for her hands, which she clenched together and then unclenched almost rhythmically.

Gabe intruded on the silence. "Uh, at what point did you become aware that your husband was in difficulty, Mrs. Harwood?"

"Not until . . . until just minutes before he died. We had all gone into the dining room by then. And while the champagne was being poured, I chatted with my daughter, who was seated on my left. My husband was at the head of the table, naturally—to my right. Then, my cousin Simon, who was also Rob's close friend, stood up to make a toast, and I was focused on him—he was down at the other end of the table. Well, Simon had just said something amusing, and I turned to Rob to see his reaction. The instant I did, I could tell that something was terribly wrong. His face was all red, and he was gasping for breath. He seemed to be trying to say something, but I couldn't make out the words. I screamed for somebody to call nine-one-one and—" She broke off, and her hand flew to her throat. "Well, you know the rest," she said, her voice a mere whisper.

"This must be extremely painful for you, Mrs. Harwood, and I'm sorry to trouble you any further, but there are one or two more questions I have to ask you."

The widow eyed him warily.

"Are you aware of anyone who might have had a grudge—no matter how minor—against your husband?"

Tess's chin jutted out. "There was no one like that; Robbie was very well liked. Besides, the people who were in our home that night? They were his *friends.*"

Gabe shifted uncomfortably in his seat. *Now for the tough one.* "Forgive me for asking you this, but I wouldn't be doing my job if I didn't. Were you and Mr. Harwood having any marital problems?"

"No, we were not. We got along very well. I loved my husband," Tess declared emphatically, "and he loved me."

At this juncture, Gabe determined that she'd disclosed as much as she was likely to—for the present, at any rate—and after he'd thanked her for her cooperation, the two men rose almost simultaneously. Tess, who looked as if she'd just survived the Spanish Inquisition, wasted no time in getting to her feet. "You also wanted to speak to my sister and my daughter. I'll send in whichever one you'd care to see first."

"Either would be fine," Gabe told her.

Catherine Feller closed the door carefully behind her, crossed the room, and sank into the very cushion her sister had so recently vacated. Then she tucked her legs under her and tilted her head in anticipation.

It was at this moment that the phone rang. The instant I heard the voice, my stomach flipped over, and I could feel this stupid smile spread across my face.

We each inquired as to the other's well-being, after which Nick told me, "I just wanted to say hi."

"Hi, Nick," I simpered.

"How are you making out with that big-money case of yours?"

"So far, I'm completely in the dark, but I haven't been able to read that much of the manuscript yet. Belle—you know, the author—took me to lunch yesterday and presented me with my first clue. Right now, though, the clue's as much of a mystery to me as the mystery itself. I'll fill you in when I see you."

"Speaking of *that,* I figure if we leave at five thirty it should give us time to get to Princeton by eight, even if we run into a little traffic. Is five thirty okay with you?"

"It's fine."

"I'm really looking forward to the weekend, Dez." His voice, when he said this, was soft, intimate. And that susceptible stomach of mine did another somersault.

"Same here," I murmured.

"Well, see ya."

"See ya," I echoed. But he'd already hung up.

I picked up the manuscript again and began where I'd left off—with the detectives about to question Catherine, the widow's sister.

"There are just a few matters we'd like to cover with you," Gabe began. "I promise we won't keep you long."

"Shoot," Catherine replied succinctly.

"Did anything unusual occur the night of your brother-in-law's death?" Gabe asked.

Catherine shook her head. "Not that I know of—aside from his dying, of course."

"Let me ask you this, then. Just prior to going upstairs to change his clothes, he placed his champagne glass on an end table. Are you aware of this?"

"I am. I walked over to Tess soon afterward. And, for a while, I was standing not more than three or four feet from that table, talking to her and Anne—my niece—and some other people: Eleanor and Philip White and this cousin of Rob's, Elaine somebody-or-other. But I didn't notice anyone monkeying around with his drink, if that's what's on your mind."

"Did you see anyone entering or leaving the dining room before dinner was served?"

Catherine shook her head. "I'm afraid I can't help you there, either." Seconds later, looking reflective now, she murmured, "So it's been definitely established that he was poisoned, has it?"

"No. We'll have to wait for the autopsy findings to learn what it was that killed your brother-in-law. Poison *is* a possibility, though."

"Oh."

"Uh, you don't sound too surprised that Mr. Harwood might have been murdered," Ray observed.

"I imagine it's because I'm not."

"Why is that, ma'am?"

"Listen, Rob was a player. Are you familiar with the term, Detective Carson?"

Ray smiled. "I think so. Would you have the names of any of the women he was involved with?"

"I'm only certain about two of them, although I don't doubt there were others—*many* others."

"And the two you're certain of—who would they be?"

"One is a woman who used to live in the same building. But that was a couple of years ago, and since then she's gotten married for the third time and moved to the Bahamas."

"And you're sure Mr. Harwood was in a relationship with this particular woman . . . how?" Gabe interjected.

"I saw Gwen and Rob together, that's how," Catherine responded dismissively.

"Where was this?"

"At the Four Seasons, of all places. My ex-husband and I arrived there just in time to get a load of them kissing passionately. I couldn't believe my eyes! It was as if they were alone in the room, for crying out loud!" And turning to Ray: "Are you familiar with the Four Seasons, Detective Carson?"

"No, I'm not."

"Shame on you! It's an excellent restaurant, one of the finest in town. You ought to give it a try one evening. I'll bet you're acquainted with any number of pretty ladies who'd be only too happy to keep you company there." She continued talking before Ray had the opportunity to react. "You'd think they'd have chosen somewhere a little less public, wouldn't you? I have to concede, though, that that evening there wasn't as large a crowd there as usual—the weather was abysmal. But still . . ." She rolled her eyes. "At any rate, it was a very rash, very *stupid* thing for them to do, particularly on Rob's part. Gwen, at least, was single then—this was before she acquired husband number three. At any rate, Rob evidently realized he'd been a twenty-four-karat-gold jerk, because the instant he and his sweetie came up for air, he began to look around the room. Obviously, he was hoping not to spot anyone there who might recognize him."

"Did Mr. Harwood see you?" Ray asked.

"No. That disgusting demonstration occurred when we were about to be shown to our table. And before Rob turned in our direction, I grabbed Ted's arm, and we ducked out—fast."

"Uh, this other lady you mentioned, ma'am . . . ?"

"Her name's Megan Riley. She's the wife of a friend and business associate of Rob's. And incidentally, the husband does his share of bed-hopping, too. You'll probably be interested to know that this devoted couple was at the party Friday night. Of course, Megan and Rob's little fling was over ages ago. But, hey, it's quite likely that she wasn't the only one of Rob's bimbos who was at his birthday celebration." Then, her eyes flashing, Catherine fumed, "And stop calling me ma'am, dammit! You make me feel a hundred years old."

Ray colored. "Sorry. I was brought up down South," he lied. "How did you learn about Ms. Riley?"

"The three of us—Megan, Tess, and I—shared the same cleaning lady then; this goes back a little over two years. At any rate, one Saturday morning Francesca—that's the cleaning lady—arrived at the Rileys' apartment somewhat earlier than usual, and she walked in on that slut Megan under the sheets with guess who. Rob made Francesca swear she wouldn't tattle to my sister, who was out of town for the weekend—the two of us were visiting our mother in the hospital. I have no idea where the hell Walt Riley was at the time. Anyway, when she came here a couple of days later, Francesca could hardly wait to let me know what she'd seen.

"Naturally, I, too, made her swear she wouldn't blab to Tess. But listen to this: She was actually insulted that I'd even consider her *capable* of doing something so terrible! She also said she'd already promised 'the mister' that she wouldn't tell his wife. I had a strong feeling that Rob must have bribed her to keep quiet, so I asked how much that promise of hers had cost him. At first, Francesca denied there was any money involved, but she finally admitted that he'd given her two hundred dollars. Apparently," Catherine added, her voice dripping with sarcasm, "the woman regarded that two hundred as only buying her silence when it came to Tess."

"Did you ever confront your brother-in-law with his infidelity?" Ray asked.

"Not on your life! It would just have led to a blowup between the two of us, and I felt that, sooner or later, it would result in Tess's learning what I was so anxious to keep her from learning."

"This Francesca, how can we reach her?"

"Beats me. She no longer works for me—or for Tess, either. She's originally from Honduras, and a few months after she walked in on Rob and Megan, she went there to visit her family, ostensibly for a couple of weeks. She wound up staying three months. By the time she came back, I'd found someone else, and so had Tess."

"Do you still have her address?"

"I never did have it. She'd given me her telephone number, though, and I wrote it down in my address book. But the book filled up last year, and I bought a new one. By then, there was no reason to include Francesca's number."

"What's her last name?"

Catherine shrugged. "Who remembers? The only thing I recall is that it was Hispanic." But two or three seconds afterward: "Wait! It's Garcia." Then directly on the heels of this: "It might have been Lopez, though." She shrugged. "Well, one or the other . . . at least, I think so."

"Evidently, you don't believe your sister was aware of her husband's infidelity," Gabe commented.

"If she was, she never said anything to me about it—and I'm family. So I'm pretty positive she was in the dark when it came to lover boy's extracurricular activities."

"You and your sister are close, then?"

"Well, I don't know if 'close' is the right word. I love Tess, Sergeant Wilson, and I have no doubt that she loves me. But we're very different. Maybe because we had different fathers. Anyhow, Tess is a lot more reserved than I am—in case you haven't been able to tell." Then, smiling coquettishly, she turned to Ray. "Well, have you had enough of me yet?"

Ray blushed and seemed temporarily at a loss for words, so Gabe stepped in. "You've been very helpful, Mrs. Feller. We appreciate your time."

"Thanks," the younger detective murmured to his partner after Catherine had made her exit.

"It was nothing," Gabe told him, grinning. "You can do the same for me sometime."

Anne Harwood was a very pretty girl, a younger, slightly taller, and—presently, at any rate—a much more cheerful version of her mother.

She was dressed in tight jeans and a loose, light blue man-tailored shirt. Her long auburn hair, her most striking feature, was pulled back and tied with a ribbon. She looked to be in her late teens and was, in fact, nineteen years old.

"I guess this is the hot seat," she joked, plunking her bottom down on the sofa.

Both men smiled politely. "I'm Sergeant Wilson, and this is my partner, Detective Carson," Gabe said.

"Hi," the girl responded amiably. "I'm Anne."

"Uh, we're very sorry for your loss, Anne."

"That's okay. It's not as if Rob were actually my father, you know," she volunteered. "He adopted me when I was three years old, the year after he married my mom."

"I see. I gather the two of you didn't have a particularly loving relationship."

"No, I guess not."

"Any special reason?"

"Nope. We never really bonded, that's all."

"How did your mother feel about that?"

"Well, my mother would have preferred our having a real father-daughter kind of bond. But it wasn't as if I hated Rob or anything," Anne stated firmly—perhaps a shade too firmly, Gabe thought. He noted, too, that her cheeks were slightly flushed now. "He didn't hate me, either," she added hastily. "Like I told you, we just never really bonded."

"And your biological father?"

Anne shrugged. "I've never met the man."

"Do you live at home, Anne?"

"Yeah, but most of the time I'm away at school—Yale School of Drama. And this year, when the semester was over, I went up to the Poconos to do some summer stock."

"But you came in for the party."

"Well, it would have been pretty crappy of me if I didn't show. Plus, my mom would have gone ballistic." There was a pause before she put to him, "Look, you keep asking me questions. Is it okay if I ask *you* something now?"

Gabe suppressed a grin. *Like mother, like daughter,* he said to himself. And to Anne: "What would you like to know?"

"My mom told me Rob may have been poisoned, but that you can't be sure until the autopsy's completed. What do you *think,* though?"

"I think it's a possibility," Gabe answered with a straight face.

"Very funny." But she said it good-naturedly. She looked at Ray then, and her voice grew softer, more intimate somehow. "What do *you* think, Sergeant Carson? And I hope you'll be more up-front with me than your partner was."

"I honestly have no idea. And incidentally, it isn't *Sergeant* Carson; it's Detective Carson. But thanks for the promotion."

"Oh, I'm sorry."

"So am I," Ray told her, smiling.

After this, the conversation centered around the surprise party. But Anne was unable—or perhaps unwilling?—to provide any meaningful information.

Gabe concluded it was time to call it quits. So he stood up and thanked the girl for her time.

"No problem. Listen, let me give you a number where I can be reached—just in case." She rattled off the number, and Gabe obediently jotted it down in his notebook. "Call me if you think of anything else you want to ask me," she said. But she was looking at Ray when she said it.

"You made quite a hit with the ladies today, partner," Gabe teased when he and Ray were in the elevator on their way downstairs.

The younger man's face turned bright red.

Gabe tilted his head. "What do you call that hair color of yours?" he asked.

"My hair color? It's brown. Why?"

"I'm seriously considering dyeing mine that same shade."

Chapter 12

Belle's clue popped into my head again while I was in the taxi on my way to work on Thursday. (I always take taxis when I'm late—and when aren't I late?) But her words were no clearer to me this morning than they'd been on Tuesday when she'd said them. *Think the way the French do?* I mean, exactly how did the thought processes of the French differ from those of us inhabiting the rest of the planet?

I continued to ponder this question, when suddenly the cab, having taken a corner on two wheels, slammed into a garbage truck. I was thrown forward and hit the partition, winding up with what would soon turn out to be a decent-size bump on my forehead. Both drivers immediately opened their windows and began screaming some choice expletives at each other. I tried to get out of the car, but Hector—the cabbie—had locked the back door. Before he'd open it and allow me to leave, I had to swear that I didn't plan to sue.

I'd no sooner walked away than Hector switched the target of his anger to my retreating back. Apparently, it had just occurred to him that I hadn't paid my fare (fat chance of my doing that!), and he was determined to collect—my lumpy forehead notwithstanding. I picked up the pace now, putting as much distance between us as my normally sedentary body would allow. I could still hear him carrying on when I was half a block away, and I stopped long enough for a quick glance over my shoulder. He was out of the taxi now, shaking his fist at me, while the driver of the garbage truck—who was maybe a foot taller than Hector—stood over him, poking a finger in his chest. Which, no doubt, was what prevented Hector from taking off after me to extract that fare.

Anyway, I now had to hike eight blocks to get to the office—two of them excruciatingly long ones. And for someone who's as allergic to exercise as I am, this was practically corporal punishment—especially when you factor in that the temperature had already climbed to seventy-nine degrees while I was still in the apartment. *Plus,* I had on a pair of never-before-worn high-heeled, faux-crocodile sandals that proved to be much too tight a fit.

The instant Jackie saw me, she aborted her conversation with Derwin. (At least, I assume it was with Derwin—her elderly, tightfisted beau—because she'd been making these adolescent little kissing sounds before she spotted me.)

"What happened to *you*? You look like you're about ready to keel over."

"There's a fifty-fifty chance I'll survive." I flashed her a reassuring smile. "I was in an accident. That is, the cab I was in had the accident—with one of those big garbage trucks, no less. I got this"—I touched the appropriate spot on my forehead—"when my head hit the partition."

"You'd better wash off that bump. Wait. I think I have some antiseptic in my desk somewhere." She pulled open a drawer and began rummaging through its contents.

"Why would I need an antiseptic? The skin isn't broken. I checked the mirror in the lobby."

"Because," was Jackie's response. (Now, I dare anyone to dispute logic like that.) "I was really getting worried," she informed me without raising her eyes from the drawer. "I tried your apartment a little while ago, but I got your answering machine." Then, almost in the same breath: "Ahh, here it is. And I have some cotton, too. So go clean the wound."

"It's not a wound, Jackie; it's a little bump, for crying out loud!"

Ignoring the protest, she handed me a bottle of witch hazel and some cotton balls, which I reluctantly accepted. It was easier than arguing—and losing.

"Thanks, Jackie."

"And what's with the limp?" she called out as I started to leave.

I turned and stuck out one of my legs, so Jackie could have a good look at what was adorning my feet.

"Those are stunning!" she said of the cause of my pain.

"Yeah, and they hurt like hell," I grumbled. "I bought them on sale at Bloomingdale's a couple of months ago, and I *was* planning to wear them over the weekend. Only I'd never gotten around to breaking them in. As it turned out, though, today wasn't the ideal day to do it."

I headed for the ladies' room with every intention of dabbing my forehead with the witch hazel. Listen, since Jackie had gone to the trouble of searching for the stuff, I figured I owed it to her. (Which, come to think of it, doesn't make a lot of sense.) At any rate, I'd just unscrewed the bottle cap when I noticed the expiration date: December 1999. I screwed the cap back on.

The first thing I did when I sat down in my cubbyhole was to kick off my killer shoes and slip on the emergency pair I keep in the bottom drawer of my desk. They'd been an impulse purchase years ago, and I'd never liked them very much. But at that moment, I adored them. While it's true they were old and torn and ugly, they didn't pinch—not even a little bit.

I wasn't up to reading the manuscript; I'd been challenged enough for one morning. So I did what I often do when I should be attending to something I prefer to postpone: I polished my nails. I was about to apply a second coat when Ellen called.

"I have to talk to you, Aunt Dez," she said flatly, sounding very un-Ellen-like. I mean, there was no cheerful little "Hi." No chirpy "How are you?"

"What's wrong, Ellen?"

"You know how my mother kept bugging me to get pregnant?"

"Sure," I answered cautiously. I was half expecting a big announcement.

"And you suggested that if I told her we were trying, it might get her off my back for a while?"

Nope. There wasn't going to be any big announcement. "I remember that, too." Margot—mother of this darling niece of mine; sister of my beloved deceased husband, Ed; and an individual I truly, and without apology, absolutely despise—began nagging Ellen about having a baby when she and Mike had been married for less than three months! And I'd hoped that this little fib I was recommending would prompt the woman to turn off the pressure for a while. Apparently, it hadn't worked—at least, not for long.

"We *want* children, Aunt Dez," Ellen declared (as she had many times before), "only we're not ready yet to take on the responsibilities of a family."

"I realize that," I assured her. "Besides, the decision about when and even *whether* to have children is yours and Mike's. Period."

"Evidently, my mom doesn't agree. I just had a long conversation with her, and listen to this: Now she's after me to convince Mike to have his sperm tested."

The idea was so outrageous that it took a second or two to process the words. "She's after you to do *what*?" I blurted out. "You're kidding, right?"

"I wish."

"She didn't urge you to get tested, too?"

"*My* mother? It would never occur to her that I could be the one with the problem, not in light of the wonderful genes I inherited. Hey, I'm Margot Kravitz's daughter, aren't I?"

"What did you tell her?"

"That I was late for a meeting and had to get off the phone. I promised I'd talk to her tonight. I have no idea how to handle this, though. For some reason, she's obsessed with the idea of becoming a grandmother again.

I guess it's because Steve and Joan haven't presented her with a new grandchild in years," she speculated. (Steve and Joan are Ellen's brother and sister-in-law, and all three of their children are practically grown now.)

"Maybe. But it's more likely that what she wants is to be a grandmother to a child of *yours*—specifically. You know how much she loves you, Ellen." Now, this wasn't intended as a defense of Margot—not directly, that is. I'd presented this rationale in the hope that it might lead Ellen to regard her mother with a little less hostility, since she did happen to love the woman.

"Oh, I don't know . . . that could be, I suppose. But anyhow, Aunt Dez, what can I possibly tell her? What she's asking—*demanding*, practically—is way out of bounds! Still, the thing is, I don't want to alienate her. She *is* my mom."

"I'm the last person you should be coming to for advice. That's what got you into this pickle in the first place."

"Don't be silly. She was already on my case before I took your suggestion. In fact, it even bought Mike and me some time."

"Speaking of Mike, he's the one you should be discussing this with."

"I agree. And I've been trying to contact him. I left a message, and I'm sure he'll get back to me later. Believe me, there's no way I'll speak to my mother before I've gone over everything with Mike. But I could really use your input."

I wasn't off the hook yet, it seemed. I considered equivocating, but in the end, I said what I thought. "I may be wrong, but I don't believe you have much of an option."

"Meaning?"

"Meaning that if you want her to butt out of what is a very private matter, I can't see how—short of pointing out that this is none of her business—you can avoid telling her the truth: that the two of you simply aren't prepared to start a family yet."

"But I've already been through that with her," Ellen protested. "She refuses to accept it."

"Well, you'll just have to be more firm—*very* firm. At the same time, you might want to let her know how much you hate to disappoint her. But look, when you talk this over with Mike, he may come up with a better solution."

"I doubt it. Anyhow, thanks, Aunt Dez."

"Call me later and let me know how you made out, okay? And good luck."

Ellen managed a faint little chuckle. "I've got a feeling I'll need it."

After finally applying that second coat of nail polish, I decided to have lunch in the office. It was much too hot to venture outside this afternoon. Besides, if I went out to eat, there was the problem of how to get around. Should I attempt to squeeze back into those lovely faux-crocodile sandals? They were killers. How about this pair of "emergency only" shoes I was wearing? Well, as beautiful as they'd suddenly become in my eyes, I had no illusions about how others would see them. So I ordered a BLT (without the L) and a black-and-white soda and ate at my desk.

At two thirty or so, almost the instant I'd finished the last bite of my sandwich, the phone rang. It was Pat Sullivan, one-half of that pair of absolute sweethearts who rent me my office space.

"Would you have the time to handle an investigation for a client of mine, Desiree?" he asked.

Would I have the time? "Sure, Pat. What's it about?"

"She's discovered that her recently acquired, very expensive, *and* not yet insured diamond bracelet is missing—almost certainly stolen. Will you be around in about an hour?"

"I'll be here."

"Good. I have an errand to run first, but I'll pop in then and fill you in on the details."

Forty minutes later, Pat called again. "I just got back, and there was a message for me," he said sheepishly. "It seems my client's twenty-three-year-old daughter stopped by the house the other evening when Julia—my client—

wasn't home. The daughter saw the bracelet and borrowed it. She left a note, but Julia didn't come across it until about ten minutes ago.

"I'm terribly sorry about this, Dez. Julia was willing to pay quite a nice fee for your services, too."

"No problem; these things happen. Thanks anyway, Pat."

All in all, it had been a pretty crummy day. So while gathering my stuff together for an early departure, I attempted to cheer myself up a little.

The cab accident wasn't that big a deal. I mean, it wasn't as if I'd actually been injured or anything. As for the beating my poor feet took traipsing to the office in those sandals, they'd feel better once I soaked them in hot water, right? (I'm talking about soaking the feet, not the sandals.) Besides, I supposed all that walking wasn't exactly a *bad* thing. I was still steaming over my overbearing sister-in-law's ludicrous suggestion (read "demand"). But Ellen would be setting her straight tonight—I hoped. And so what if the case Pat had had in mind for me evaporated? There'd be other cases—sooner or later, anyhow.

Listen, I told myself, *maybe it's true that this wasn't the best day you've ever had. But there are bound to be worse ones.*

Which somehow wasn't as uplifting a thought as I'd intended it to be.

Chapter 13

By the time I got home, I was feeling really guilty about not having so much as removed the manuscript from my attaché case all day. I mean, it wasn't as if I had a bunch of other cases to occupy my time. (Or, for that matter, even *one* other case.) So I ate an early supper—a really quick one—and took an even quicker shower (instead of the nice, relaxing bubble bath I figured I was entitled to that evening). After which I decided I'd get down to business.

I turned to the fourth chapter of part two, but it was a while before I looked down at the book. I was thinking about Ellen. I was very concerned about how Margot would react to her dutiful daughter's asserting herself like this. Well, I'd find out soon enough. Still, I had my fingers crossed when I began to read. . . .

"Well? Who wasted our Romeo?" a grinning Gabe put to his partner.

"Hey, a guy with all your years of experience on the force? I've been waiting for *you* to tell *me.*"

The two men were in a local fast-food restaurant, seated at a small table. Neither had eaten since early morning, and at the moment, they were alleviating their hunger pangs via plates piled high with Southern-fried chicken and mashed potatoes drowning in gravy. Before long, they would be visiting one of the remaining nine people on their still-daunting list of suspects.

"Wouldn't it be nice if all of these folks we have yet to talk to lived at the same address?" Ray murmured, stifling a yawn.

Gabe chuckled. "Dream on, Ray, dream on. There were mostly couples at the party, though, so it's not as bad as it could be. Also, the majority of them live right here in town. That's another plus."

"Why? I don't know about you, partner, but I wouldn't mind one bit if we had to interrogate someone in . . . say, Hawaii."

"Like I said, Ray, dream on."

A short while later, the pair stopped at a Baskin-Robbins for sugar cones—and, once again, revealed their similar tastes in food, rocky road being the flavor of choice for both. Gabe stopped licking his cone only long enough to offer a rationalization for the indulgence. "Gives my energy level a little boost," he pronounced. Mainly for his own benefit.

Within fifteen minutes, the officers were seated in the living room of the most elegant home either of them had ever visited. The uniformed maid who'd admitted them to the town house had just advised that, "Mrs. Clarke will be with you shortly," before making her exit.

"Wow!" Ray exclaimed—but softly—as he appraised his surroundings. Gabe nodded in agreement. The deep cream-colored carpeting was thick and luxurious. The furnishings—most of them almost certainly antiques—were all silks, velvets, and rich, burnished woods. And decorating the light cream walls was an eclectic display of handsomely framed artwork that extended more than halfway up to the high, vaulted ceiling. Staring at this extensive and obviously very costly collection, Ray commented in a hushed voice, "I feel like I'm in a museum, for Christ's sake."

After a quarter of an hour's wait, Gabe glanced at his watch. " 'Shortly' seems to be open to interpretation," he groused. As if on cue, the two men got to their feet then and headed for the paintings. Not that either of them could, by even the most elastic of imaginations, be considered an art lover. It was simply something to do. They didn't have to do it for long, however, because in less than two minutes, Elaine Clarke put in an appearance.

And what an appearance!

She stood in the doorway, posing, her right arm above her head, resting on the door frame. Medium height and almost pathetically thin, the woman—who might have been anywhere from age sixty upward—was heavily made up, with a foundation that was far too dark for her pale skin, two red circles decorating her cheeks, and bright green eye shadow. Her thick, orangey-red lipstick extended slightly beyond her lips—and was a near perfect match to the orangey-red hair that fell to her shoulders. Most jolting of all, however, was her silk, ankle-length, yellow print cheongsam, its side slit extending almost to the top of her thigh!

Both men hurried toward her, and she held out her hand to the first to reach her, fluttering her lashes at him. Gabe shook the hand politely. When she frowned, then turned abruptly to Ray, Gabe suspected that he hadn't reacted as he'd been expected to. And in seconds, there was no doubt in his mind that he'd committed a grievous faux pas. Elaine had just offered that same hand to Ray, who, it seemed, was savvy enough to press it to his lips. She smiled warmly at the young detective before declaring, "Well, gentlemen, let's not just stand here; let's get comfortable." So saying, she sashayed over to a dark green velvet settee, and after carefully smoothing the cheongsam, sank down into the cushion with a remarkably fluid motion, her long, still-admirable legs stretched out to the side, her right arm across the back of the settee.

Once settled, Elaine motioned the police officers to the green and white striped silk armchairs opposite the settee. "Would you care for anything to drink before you begin giving me the third degree?" She tittered at her own use of the term. "A little vino, perhaps?"

"Uh, thank you, Mrs. Clarke, but we're fine," Gabe answered.

"That's right; you can't indulge while you're on duty. Well, then, you might as well start your questions."

There was, however, no time to comply. "Tess tells me you suspect that Robbie may have been poisoned," she pronounced.

"We don't actually *suspect* poison; we're counting on the autopsy to provide us with the cause of death. But in the meantime, we can't afford to overlook any possibility," Gabe explained.

"I see. And you're about to ask if I saw anyone drop a little something into Robbie's champagne flute when no one was looking, correct?" Obviously, this, too, didn't call for a reply, because the woman continued without pausing for breath. "Or if I noticed anyone entering or leaving the dining room before dinner was served—although you don't consider it likely that this is where the poison was dispensed. You get two nos, I'm afraid."

Gabe grinned. "Mrs. Harwood also mentioned we'd be asking you about those things, I take it."

"No. Anne did."

The grin broadened. "Well, I wasn't that far off. But tell me this: How well did you know Mr. Harwood?"

"Quite well. We were first cousins, and our parents were very close."

"You and he were close, too?"

"I suppose we were, in a way—although there *was* friction between us at times, even while we were growing up. Or perhaps I should say, *especially* while we were growing up."

"Why was that?"

"I babysat Robbie when we were young—I'm a few years older than he is." She bit her lip now and shook her head sadly. "I mean, than he *was*. And I admit to having been somewhat bossy in those days. Most likely, I still am. I'd tease him, too. I used to call him Pudgy-wudgy—he was *such* a tubby little boy—and he'd put his hands over his ears. Once, he actually punched me! Also, in light of his having been christened Robin, I gave him the nickname Little Robin Redbreast, as well. He wasn't terribly pleased with that one, either. 'I'm not some crappy bird!' he'd scream at me.

"Then, as adults, he resented me for sticking my two

cents' worth into his personal life. Can't say I blame
him, either. I didn't approve of his getting involved with
Tess, and I said so. You see, throughout his life—and,
frankly, for reasons that have always eluded me—Robbie
was a great success with the ladies. And I couldn't understand why, when he finally decided to settle down,
it would be with the unwed mother of a small child. I
hate to admit it, but I was wrong there." A second or
two elapsed before she added with a wink, "Of course,
this was the one and only time."

"I take it that at some point you revised your
opinion."

"Definitely. Tess turned out to be a wonderful wife
to Robbie."

"What about more recently, ma'am?" Ray interjected.
"Had you and Mr. Harwood been on good terms?"

"Reasonably good, I suppose. But the fact is, he was
a philanderer. And, to be very frank, I don't approve of
married men who can't keep it in their pants." Each of
the detectives noted a look of surprise on the other's
face now. Evidently, Elaine saw it, too. "Sorry to have
shocked you, gentlemen, but I believe in telling it like
it is."

"No, no," Ray said hurriedly. "We weren't—"

Elaine put up her hand. "Listen, I've *been* where Tess
was. My second husband, Mr. Byrd, played me dirty.
Only I didn't take it lying down." She chuckled. "No pun
intended. At any rate, I became suspicious when he
began coming home from work at all hours. And as
soon as I learned it was his secretary that louse was
working on, it was 'Bye-bye, Byrdie.' His little affair cost
him, too—big-time." She waved an arm around the
room. "I was able to acquire many of my most prized
possessions because Harvey Byrd ended up being such
a generous fellow—under duress, of course."

Ray thought he should say *something* to this. "Well,
things seem to have turned out pretty nicely."

Elaine nodded. "With the exception of Mr. Byrd, I've
been quite fortunate in the romance department. I've
attracted some wonderful gentlemen, all of whom also

happened to be comfortably fixed. I believe I can attribute at least part of my good fortune to having been in the theater. Men seem to find that something of an aphrodisiac." And with more than a touch of pride: "I was even on Broadway once—in *Sweet Charity.*"

In the theatre, huh? Gabe said to himself. *That explains this getup of hers.* "So you were an actress."

"Well, no, I was a dancer. But that has pretty much the same effect on the opposite sex," she answered, sounding slightly defensive. "At any rate, what I started to say before was that having been betrayed by someone I'd put my trust in, I had great sympathy for Tess."

"Do you think she knew that her husband was seeing other women?"

Elaine Clarke's response was postponed by the ringing of my telephone.

As soon as I picked up, Ellen—dispensing with any unnecessary preamble—updated me on her current crisis. "I spoke to Mike, and it was unanimous: he had the same advice you did, Aunt Dez. Right after that, I talked to my mom and finally leveled with her. Well, as you can imagine, she was positively livid. First, because I admitted that Mike and I still weren't ready for any little Lyntons, and then because I'd lied to her about trying to become pregnant. Anyhow, she hung up on me."

"I am *so* sorry, Ellen. I was hoping—"

"Wait. It *does* get better. About half an hour later, when I'd more or less pulled myself together and was about to call you, she phoned and apologized. She actually conceded that she had no right to dictate when my husband and I should have a baby—can you *believe* it? And then she pretty much confirmed what you suspected was the primary reason she'd been that anxious for me to conceive. She insisted that the problem was, since she loves me so much, she just couldn't wait to be a grandmother to a child of mine. I could hear my dad in the background then, and that's when she tagged on—kind of sheepishly, too—'Still, I was wrong. You and Mike have to do what's right for the two of you.' I almost passed out on the spot."

"I'm very, very happy things worked out."

"Me, too. But you know something? I'd bet a million dollars that it was my dad who got her to apologize and *then* say she'd leave it up to Mike and me to decide when to have children."

"That sounds like your dad," I agreed. I refrained from adding that it sure as hell didn't sound like her mother!

Seconds later, I put down the receiver and almost simultaneously picked up the manuscript again, reminding myself that Elaine had just been asked whether she thought Tess knew about her husband's infidelity.

"I can't be certain, of course, but it's my opinion that she did—at least, on some level. Robbie was hardly the epitome of discretion. Nevertheless, there are women—and Tess may very well be one of them—who choose to close their eyes to their husband's shenanigans. Acknowledging the truth—even to themselves—might compel them to take some sort of action, you see. Which could result in not only destroying the marriage but, conceivably, their entire way of life."

Gabe nodded, impressed with the analysis. "You and Mrs. Harwood never actually discussed this matter, then."

"No, we did not. My feeling is that Tess was in denial when it came to Robbie's extracurricular activities."

"How did you find out about his other women, ma'am?" Ray asked.

"Actually, there had been rumors to that effect for ages. Only I refused to give them any credence. But eleven years ago, I took a two-month trip to the Orient. And before I left, Robbie asked for the keys to my apartment, so that he could 'stop in every so often and check on things.' Or so he *claimed*. I just stood there, staring at him. 'Thoughtful' was simply not a word you associated with Robbie. Well, at least he was embarrassed enough to blush. 'I know why you want those keys,' I finally told him, 'and I have no intention of giving them to you.' "

"Just one more question. Did your cousin have any enemies that you're aware of?"

"None I'm actually *aware* of. But it would have been a miracle if his bedroom antics hadn't earned him the wrath of at least one angry husband, not to mention their impact on a jilted lover or two."

The officers were ready to leave now. Elaine remained seated, so they approached the settee and thanked her for her help.

And this time, when she extended her hand to Gabe, he knew exactly what to do.

Chapter 14

The best thing about today's being Friday was that the very next day would be Saturday. And this particular Saturday couldn't get here fast enough—from where I sat, anyhow.

In spite of the fact that we live in the same building, I hadn't seen Nick for two weeks. One of the reasons is that he's a devoted father, who often spends evenings with his diabolical little offspring. Also, although it wasn't something we'd ever discussed, there seemed to be a kind of tacit agreement that we wouldn't just drop in on each other. Which does have its pluses. I mean, in spite of missing the man like crazy, I'd have hated to answer the bell one day when my face was slathered with gook and my glorious hennaed hair was all decked out in rollers—to find Nick on the other side of the door.

Anyhow, soon after I got to the office that morning, I buried my nose in Belle's manuscript. I'd barely scratched the surface of part two, by far the longest section in the book. And since I had something even more exciting to do this weekend than attempt to decipher the clue to a $24,940 mystery, I was hoping to make up for my projected absence with a concerted effort now.

You'll just have to stop daydreaming about Nick and stay focused, I instructed myself. And guess what? My powers of concentration proved to be a revelation.

I opened to chapter five:

Promptly at eight a.m. on Monday, Ray picked up Gabe in front of his building. Before paying a visit to numbers five and six on their list—who weren't expecting them until nine—they stopped at a local coffee shop for breakfast. Neither man was in a particularly good mood.

"You know," Ray grumbled, "I can see us investigating Rob Harwood's death till hell freezes over. And who knows if we'll ever get anywhere?"

But while Gabe privately shared these sentiments to some degree, he tried to be encouraging. "You know, right from the onset, I had this strong sense that if we were going to solve this one—which I believe is something we're both committed to doing—it wouldn't happen just like that." He illustrated the words with a snap of his fingers. "I'm sure you weren't counting on any instant revelation, either." Then, without pausing for confirmation: "I fully expect that we're going to have to do a lot of digging in order to get at the truth here."

Ray nodded. "Don't mind me," he said. "I'm a little hungover this morning. Hey," he added a couple of seconds later, "want me to tell you what would really be a kick in the head? If, after we knock ourselves out for two, three, maybe even four weeks, the autopsy reveals that Harwood died of natural causes."

"It would be a kick, all right," Gabe muttered. "Only not in the head."

Simon Cooper was Tess's first cousin. A tall, good-looking man with dark, wavy hair and almost coal black eyes, Simon and his wife, Helen—who also had dark hair and eyes, along with a creamy olive complexion—were a striking pair. Also present on the terrace of the Coopers' very pleasant apartment that morning was their daughter, April, a gawky fourteen-year-old with braces on her teeth, zits on her face, and watery blue eyes. (Yes, blue. But while it was certainly *possible* the color was the result of recessive genes, the officers would later agree that it was more likely the teenager had been adopted and that she was actually the progeny of two extremely annoying and unattractive people.)

In view of the nature of their visit, both Gabe and

Ray were uncomfortable with having the girl there. But April had vigorously rejected her father's dictate that she excuse herself, and Simon had finally given in. "You can only stay as long as you behave yourself, though," he'd warned her.

The detectives had been persuaded to join the couple in their morning coffee, which featured the added bonus of some tiny but really tasty Danish pastries.

Helen had just broached the subject of that fateful Friday evening. "Do you really believe that Rob was poisoned?" she'd asked. Then, responding to the question Gabe was about to pose: "Catherine told us you appeared to be leaning in that direction."

"I wouldn't exactly say 'leaning,'" Gabe contradicted, "but poison *is* a possibility." He turned to Simon. "I understand you and Mrs. Harwood are cousins."

"That's right."

"And, apparently, you were close to *Mr.* Harwood, as well. Unless I'm mistaken, you gave the toast at the birthday dinner."

"You're not mistaken. I liked Rob very much. We used to play tennis together, and occasionally we'd go to dinner—Helen and I—with Rob and Tess. He was very good company—Rob had a terrific sense of humor. We used to laugh a lot, the four of us. He had a really great laugh."

"So does a hyena," April quipped.

"April," Simon cautioned, "you promised you'd sit there quietly if we permitted you to remain. Keep this up, and you're headed for your room."

"What did I say, anyhow?" the girl mumbled petulantly. Noting her father's expression, however, she quickly added, "Okay, okay, I'll shut up."

Well, as long as the kid's here . . . "It doesn't sound as if you liked Mr. Harwood very much," Gabe put to her.

"That's because I didn't. He came over the night of my birthday last year. And do you know what he gave me for a present?" April challenged.

"Uh, no, I don't."

"Nothing, that's what. A big, fat zero!"

Helen shook her head in exasperation, and Simon, with an obvious attempt at controlling his temper, said quietly, "I've told you a dozen times, April, that Rob had no idea it was your birthday." He turned to the detectives. "On his way home from work that evening, Rob stopped in to return a book he'd borrowed from me. He was here for all of about three minutes; he wouldn't even stay for a drink."

Gabe looked at to his partner and nodded. It was a cue for Ray to take up the questioning. "And you, ma'am?" the younger man inquired. "Were you also good friends with the deceased?"

"I liked him well enough, but to be honest, I never felt completely at ease with him."

"Why was that?"

"Rob was . . ." She glanced at her daughter and hesitated for a second or two before continuing. "He was, well . . . he was a little too touchy-feely for my taste."

"Touchy-feely?" Ray echoed.

For a moment, a small smile turned up the corners of Helen's mouth. "That's right. Whenever we were standing and talking—even if there were other people present—he'd casually drape an arm across my shoulders or put his hand on my back. Once, he even *rubbed* my back! Listen, I'm not claiming any of this was actually out-of-bounds; nevertheless, I didn't appreciate his actions. Sy always maintained that these were innocent gestures, and that might have been true. Only . . ." Her voice trailed off.

"I kept telling Helen that Rob wasn't being a letch, not with her," Simon insisted. "Our friendship—Rob's and mine—precluded anything like that. The fact is, he was by nature a warm, outgoing person. But Helen never quite accepted this."

Gabe hesitated. He was feeling particularly uneasy about posing his next question to the couple in the presence of the fourteen-year-old April when the teenager piped up with, "Warm and outgoing my ass"—a pause here—"-pirin," she added with a smirk. "The guy was a shit." And before either parent could demand she absent herself, she put in hastily, "Okay, okay, I'm going," and bolted from the room.

"Are you aware that the deceased had a reputation as a playboy?" Gabe brought up at this point.

Helen was the first to answer. "We were fairly certain he was cheating on Tess, although we didn't actually *know* it. But this was another reason I was so uncomfortable when he'd touch me like that."

"That still doesn't mean he was making a pass at you," Simon countered. "I just can't see Rob attempting to seduce my wife."

"It sounds as if you were closer to the deceased than you were to his widow—your cousin," Gabe observed.

"I imagine in a way that's true. But this doesn't mean I'm not fond of Tess, as well. Listen, it's as Helen said. We don't really *know* that he was cheating on her."

"Do you think Mrs. Harwood suspected that her husband was unfaithful?" Gabe asked.

"Not as far as I could tell," Helen offered.

"And you, Mr. Cooper?"

Simon shrugged. "All I can say is that I hope not. Tess deserves to have some happy memories, at least."

"Amen," his wife murmured.

"Can you think of anyone who might have wanted Mr. Harwood dead?"

"No, I honestly can't," Simon responded, as Helen simultaneously shook her head.

"Uh, just one or two more questions, I promise. Shortly after he arrived at his home that evening, Mr. Harwood went upstairs to change his clothes. The—"

Before Gabe could finish the preamble, Simon volunteered, "Neither of us saw anyone drop something into Rob's champagne glass in his absence, I assure you."

"I suppose it was Catherine who enlightened you with regard to the champagne glass, too." Gabe couldn't quite suppress a smile.

"You're right," Simon verified. "She also told us you'd be asking if we noticed any of the guests enter or leave the dining room before dinner. And I'm sorry to say we can't help you there, either."

"I'm sorry, too," Helen said earnestly. "I wish we could have been of some assistance."

A few minutes later, the detectives left the apartment.

When they reached the elevator bank they spotted a large piece of paper Scotch taped to the wall. Printed on the paper in huge block letters was a brief message. It read: "Rob Harwood was a shit!!!!" (The "was" had been underlined six times.)

Gabe's grin seemed to spread all the way across his face. "It isn't signed, but I think I may have an inkling as to who wrote this anyway."

"I guess," Ray deadpanned, "that's why you're the one who made sergeant."

I put away the manuscript at this point, but within minutes I took it out again and skimmed over it. Then, for quite some time, I sat at my desk, thinking.

Could Rob's killer be one of the Coopers? It wouldn't be too difficult to make a case for them both.

Take Helen. Suppose her objections to the deceased were a cover, and she'd actually been having a little fling with the man. And now suppose that he'd dumped her for another woman. Well, maybe she expressed her displeasure with him by getting her hands on a little arsenic (or whatever).

How about Simon? I put to myself. Coming up with a motive here was a cinch. He learned that Rob, his cousin by marriage, as well as his good buddy, was having an affair with Helen. Not surprisingly, he wanted to put a stop to it, which he did. Permanently.

I speculated about the dead man's immediate family then. Let's assume that Rob *did* have a wandering eye (not to mention those other parts of his anatomy that also seemed to get around pretty well). And let's say that Tess was aware of her husband's cheating ways—which didn't appear to be much of a reach. Well, I could appreciate how she might have gotten so tired of her victim status that she elected to pass that designation along to her husband.

Anne? She made no bones about not being overly fond of her stepfather. But maybe she had a much better reason for feeling as she did about him than the one she gave the police. I mean, all she told them was that she and Rob had never bonded. But it wouldn't exactly shock me if dear old stepdad had been making a play for her—and she finally decided there was only one way to be certain he'd leave her alone.

Which brought me to Catherine. It wasn't inconceivable that her brother-in-law came on to her—or vice versa—and that the two of them wound up playing house together. It also wasn't inconceivable that, at some point, Catherine regretted betraying her sister, but Rob wouldn't allow her to call it quits yet. Or possibly the only thing she regretted was Rob's dumping her for someone new. Well, I just couldn't imagine Catherine's taking either of those possibilities with a grain of salt . . . can you?

And then there was Elaine. Actually, I never bothered to work out any kind of script for her. The truth is, if Rob's colorful cousin *did* turn out to be the killer, I'd probably have fainted dead away.

At a little after two I put an end to my ruminating. And it was about time! I mean, I'd almost certainly been racking my brain for nothing, since Belle had stressed that in order to solve the mystery, it would be necessary to think the way the French do. But despite being of French descent (my maiden name was Soulé), I wasn't French enough to have the vaguest idea what she was talking about. And anyway, I realized now that I was hungry.

I ordered in and had a sandwich and a Coke at my desk, following which I collected my belongings, stopped off to wish Jackie a good weekend (I'd have been toast if I hadn't), and then left for the hairdresser's.

Emaline has been doing my hair for I don't know how many years, and she never fails to brag that she has "golden hands." But you can always get an appointment with Emaline, even at the last minute—which should give you some idea of just how golden those hands of hers *aren't*. The thing is, though, this same availability is also a big plus. So is the fact that her shop is only a couple of blocks from my office. Add to this that I'm used to her. *And,* as I've tried to explain to Jackie at least a dozen times, with Emaline, my expectation level is so low that she rarely disappoints me.

At any rate, that day I walked out of there looking somewhat better than I had when I walked in. And certainly, I was a lot more presentable than I'd been on the afternoon of New Year's Eve, when—thanks to Emaline's handiwork—I wound up bearing a striking resemblance to a French poodle.

Chapter 15

Instead of going straight to the apartment, I stopped in at Jerome's, this coffee shop in my neighborhood that I visit whenever there's nothing very tempting in my freezer or if I'm too tired or lazy to prepare whatever *is* in there. That Friday, all of the above applied.

As soon as I was seated—and in a nice, big booth, too (Jerome's does get busy at times, but not too often)—I surveyed the room. Yep. There was Felix. He spotted me, and we waved to each other. Well, Felix's presence meant one thing: I'd be having a cheeseburger—whether I wanted to or not. Lucky for me, this was one day I *did* want to. But about Felix . . .

By now, he has to be pushing eighty from one side or the other, and he takes a great deal of pride in his memory. He never asks for my order; he just rattles off the choices I made the first night he ever served me, which seems like forever ago.

"Don't say nuthin', you hear?" he almost invariably instructs me. "You want the cheeseburger deluxe, only it should be well done. The fries, they gotta be well-done, also. And you'll have a Coca-Cola, but I shouldn't bring it before the burger comes out." Then he stands there and grins, waiting for confirmation. "So, am I right?" he says.

And I never have the heart to contradict him—even when I'm dying for the sliced-steak sandwich.

Now, though, I could sense there was something different about the man the moment he approached the booth. I was certain of it when he opened with a listless, "How are you today, Desiree?" followed by a disinterested,

"So? What can I get for you?" I damn near fainted! And before I could recover: "You would like to see a menu maybe?"

A menu? *This,* from Felix? "No, that's all right." And I proceeded to recite the order he'd been reciting to me ever since that first, long-past evening. He nodded in response and began to walk away. "Wait, Felix!" I called out.

He doubled back. "You changed your mind?"

"No, nothing like that. It's just that you don't seem like yourself. Is anything wrong?"

"*Everything* is wrong. But better I don't talk about it."

"All right. If I can help in any way, though, let me know, okay?"

He nodded. "Thank you, Desiree."

In about ten minutes, he returned with my food, and after setting down the platter and the drink, he turned to leave. Then he turned around again. "Uh, you said before something about . . . about helping?"

"That's right, I did. I meant it, too."

"Yes, well, I thank you. What I need is—and never in a million years could I have imagined something like this—but I got to get one of those private investigators. You wouldn't, by any chance, know of such an individual?"

Now, I'd more or less taken it for granted that after all this time Felix was aware of how I earned my living. But could be the subject had simply never come up. Either that, or he'd forgotten what I'd told him. Knowing Felix, however, my money was on the former. "*I'm* a private investigator, Felix."

The old man stared at me with more than a little skepticism. "No offense, Desiree, but you don't look like it."

"No offense taken, Felix, but this is what I am."

For the first time since I'd sat down here, I actually saw him smile. "Well, how do you like that! Listen, we could maybe talk in a little while?" He checked his watch. "Usually, when we're not too busy, I take a fifteen-, twenty-minute break at five thirty. And it looks to be pretty quiet so far. You wouldn't mind if"—he automatically glanced at his watch again—"if in one-half hour we go sit in the back of the kitchen, and I tell you my troubles?" He smiled again when he said this, but his eyes seemed to be pleading with me.

"I wouldn't mind at all."

Suddenly, Felix snatched up my plate. "Is cold already," he muttered, frowning.

"That's okay. I'm sure it'll be fine."

"Fine, it's not no more. Is like ice." Then he put his hand on my soda glass. "Warm like bathwater," he reported, appropriating the Coke now, too. "Three, four minutes, and I bring back everything like it should be." And with this, he hurried away.

Twenty minutes later, after I'd all but licked my refurbished platter clean, I glanced around the room, searching for Felix. I caught his eye and signaled to him as he was handing out menus to some people at a table in the rear. He hurried over. "You gotta leave now?" he asked, looking disheartened.

"Oh, no, I can stay," I assured him. "I just thought that as long as I'll be sitting here a while longer, I might as well have a cup of coffee and, um, something sweet. You wouldn't, by any chance, have any of that wonderful strawberry cheesecake today, would you?"

"No, today we got *cherry* cheesecake." He lowered his voice. "This is better than the strawberry. You take my word for it."

So I had the cherry cheesecake. And while I can't say that it was actually *better* than the strawberry, it did give those strawberries a run for their money.

I'd just consumed the last crumb of cheesecake when Felix called for me at my booth (sort of like a date) and ushered me into the kitchen. There were four people in the room, two of them presently standing at the stove, while a third was cutting vegetables, and the fourth was washing dishes.

We walked right by them, as Felix led the way to a small table in the rear.

"You'd like something to drink, maybe?" he asked, as

soon as we'd planted our derrieres on the two spindly chairs at the table.

"No, thanks, Felix. Right now, I'd like to hear about what has you so upset."

And I did. I mean, I'm sure the man didn't leave out even one tiny detail when he recounted all the things that had contributed to his suspicion that Shirley, his wife of fifty-three years, had been cheating on him.

It began, Felix told me, one afternoon about a month earlier. He was in the bedroom, getting dressed for work—he started at three—when the phone rang. Shirley, who was in the living room then, picked up. But she started speaking very softly, so softly that Felix's curiosity was piqued. And he went to the bedroom door to listen. He heard his wife say something like, "It was good seeing *you* last night, too." And then in a voice so low that it was a strain for him to make out the words, she murmured, "Thank you, Tony. I had a wonderful time, too."

A few minutes after Shirley hung up, Felix asked her "real casual-like" who she'd been talking to. She claimed it was her sister, Henrietta. "I ask you, Desiree," Felix challenged, 'Henrietta' sounds to you like 'Tony'?"

About two weeks went by, and then one evening Felix called Shirley from the restaurant to tell her they'd had an overflow crowd that night, and he'd be slightly delayed in getting home. "Almost always I walk in the door by fifteen, twenty minutes past eleven, so I didn't want she should worry," he explained just a little self-righteously. But Shirley didn't answer the phone, and Felix wound up talking to the answering machine. When he arrived at his apartment close to an hour later than usual, he told his wife that he'd tried reaching her. "Of course, she had an answer for this; my Shirley, she's got an answer for everything," the distraught man muttered. "She was in the shower, she said to me. But after a couple minutes, I went into the bathroom. Her towel was still folded up, like it just came off from the shelf in the closet. And when I felt it, that towel was dry like a bone."

It was close to three o'clock this same morning, and he was still trying to fall asleep, when Felix remembered that during that suspicious telephone conversation of Shirley's, which had taken place on a Thursday, he'd overheard her mention something about "last night." And now it was on a Wednesday that he hadn't been able to get in touch with her. So he suspected Shirley's rendezvous (my word, not his) were taking place on Wednesdays. And this being the case, he decided to leave work early the following Wednesday.

"At eight thirty I said to the boss that I wasn't feeling too good. He's a very nice man, Mr. Chapin, and he said for me to go right home. Believe me, I don't like that I lied to him. But you tell me, Desiree, what else could I do?" In a gesture of helplessness, he shrugged and held out his arms.

"Was your wife at the house when you got there?" I asked.

"Nope. She walked in about forty-five minutes after I did, looking innocent like a baby."

"Did she tell you where she'd been?"

"She told me where she wanted me to *believe* that she'd been. Which was at some friend's house—Estelle, the name is. She said to me that Estelle invited her for dinner so she could show her the pictures from her new grandchild. Baloney! Little Allison is six months old already, and all of a sudden Estelle needs to show her the pictures? They went shopping together a couple weeks ago, even. Why didn't Estelle show her the pictures then? Anyhow, I asked Shirley, 'How come you didn't mention to me that you were going there?' And she claimed she told this to me the other day, but I must have forget about it. But I didn't forget nothing, Desiree, honest to God.

"So?" Felix put to me abruptly. "Will you find out if Shirley has got herself another man?" Without pausing for breath, he segued into, "Don't worry. I can afford to pay whatever you charge; I make decent money—pretty decent, anyhow." And then, almost timidly: "Uh, how much *do* you charge?"

I quoted him an hourly rate that was considerably lower than my usual fee. (After all, considering the number of cheeseburgers he'd served me through the years, Felix was an old friend by now.)

"Okay," he said. I thought he looked a little relieved.

"By the way, what time do you normally leave the house for Jerome's?"

"This other waiter—Manny—he picks me up at quarter of three like clockwork."

"Fine. I'll be sure to station myself there by then. One other thing: Do you have a picture of Shirley?"

He nodded, fished around in his wallet, and finally extracted a dog-eared snapshot of a rather small blond woman standing at a table, slicing into a large cake. There were a number of people in the background, none of whose faces were clear enough to be recognizable from the photo. I could only hope that Shirley was the central figure here. "This is Shirley—the woman cutting the cake?"

"That's right. It was her birthday. Number sixty."

"How long ago was this taken, Felix?"

He scrunched up his forehead as he thought for a moment. "It will be fourteen years in September." And noting my expression: "Believe me, she looks the same today like she did then, almost."

"You have nothing more recent?"

Felix shook his head. "Shirley, she don't like anybody should take her picture."

I shrugged inwardly. Well, I'd just have to go with what I had. I mean, what choice was there? So I got Felix's address and assured him I'd be in touch. "I assume it's okay to phone you here?"

"Sure. I'll give you a card from the place; they got bunches of them in the front."

I began digging around in my bulging, suitcase-size handbag for a good minute or two before I was finally able to locate my own cards. "This is in the event you want to reach me before I call you," I explained, extracting one of the cards from the card case and handing it to him. Then it dawned on me: I'd known Felix all these years and had no idea of his last name!

"Is Lugash," he informed me.

We were just leaving the kitchen when he stopped short. "Wait. You forgot something, Desiree."

"I did?"

"Sure, the deposit. I didn't give you nothing yet."

I'd never heard it referred to as a deposit before, but deposit, retainer—*whatever*—it's not that often anyone volunteers the money. "I don't need a deposit, Felix; you'll pay me when I find out what's going on here."

And now I mentally crossed my fingers. Felix was *such* a nice man. I could only hope that things wouldn't turn out to be as bleak for him as I feared they would.

Chapter 16

When I got home from Jerome's, I packed some of the things I planned on taking to New Jersey. These included a gorgeous black lace nightgown and peignoir set that, with my appalling lack of willpower, I'd bought on a whim a couple of years ago in the hope that there'd be an occasion worthy of it one day. And hallelujah! That day was tomorrow!

A lot of the smaller items I'd have to leave out until the last minute. You know, stuff like my eye makeup and my eyelash curler and my lip gloss, and all those other absolute necessities I didn't dare face the world—and especially Nick—without.

Anyhow, it was close to midnight when I got into bed. But I wasn't really sleepy, so I had Belle's manuscript keep me company for a while.

Shortly after leaving Simon and Helen Cooper, I read, the two men paid an unannounced visit to Rebecca McMartin. The decision to stop in at her office just then was prompted by proximity; she worked only three blocks from the Coopers' apartment.

Apparently, the woman hadn't expected to be questioned by the police at all. When the receptionist (the nameplate on her desk read, CANDY) buzzed Rebecca to inform her of their presence, Ray overheard Candy mumble, "Geez, Rebecca, how the hell do I know?" After which, almost as an exclamation point, she cracked her gum.

And now Candy, very obviously feeling put upon, led the way down the hall to Rebecca's inner sanctum. Holding open the door, she motioned for the officers to enter. Then she cracked her gum again and made a hasty retreat.

Once inside, the pair were greeted by the room's sole occupant, a pleasant-looking, slightly overweight middle-aged woman, who was seated behind a handsome mahogany desk. "What's all this about, Detectives?" she said, frowning, while simultaneously getting to her feet and extending her hand.

Both men quickly shook the outstretched hand before Gabe replied, "We'd like to ask you a few questions about the evening of Rob Harwood's death, Miss McMartin. We promise not to take up much of your time."

"It's *Mrs.* McMartin, but call me Rebecca." Then, once she was back in her chair and Gabe and Ray were seated opposite her, on the other side of the desk, she demanded, "Why would you want to ask me about that? I understood Rob died of a heart attack." There was a protracted pause before she added, "Didn't he?"

"It's very possible that he did," Gabe told her. "But we can't overlook the possibility of foul play, either. We won't know for certain what killed Mr. Harwood until we see the autopsy report—and that's very likely weeks away. In the meantime, we felt it would be best to talk to everyone who was at that party while the details are still fresh in their minds."

"And you think that Rob may have been . . . may have been *poisoned*? Is that it?"

"We don't really think anything right now. It's just something we have to check into."

"Oh, my God," Rebecca said softly. "Oh, my God," she said again, the words barely audible now.

"Did you happen to notice Mr. Harwood's champagne glass sitting on a table while he was upstairs changing clothes?"

Looking as if she were in shock, Rebecca shook her head. "I was aware that Rob had changed his suit at some time or other, but I don't know anything about his leaving his glass on a table. Do you . . . do you believe that somebody poisoned his champagne?"

"There's also a possibility that the perpetrator—

assuming there *was* a perpetrator—slipped into the dining room prior to the meal and dropped the poison into his water glass. Did you notice anyone entering or leaving the dining room before you were all called in to dinner?"

"No, no one."

"How well did you know Mr. Harwood, ma'am?" Ray asked gently.

"Oh, I believe I knew him very well. We met about twelve years ago, when I took a job with this company. Rob was already employed here then."

"How long did you work together?"

"A little under a year."

"And the two of you kept in touch after Mr. Harwood left the firm?"

Rebecca nodded. "We spoke on the phone a couple of times a month. And every once in a while, we'd meet for lunch, as well."

"Are you aware of anyone he might have been having problems with—either personal or business related?"

"No, I'm not. And I doubt there *was* anyone like that. Rob was *such* a likeable person."

"I gather you were quite fond of Mr. Harwood," Gabe observed.

"You have that wrong. I was *very* fond of him." She went on to paint a glowing portrait of her former co-worker, describing him as one of the most charming and considerate men she'd ever known. She lauded his sense of humor, his intelligence, his passion for living. "I'll really miss him," she murmured, brushing away a single tear. Then, noticing Gabe and Ray exchange knowing looks, her hand flew to her mouth. "Oh, no," she said incredulously. "You can't possibly be thinking what I think you are. Our relationship wasn't anything like *that.*" And when neither officer responded: "I had only recently lost my husband— my *wonderful* husband—when I joined this firm. And believe me, I wasn't interested in replacing Warren with another man. Besides, why would Rob want *me* when he had a gorgeous wife at home? He was just a great friend to me at a time when I really needed a friend—and ever since."

"Uh, ma'am?" Ray began, attempting to choose his words carefully. "You do know that there are rumors Mr. Harwood may occasionally have gotten romantically involved with other women—other than his wife, I mean."

"I'm well aware of that," Rebecca responded sharply, her eyes blazing now. "But as far as I'm concerned, that's all they are: rumors. I have serious doubts that Rob was the womanizer he was purported to be."

In view of how upset Rebecca had evidently become over this line of questioning, Gabe nodded. "You could be right," he told her in his most conciliatory manner. After which he moved off the subject. "You attended the party with a gentleman, I understand."

"Correct."

"Was he also acquainted with the deceased?"

"Uh-uh. In fact, this was the first time Mickey had visited our fair city."

"Ever?"

"Ever. Mickey and I met at college—Ohio State. And don't you dare ask me the year," she added, with a mischievous little grin.

Gabe grinned back at her. "And you invited him here to escort you to the party?"

"Actually, no. He wrote that he'd be in town for a friend's wedding—which was this past Saturday evening— and asked if I was free to have dinner with him Friday night. I hadn't seen him in quite some time, and I was anxious to get together with him again. But I also hated to miss Rob's birthday celebration. So I called Tess about the situation, and she very graciously insisted that I bring Mickey to the party."

"Would you mind telling us how we can get in touch with your friend," Gabe said. It wasn't really a question. "There's always the chance he might have noticed something that evening that's relevant to the investigation."

"No problem." Rebecca tore off a sheet of paper from the small notepad on her desk and jotted down the information.

"You're certain he and Rob had never met before?" Gabe asked as he pocketed the paper she handed him.

"Absolutely. I introduced them that Friday night. They'd never set eyes on each other until then."

"Seems like a very nice lady," Ray remarked, as he and Gabe were walking to the car. "And she had an unusually high opinion of the deceased, wouldn't you say?"

"Yep," the other agreed. "Either that, or Rebecca McMartin is one savvy perp."

I put down the manuscript at this point and turned off the light. But I was too excited about tomorrow to sleep. And before I knew it, I was trying to come up with a motive for Rebecca to murder her good friend. I was aware that without deciphering that damn clue, this was almost certainly a waste of time. But old habits die hard. And besides, it was something to do.

Who's to say that Rob Harwood, who seemed to have had his pick of beautiful women, didn't find something appealing about this overweight, middle-aged lady? I mean, those things *do* happen. (At least, I like to think so.) Besides, if Rebecca and Rob had begun fooling around fairly soon after they met, she would have been twelve years younger and maybe even a little slimmer. As to what had motivated her to get involved with him in the first place, she'd recently been widowed, right? And Rob (according to this particular scenario of mine) had been a very good, very comforting friend. Then one day he comforted her right into the bedroom! At any rate, the affair went on for years, but recently Rob broke it off for some reason. Maybe Rebecca had been after him to leave his wife, and, tired of the nagging, he ended it with *her,* instead. Or possibly it was his philandering that brought her to the boiling point. In either case, she finally did what any self-respecting woman in her shoes would have done: She killed the louse.

Satisfied now that *something* could have driven Rebecca to murder her old friend, I closed my eyes. And before long, I was fast asleep.

Chapter 17

I was a nervous wreck on Saturday.

It was a good thing I'd slept late that morning, since there was that much less of the day for me to mess up.

Things began to go wrong as soon as I finished breakfast, when I broke a plate. *No big deal,* I told myself. I mean, we're not talking fine china here.

Then, not much more than an hour after this, there was that nail polish business. Now, while I'd put on fresh polish only the other day, I decided I needed a *real* manicure. Of course, I could have gotten one yesterday from Emaline's cousin Ernestine, who's a manicurist and works out of Emaline's shop a couple days a week. But I'd availed myself of that woman's services once before, and she cut so deeply into my cuticle that I almost bled to death. (Okay, so I'm exaggerating a little.) Anyhow, I elected to do my own nails today. I figured I couldn't make a worse job of it than Ernestine had. I was wrong. I wound up spilling some of the polish on the cushion of one of the kitchen chairs. Fortunately, the cushion's red, so the coral polish didn't really show—not from a distance, anyhow.

The coup de grâce, however, was when I poured shampoo instead of bubble bath into my bathwater. (You probably won't believe me, but the bottles *were* very similar.)

Somehow, though, once the bath disaster was over, I managed to calm down. And from then on, things actually went pretty smoothly. I brushed my hair until I could barely lift my arm, but I got out what little frizz Emaline had put in this time. I was able to apply my eye makeup with a steady hand, for a change. Plus, I decided I still looked damn good in the two-piece gray cotton A-line I'd gotten at Woman of Substance last year, which— although it had cost far too much even at the end of the season—I'd stubbornly refused to let myself leave behind at the store. To top everything off, when I put on the beautiful gold charm bracelet with the ruby heart that Nick had given me for Christmas, I was able to fasten the clasp on the very first try.

Nick rang the bell promptly at five thirty.

When I opened the door, he just stood there for a few seconds, appraising me. "You look beautiful," he said.

"You look beautiful, too," I said back. Not only was he wearing an immaculately tailored dark gray suit (which blended very nicely with my light gray dress), but he was smiling that irresistible (to me, anyhow) gap-toothed smile of his.

"I have to admit something, Dez. Nobody has ever told me that before."

"I'm sure there were enough people thinking it, though," I offered.

He chuckled. "I wouldn't put money on that, if I were you."

"I'll go get my overnight bag." As soon as I said the words "overnight bag," I could feel myself blushing. Me! A mature, sophisticated (I like to think) woman of never-mind-how-many years.

I was about to walk away when Nick pointed out, "There's a little tan bag right in the corner there, Dez. Would that, by any chance, be it?"

God! I was such a ditz today! "Uh, yes. I can't imagine how it got in here," I mumbled.

"Gremlins," he pronounced somberly. "You never know when they'll pull that sort of thing."

The Golden Goose was a small, intimate restaurant with shiny eggplant-colored walls (which the maître d' referred to as aubergine); thick, pale pink carpeting; and subdued lighting. Moments after we were seated, the headwaiter came by to ask if we'd care for something to drink. Nick responded with, "A bottle of Dom Pérignon, please." I damn near fell off the chair.

"Are you crazy?" I demanded before I could stop myself. It was delivered in a kind of whisper, but unless the waiter—who was standing right over us—was completely deaf, he didn't miss the admonition.

Nick merely smiled at me. Then he nodded to the man, which was obviously his nonverbal way of communicating, *Don't pay any attention to her.*

"I consider this a special occasion for us, Desiree," he said when we were alone again.

"I'm sorry I blurted that out, but the Dom Pérignon is *such* an extravagance."

"Let me worry about that, will you?" he countered, his tone a shade testy now. But he mellowed almost instantly. "I appreciate your concern, Dez; I really do. Once in a while, though, it feels good to splurge. I want to celebrate the fact that for the first time, we're spending an entire weekend together."

I refrained from pointing out that, in terms of hours, it was closer to a day than a weekend. Still, until tonight, we'd never been away before, the two of us. So even though we'd traveled only across the river to New Jersey, I determined that Nick was right: We did have something to celebrate.

While we were sipping our champagne and nibbling on some hors d'oeuvres, Nick asked if I'd made any headway in solving Belle's mystery.

I shook my head. "I don't seem to be getting anywhere at all."

"You'll figure it out; you always do," he offered encouragingly.

"Easy for you to say," I retorted—but lightly.

"Do you think it might help to talk about it?"

I shook my head. "I'm happy to get away from it for a while. Maybe another time, though—that is, if you don't mind my rambling on and on . . . and on."

"Hey, I asked *you,* didn't I? But don't shoot me if—as I anticipate will be the case—I prove to be no help at all. Okay?"

"It's a deal."

This led to Nick's mentioning *The Da Vinci Code.* "I'm about halfway through, and it's really fascinating. Have you read it, Dez?"

"Not yet, but I will. Probably by the time I do, though, almost everyone else in America will have read it twice."

"I'd let you have my copy when I'm finished, but it's not really *my* copy. Emil lent it to me," he explained, referring to the man who works for him at the flower shop.

"How *is* Emil?" Then, being an incorrigible busybody: "Is he still seeing that woman—Bev?" Now, Emil's a widower in his early fifties, while Bev is sixty-eight. And although Emil was apparently unbothered by the age difference, his brother and sister—both of whom he's very close to—were having fits about the match.

"He certainly is. In fact, I have a feeling it's getting pretty serious."

"Have you met her yet?"

"Just once, when she stopped in at the shop. She seems like a very nice person. Maybe we could go out one evening, the four of us."

"I'd like that."

It was then that the waiter brought us the menus, and when I opened mine, I had to blink a couple of times to be sure I was seeing what I thought I was. A whole bunch of my very favorite dishes were right there, in black and white. (So to speak, that is. The script was actually printed in aubergine.) I wasted no time in designing my dinner. I'd begin with the escargot. After that, of course, I'd move on to the roast duckling à l'orange, accompanied by wild rice with mushrooms, plus a side dish of broccoli with hollandaise sauce. And I'd end this perfect meal with the perfect dessert: a profiterole filled with vanilla ice cream and topped with a warm, bittersweet chocolate sauce. Dedicated foodie that I am, I wasn't in Wheeler, New Jersey, just then; I was in heaven!

Nick was pleased with the available choices, too. He ordered the onion soup, followed by a steak with béarnaise sauce and French-fried potatoes, then ended up where I did: with the profiterole and a cup of really good coffee.

Over this marvelous food, we talked about all sorts of things. But neither of us mentioned Derek. Knowing how much his son meant to Nick, I kept telling myself to ask how he was getting along, but I just couldn't convince myself to open that door. I mean, what if Nick took this as a sign that I might be willing to give that rotten little apple of his eye another chance? At one point, thinking Nick was about to bring Derek into the conversation, I had this weird desire to gnaw on my fingernails. (And I've *never* gnawed on my fingernails!) But, thankfully, he didn't so much as mention the name. Sure, I realized— and I'm certain Nick did, too—that sooner or later, this Derek thing would have to be dealt with. But I was hoping for later. Much, *much* later.

We arrived at the bed-and-breakfast before eleven thirty, as mandated. Practically the instant we walked in I could verify that the place lived up to the one-word description that whoever-it-was had related to Nick: "charming."

The owners, a handsome older couple, graciously welcomed us into their home, a spacious, five-bedroom colonial house, the main floor of which was tastefully, although not elaborately furnished in polished woods and colorful chintzes. Mrs. Knudson, the wife, showed us to our room, which was on the third floor, the bedrooms on the lower floors having already been grabbed up by the time Nick made the reservation. My knees started to give out when I reached the second landing. But I lectured myself that if the proprietress—who appeared to be in her sixties, and who, like yours truly, could hardly be called svelte—was able to lug her considerable poundage up another flight, so could I.

Our room, when we finally made it there, was well worth the exertion. Not only was it unusually attractive, but the space practically oozed comfort. About twice the size of my own bedroom, it contained a couple of easy chairs that were pulled up to a small cherry table. It also included both an armoire and a chest of drawers, along with a dressing table and even a fairly well-stocked bookcase. There were crisp white crisscross curtains at the two windows and a fluffy, fairly large beige and white rug on the floor. But the pièce de résistance here was at the center of the far wall, opposite the door: a huge cherry four-poster, with white bedding and a white eyelet canopy.

"What a charming room!" I told Mrs. Knudson. (There was that word again! But it really did fit.) She beamed with pleasure.

"Do you honestly like it?" Nick asked anxiously when she'd left us.

"I love it. Why, don't you?"

"I think it's great. I was double-checking, that's all." Then, with a grin: "There's one problem, though. Look at the size of that bed! I'll never be able to find you in there."

I laughed. "You will if you really try."

It wasn't long afterward that I was proved right.

He really tried. And happily for us both, he found me.

Our Sunday morning began with a wonderful breakfast at—where else?—the bed-and-breakfast.

Genevieve Knudson looked as if she'd be a good cook—and she was. There was another couple seated at the table when we came downstairs that morning, and we chatted with them for a while over raspberry pancakes, ham and eggs, homemade pastries, and some good, strong coffee.

Our fellow guests mentioned that Wheeler Center was really worth visiting and that it was only a few blocks from the Knudsons'. So when we finished breakfast, we headed over there and—we hoped—walked off a fraction of what we'd just taken in.

*   *   *

My first thought on approaching the picturesque area known as Wheeler Center was that it looked as if it had been transported here from another century. It consisted of four short blocks of tree-lined cobblestone streets; narrow, brown-shingled buildings—most of them complete with turrets; and one funky little shop after another. At the second shop we visited, I came across what I decided was the perfect gift for Nick: the world's ugliest little ceramic monkey—which also happened to be a pencil sharpener. (You stick the pencil into the monkey's belly button!) Nick reciprocated with a nail kit containing green, purple, chartreuse, and black polish.

After browsing for about an hour, we stopped for ice cream and then sat outside on a bench for a while, holding hands, licking our cones, and people watching.

Late in the day, when we were heading home, Nick told me he'd never had a better time.

My stomach did a somersault. "Funny you should say that, Nick," I responded when it was right-side up again. "That's exactly what I was going to say."

Chapter 18

I came home feeling girlishly giddy and *wonderful,* my feet barely touching the ground. All I could think of was Nick—and what an incredible time we'd had together.

But later, when I went to bed, I couldn't fall asleep. And it wasn't pleasant thoughts that had me tossing and turning. I was focused now on the one subject neither of us had wanted to broach during our mini-getaway: Derek.

Yes, I had a great deal of animosity toward Nick's little progeny. But, trust me, it was well-founded. This is a boy who, right from day one, was determined to push me out of his father's life. And if you think I'm exaggerating, listen to the stuff he's pulled.

During our very first meeting, Derek deliberately poured a frozen hot chocolate in my lap—and swore it was an accident. Then two months later, there was a second incident. I'd asked Nick to dinner at my apartment. And when Derek unexpectedly wound up in his father's care that evening, I included him in the invitation. I even prepared a special menu for that dear, sweet child. And how did he respond? Well, this time I caught him in the kitchen, dumping half a bottle of black pepper into the boeuf Bourguignon that was simmering on the stove!

The really frustrating thing, though, was that on both these occasions I had to cover for The Kid From Hell (TKFH in its abbreviated form). I mean, say I'd disputed his account of the frozen-hot-chocolate episode. Who do you think Nick would have believed: his own flesh and blood or a woman he'd just recently begun dating? As for the Bourguignon, the explanation I gave Nick was that I'd intended to pour off some of the fat, but I lost my footing and our dinner ended up in the sink.

I never did tell him the truth with regard to those two little "mishaps." Listen, even if he accepted my versions, I'd have been forcing a doting father to view his only son in a very unflattering light. And I can't imagine him thanking me for it.

At any rate, after the untimely demise of my boeuf Bourguignon, the three of us adjourned to a nearby Chinese restaurant for some sustenance. And it was here that TKFH wound up cooking his own goose (figuratively speaking, of course).

An offhand remark by one of the other customers resulted in his throwing a tantrum and telling his father—along with the rest of the diners at the establishment—what he *really* thought of me. And, believe me, there was no mistaking him for a fan.

As a result of that outburst—and maybe some other stuff I'm not even aware of—Derek ended up in therapy. But after only a few months, he claimed to have made great progress. He told his father he sincerely regretted his behavior toward me and was, in fact, eager for us to be friends. Not surprisingly, the doting dad bought this little fairy tale. In fact, he even went along with Derek's suggestion that we go out one day, the three of us. Would I consider it? Nick asked. I didn't have to let him know right then and there, he said. I was to think about it.

Naturally, this was a question I'd expected to be faced with one day. But I kept hoping that day would be in the distant future. The thing is, whatever decision I finally made was bound to be the wrong one. Look, I couldn't imagine this pocket-size Satan's ridding himself of all those negative feelings about me after such a brief time in analysis. I mean, he'd made it all too obvious that he considered me to blame for the fact that his parents weren't together. It didn't matter that they were already divorced when his father and I met. Derek was convinced that if I were out of the picture, they'd go back to being a family again. Which is something Nick maintained could never, *ever* happen.

Anyway, I knew then what it was like to be faced with a Hobson's choice.

Let's say I agreed to this threesome business. It would only give The Kid From Hell yet another opportunity to put one of his nasty little schemes into motion. And if things didn't work out as planned during our first outing, there was always the next time and, if necessary, the time after that. . . . At any rate, sooner or later Nick would recognize that it was impossible for his son and me to coexist in his life. And which one of us do you think would have to go?

On the other hand, suppose I declined to go out in Derek's company. Wasn't Nick bound to regard this as an unwillingness to allow the kid to make amends? And wouldn't that, too, result in alienating this man I cared so much about?

For weeks I put off addressing this dilemma of mine, but at last I forced myself to deal with it. Over dinner one evening, I finally made contact with my missing spine and told Nick I didn't feel that such a short time in therapy was sufficient to overcome Derek's deep-seated hostility toward me. I said it was conceivable that the boy himself might not be aware that he'd retained this animosity (although, of course, I didn't believe this for a second). I went on to express my concern that an attempt to socialize prematurely could jeopardize any chance for a friendship that Derek and I might have later on. (I admit, though, I was actually skeptical—*very* skeptical—that there was even a remote chance of our ever developing an amicable relationship.)

Nick appeared to understand my decision. "That makes sense," is what he told me. His main concern, he said, was trying to explain things to Derek. Nevertheless, later that night as I lay in bed (alone), it crossed my mind that the brief, but warm kiss Nick had planted on me at the door might not have been saying good night, but good-bye.

Thankfully, I was wrong. Still, there was no getting away from the fact that sooner or later I'd have to deal with this same question again—and that I couldn't possibly come up with the right answer.

Because there wasn't any.

Chapter 19

The last thing I remember before I finally drifted off that Sunday night was turning toward the window and seeing that daylight had begun to creep into the bedroom under the shade.

My detestable alarm clock jolted me awake what seemed to be only minutes later. I opened one eye, reached over, and shut it off. Then, being the well-grounded grown-up that I am, I *sneered* at it. After which I closed the eye and went back to sleep.

Naturally, when I finally woke up again—it was almost ten thirty by that time—I didn't waste a minute in phoning Jackie. (To fail to touch base with her would have put me on her *s* list, where no one in her/his right mind would care to be.)

"The bathroom sink overflowed this morning, and I have a terrible mess to deal with here," I told her. (That wasn't *exactly* a lie. It actually happened, only it was a couple of months earlier—on a Saturday.)

"You could have called," she scolded. "I was just about to try *you*."

"I am calling," I reminded her.

"Did you have to wait this long? I was worried."

"I'm sorry, Jackie, honestly. But between trying to reach the super and toting around buckets and mopping up the floor—the water even made it into the foyer—I was really frantic, and everything else kind of flew out of my head." I managed to sound so convincing that *I* almost believed me. (Listen, I wasn't a member of my high school thespian society for nothing.)

"I suppose you did have your hands full," Jackie admitted grudgingly. Then, more amiably: "How's everything now?"

"Wet. But I finally got the super to come up here. He told me a pipe had burst. Anyway, things seem to be under control at last—under control, but waterlogged."

"Well, as long as the problem's been fixed . . . Uh, look, I'm sorry I lit into you like that."

"That's okay. Hey, what are friends for?" We both laughed. "I'll see you tomorrow."

Now, since technically I'm *her* boss (although I myself often fail to remember that this is the case), you might wonder why I'd need to concoct an excuse like that in order to work at home—which was what I intended doing. In fact, I could hardly wait to dig into Belle's manuscript again.

The thing is, though, every so often—and you can never tell when the mood will strike her—Jackie goes on a little crusade about work ethics. And apparently she doesn't always find me that credible. So, not feeling all that confident that she'd believe me if I leveled with her, I opted not to.

Listen, it's very likely that this woman is the bossiest, most opinionated, most irascible secretary in New York. And I admit it, she intimidates me—as you've no doubt gathered by now. (My being a PI doesn't necessarily mean I'm the bravest individual on the block, you know.)

So why do I put up with that sort of thing? you might ask. Well, aside from having acquired her services along with my office space, it's because she's also an extremely competent individual. But more important, Jackie's like family to me. Which is why, if it takes a little white lie— or even a more elaborate one—to keep the peace, so be it.

After breakfast—or, considering the hour, I suppose you could call it brunch—I adjourned to the living room sofa with the manuscript, opening to where I'd left off on Friday, with the detectives having just paid a visit to Rob's old buddy Rebecca McMartin.

They were no sooner back in the car, chapter five continued, than Gabe and Ray decided it was time to break for lunch (pepperoni pizza and Rocky Road ice cream). Then they took a thirty-five minute drive to the outskirts of the city to have a talk with Tess's very good friend Eleanor White and her husband, Philip.

The couple lived in a modest brick house on a street of almost identical modest brick houses. The doorbell was answered by a tall, good-looking blonde of indeterminate age, dressed in formfitting jeans and a loose white shirt.

"Mrs. White?" Gabe asked.

"That's me, Eleanor White," she verified with a tentative smile. "But everyone calls me Ellie."

"I'm Sergeant Wilson, and this is my partner, Detective Carson."

The woman nodded. "Please come in."

She led the way into the living room, which was furnished with worn, mismatched pieces and a faded and soiled rug. It was a home in sharp contrast to the others the detectives had visited these last two days.

"Have a seat, won't you?" Ellie invited. "Um, better take the club chairs," she suggested, indicating the two discolored corduroy chairs at right angles to the sofa. "The couch is kinda lumpy; we're going to have to treat ourselves to a new one pretty soon. Can I get you something to drink—coffee, maybe?"

"Thanks very much, but we've just had some," Gabe told her.

"Oh. Well, let me get my husband. He's in his studio, which is at the rear of the house, and when he's working—Phil is a graphic designer—he doesn't pay a whole lot of attention to doorbells." With this, she all but flew from the room.

By the time Gabe and Ray had settled in the corduroy chairs, Ellie was back.

"Phil will be out in a minute," she informed them, plainly ill at ease. "Are you sure you wouldn't like a drink, Officers?" she offered again. "We've got Coke and Pepsi—we're a two-soft-drink family—also grape juice. My daughter *loves* grape juice. Her name's Gwen—she just turned fifteen," the woman finished lamely.

Gabe shook his head. "I'm fine, thank you," he assured her. "Ray?"

"Thank you, ma'am, but I'm fine, too." A minute or two later, Ray noticed a beautiful little spinet in the corner of the room. "Do you play?" he asked Ellie, who'd just taken a seat on the edge of the sofa. On seeing her stunned expression, he reddened. "The piano, I mean."

"Oh, no." She tittered, evidently embarrassed by her reaction. "It was a birthday present for Gwen from her father—my ex-husband. She just started taking lessons."

It was then that a tall, thin man with rimless glasses and a bad complexion put in an appearance. He was wearing baggy khaki pants and a wrinkled short-sleeved cotton shirt. From a distance, Ray had taken the new-comer for a teenager. It had even crossed his mind that this might be Ellie's son. But on seeing him more closely, the detective realized the fellow was an adult. Still, Phil White couldn't be more than thirty, Ray decided, and was, in all likelihood, a few years younger.

"We appreciate your making yourselves available today—you and Mrs. White; we'll try to do this as painlessly as possible," Gabe said as the three men shook hands.

"No problem," Phil assured him, joining his wife on the sofa. "I understand you suspect that Rob may have been poisoned."

"Word gets around, I see," Gabe commented dryly. "That's only one possibility, Mr. White, but, naturally, we can't afford to disregard it."

"No, of course not. And by the way, I'm Phil, and this is Ellie." He indicated his wife with a toss of the head. "Do you have any idea of the motive yet?" he asked, his tone suddenly confidential.

"Apparently, Mr. Harwood was something of a ladies' man. And while we can't be certain this had anything to do with his murder—assuming for the moment that he was actually murdered—it appears to be as good a place as any to start."

"Rob? A ladies' man? I'm really surprised to hear that;

I always thought of him as a pretty solid citizen. And he seemed devoted to Tess."

"How about you, ma'am?" Ray put to Ellie, who appeared to have been content to let her husband do the talking. "Were you at all suspicious that Mr. Harwood was cheating on his wife?"

She shook her head. "No, I wasn't," she answered, turning the color of her surname. "Um, are you sure it's true?"

"Reasonably sure." At this point—and independent of each other—both Ray and Gabe were entertaining the possibility that Ellie White was among the deceased's conquests.

"I understand you told the detective you spoke to on the night of the party that you and Mrs. Harwood are longtime friends," Ray continued.

Phil was the one to reply. "They've been best friends since they went to high school. That was in Huckleby, Pennsylvania."

"You moved to New York together—you and Mrs. Harwood—Ellie?"

Once again, Phil spared his wife's vocal cords. "No, right after graduation, Ellie got an offer from a modeling agency and headed for the Big Apple. My Ellie was a successful model for quite a while—one of the top names in the business. But, anyhow, three, four years after Ellie came to New York, Tess hooked up with Rob, who happened to be from Manhattan, and she moved here, too."

"Mrs. Harwood never spoke to you about her husband's infidelity, Ellie?"

"My wife's already told you she wasn't aware of anything like that, Detective. "If she'd—"

"Excuse me, sir, but we'd appreciate it if you'd allow her to answer for herself," Gabe cut in, an edge to his voice now.

Phil frowned but refrained from speaking. And, after chewing on her lower lip for a moment, Ellie responded in a near-whisper, "Tess never mentioned anything to me about Rob's doing any cheating, I swear."

"And you never heard rumors to this effect?" Ray pressed.

"If I did hear something like that, I forgot about it." Then almost at once she added emphatically, "I don't place any stock in rumors."

"Are you aware of any other reason that someone might have wanted Rob Harwood dead?"

"None, honestly."

"Neither of us are," her husband volunteered.

"We have just a few more questions," Ray informed the couple. "The night of the murder, Mr. Harwood left a glass of champagne on a small table when he went upstairs to change his clothes. While he was gone, you were standing pretty close to that table, talking to his wife and some other people. Did either of you notice anyone drop something into that glass, or even pause near it for a moment?"

"No, we didn't notice anything like that," Phil said.

"And you, ma'am?" Ray asked Ellie, ignoring the "we."

"I didn't notice anything like that, either. You think the poison was in Rob's champagne; is that it?"

"As of now, we don't actually *think* anything. But it's conceivable."

Phil checked his watch at this juncture. "Listen, guys, I have a deadline to meet, so—"

Guys? Gabe frowned. "We're almost through here, Mr. White," he retorted, deliberately reverting to the more formal form of address. "But keep in mind that we're trying to get a leg up on what could very well turn out to be a murder. However, if you'd be more comfortable answering these questions at police headquarters, that won't be a problem; *Detective* Carson and I can arrange to talk to you there."

"What else do you want to know?" Phil muttered.

"Did you, by any chance, see anyone enter or leave the dining room prior to dinner being served?"

"Not that I can recall," he answered tersely.

"I don't recall anything like that, either," Ellie seconded.

Gabe sighed. "Well, I guess that about covers it. Thank you for your time, Ellie." And, reluctantly shaking Phil's outstretched hand: "You, too . . . *guy.*"

*　　*　　*

As soon as the detectives drove away from the house, Ray—who was at the wheel—shook his head. "You let that 'guys' business really get to you. Forget it, Gabe. White's a four-star jerk."

"It doesn't have anything to do with how he spoke to *us*—not personally, anyhow," his partner retorted. "That cretin was insulting the badge."

Ray quickly changed the subject. "She was nervous as hell—his wife."

"I noticed. Got any theories as to why?"

"I'm thinking she may have had a fling with her best friend's husband at some point—or at least a one-night stand. And she felt we might regard this as giving her a motive for murder. You know, 'a woman scorned.' She could have been afraid she'd give herself away. And that's why she let her kid husband do the talking."

Gabe smiled—but inwardly. The "kid husband," could very well be the same age as Ray. "I'm thinking the same thing," he said. "And you realize, of course, that if she *was* screwing around with Harwood, and her husband learned about it, he'd also have had a motive for offing the man. You know, I don't find it at all difficult to see our buddy Phil resorting to poison."

Ray grinned. "It wouldn't be because you don't like the *guy*, would it?"

I fully intended to read more of the manuscript that day—after a short break, that is. But I'd no sooner switched on the television than the phone rang.

The "Hi, Dez" was all it took for my heart to plummet straight to my toes.

"Hi, Nick," I simpered.

"I just called your office and they said you wouldn't be in today. Are you okay?"

"I'm fine. I thought I'd work at home, that's all."

"The manuscript?"

"Yep."

"How's it coming?"

"Don't ask."

"I already did," Nick said, a smile in his voice. "Seriously, though, you can't let yourself get discouraged. This Belle Simone wouldn't be willing to pay you that kind of money to solve the mystery if it was going to be easy. But I'm confident you'll come up with the answer if you stick with it. Just keep in mind that you've tackled tough ones before—plenty of them. Like that sweet old lady who was found at the bottom of her basement steps. And how about the poor guy who was murdered before he could donate one of his kidneys to his brother? Those were very challenging cases, too. And you did what the police weren't able to do: You solved them."

"I did, didn't I?" I murmured, grateful for the reminders. "Thanks, Nick. Thanks a lot."

"Glad to be of service. But seriously, I wanted to tell you again how special this weekend was for me. It was . . . wonderful."

"Yes, wonderful," I repeated, afraid that if I said another word, I'd burst into tears. (Not that I'm emotional or anything.)

"Uh, Dez? Tiffany has a new boyfriend, but at least this one's over thirty."

"Another rocker?" (Nick's ex has a *thing* for rockers and, as a rule, the younger the better.)

"No, but close. He manages them. Anyhow, there's a pretty good chance she'll be spending all of next weekend with Toby—the boyfriend—so Derek will be staying with me. And I know you wouldn't be comfortable in his company—not yet, that is. Right now, though, things are still up in the air. But I'll call you in a few days, as soon as Tiffany's finalized her plans—if that's all right with you."

"It's fine with me. Of course, I don't know what to say to Marcello when he phones. . . ."

"You'll think of something," Nick responded, chuckling.

We hung up seconds later. And for a fleeting moment I felt all warm and cared for. Then I heard Nick's words in my head: *I know you wouldn't be comfortable in his company—not yet, that is.* And I felt sick.

"How could I *ever* be comfortable in his company?" I said aloud.

Chapter 20

As soon as I woke up on Tuesday, it began to bug me. I mean, what on earth had prompted me to give Jackie that overflowing sink story so I could spend the day working at home? After all, what could she possibly have done if I'd leveled with her—fired me?

Actually, I knew why I'd lied: I have a yellow streak—this very *wide* yellow streak—running right down the center of my back.

At any rate, when I got to the office that morning, I was feeling pretty guilty about having deceived my very good friend. That was why, when Jackie checked her watch the instant I walked in, then peered at me critically and shook her head, I let it go. I didn't so much as bat an eye, either, when she followed this with her usual lecture about my not having notified her that I'd be late. And I was positively stoic when she held up a message slip and told me, "Edna picked up this call while I was in the ladies' room," after which she proceeded to familiarize herself with its contents. But my patience finally snapped when she began to do what she's been doing more and more of lately. "It's from Ellen," I was advised. "She says—"

I held out my palm. "I know how to read, Jackie," I informed her between clenched teeth.

She handed me the slip—but not before having the last word, as usual. "My, didn't *we* get up on the wrong side of the bed today."

I read Ellen's message on the way to my cubbyhole. She'd try me again later if she got a chance; otherwise, she'd speak to me tonight at home.

As soon as I was settled at my desk, I opened my attaché case and took out Belle's manuscript. Then I stared at it for a few seconds—and promptly shoved it into the bottom drawer. I couldn't concentrate this morning. Not in light of last night's mention of Derek. Hearing Nick say that I might not be comfortable with TKFH *yet* had the effect of waving a red flag at a bull. Well, in a way, that is. Except that instead of attacking, I wanted to withdraw. To maybe curl up in a corner somewhere and suck my thumb.

I paid a few bills instead. I'd just written out the last check when Jackie came in.

"We still friends?" she asked tentatively.

"Of course we are."

"I'll stop reading your messages to you—that is, unless you're calling in or something and you ask me to. Okay?"

"Don't worry about it, Jackie. It's like you said: I woke up on the wrong side of the bed this morning." Once the words were out, I could have kicked myself. I'd actually given her permission to do something that had been driving me a little crazy for months now!

"I was wondering if we could have lunch later. You have to tell me how everything's going with Nick, and I want to hear all about that mystery you're working on for Belle what's-her-name."

"Simone," I supplied. "You seem to be so busy lately that we haven't had much time to visit."

"Yeah, I know. Elliot's defending some big-shot CEO in this fraud case, and there were piles and piles of preparation work involved. And then, whenever I got a breather, I started thinking about Derwin. For a while, there was, well, this problem. But it's been straightened out. So? Lunch today?"

"Sure."

"I do want to hear about that manuscript. Have you made much progress yet?"

"I haven't made *any* progress yet."

"You will, though; I know you will. You'll see."

It was like listening to Ellen. Only an octave lower.

* * *

We ate at a small Italian restaurant that had recently opened up a couple of blocks from the office. We each had a glass of Chianti, followed by the special luncheon of the day: green salad, mushroom-stuffed ravioli in a sage-butter sauce, and a choice of three desserts. (Jackie opted for the spumoni, while I couldn't resist the chocolate cheesecake.)

It didn't take more than three or four sips of the wine for Jackie—at my request—to begin filling me in on the Derwin thing. And from that moment until we were back in the office, the conversation was practically nonstop.

Before I go into what Jackie had to say about her longtime significant other, though, let me tell you this about him: To refer to Derwin Snyder as "cheap" isn't doing him justice. I mean, when Derwin and Jackie are out to dinner with friends, ninety-nine times out of a hundred he manages to be in the men's room when the waiter brings the check. And on those rare occasions when the bill comes to the table in advance of his vanishing act, someone else always seems to get to it before Derwin can make contact with his wallet. (I swear, that man has the world's shortest arms!)

So why does Jackie continue seeing him? Maybe it's chemistry. All I know for certain is that, for whatever reason, she's crazy about him. The feeling is mutual, too. In fact, every once in a while he'll do something really, *really* sweet—generous, even. (Although not often enough to spoil her, of course.)

Anyhow, Jackie opened with, "I came close to breaking up with Derwin this weekend."

"You *what*?"

"I can't tell you how furious I was with that man, Dez. He was lucky I didn't have a lethal weapon within reach."

"What happened, Jackie?"

"You've heard me mention my friend Sue, right?"

"I . . . It sounds familiar."

"Sue and I went to high school together, and we've been close almost from the day we met. But a while back, she married this terrific guy from San Francisco, so I don't get to see her very often. A few weeks ago, though, Tim—her husband—was scheduled to come to New York for a business convention, and Sue decided to accompany him. Well, Mary Beth and I—Mary Beth's another old high school buddy of ours—made plans to take her to La Côte Basque for lunch that Saturday."

"La Côte Basque, huh?"

Jackie nodded. "We wanted to do something extraspecial for Sue. We've both visited them in San Francisco, and she and Tim treated us royally. Well, unfortunately, on Friday Mary Beth fell and broke her ankle. I figured it would be just the two of us then. But all of a sudden, Derwin pipes up with how he'd love to meet Sue, since he'd heard me speak of her so often, and couldn't he go in Mary Beth's place?

"Now, I really thought the lunch should be a girl thing, you know? Only I didn't want to hurt Derwin's feelings. Anyhow, I checked with Sue, and she said it would be fine with her if he came along, that she'd like to meet him, too. So I told Derwin okay, but I made it very clear that Mary Beth and I had intended treating Sue to lunch and that I still planned on treating her.

"At any rate, we had a lovely meal that day, and we were sitting around and chatting over coffee when I had to go to the ladies' room. At first, I was hesitant about getting up before I paid the check. But then, I figured that since I'd been so explicit with him about treating Sue to lunch, Derwin would take care of the bill if the waiter brought it in my absence. To be *doubly* sure, though, before excusing myself, I dropped my handbag near Mr. Generosity's foot. And when he stooped to pick it up, I bent down, too. 'You'll pay the tab,' I whispered."

"But he didn't," I interjected.

"How'd you guess?" Jackie said wryly. "Later, he insisted that he thought I'd changed my mind about treating, because he could have *sworn* I'd said, 'Sue'll pay the tab.' And, what's worse, she did. My dear friend comes in from the West Coast—and winds up not only springing for *my* lunch at this expensive French restaurant, but for my cheapo boyfriend's, too. And the thing of it is, Derwin knows me well enough to realize I'd have reimbursed him. I swear, it's as if he's constitutionally incapable of picking up a check."

It was apparent that Jackie was still very upset about the incident. "Next time Sue's in town you can make up for it," I offered encouragingly.

"Oh, you bet I will. In the meantime, I sent Sue and Tim a beautiful basket of fruit last week. But to get back to Derwin . . . I decided to accept his explanation, and for a while I pretended to myself that things were just peachy between us."

At this point, I recalled how when I'd walked into the office after that horrendous taxi ride of mine, I heard Jackie making these juvenile kissing sounds on the phone to her beloved. Which, now that I thought about it, wasn't like her at all. Apparently, she'd been going all out to convince herself that her relationship with Derwin was positively blissful.

"But eventually," she went on, "I couldn't pretend any longer. I made myself accept what, on some level, I already knew to be the truth: that Derwin had lied to me. And this past Sunday, I had it out with him.

"He finally admitted that he did hear me correctly when I told him to take care of the check, but—and this is almost verbatim—he hated to see me spend so much of my hard-earned money on a fancy lunch. His rationale for letting Sue pay instead—*Sue,* who's always been so generous with me—was that her husband could afford it a lot better than I could.

"That did it. While it was hardly the first time I chewed him out for something like this, that morning I laced into him like I never had before. I told him I wouldn't put up with his penny-pinching any longer—not even for one more day. And I'm sure I finally convinced him that I meant it."

Suddenly, Jackie clamped her hand over her mouth for an instant. "God! I didn't intend to go into all of this, Dez. It's only that between the business with Derwin and that ball-breaking case of Elliot's, I never did get around to asking you about that big-bucks mystery you're working on. And I didn't want you to think it was because I wasn't interested. It was because, well, I was too damn self-involved for a while."

"Hey, don't apologize. You've had a lot to deal with lately. I hope things with Derwin go really smoothly from now on."

"Oh, I'm confident that at long last he's learned his lesson." But somehow Jackie's tone failed to carry the conviction of her words.

I wasn't the least bit anxious to talk about Nick that day, so when Jackie asked about him, I assured her that he was fine and *we* were fine. It wasn't that I was angry with him, you understand; I was just feeling miserable about the whole crappy situation. Anyhow, I immediately changed the subject by proceeding to discuss the contents of Belle Simone's manuscript.

After a brief mention of the character of the deceased, I went into a fairly detailed account of what I'd read so far of the detectives' interrogation of the various people who were present that night. "But the trouble is," I explained, "while I haven't finished it yet, I'm almost certain there's no possibility of my arriving at a solution to the mystery unless I can get a handle on the clues I receive from Belle—which she hasn't yet incorporated into the book itself."

"You're not suspicious of any particular person?" And before I could respond: "I myself am partial to the sister-in-law."

"Catherine? I certainly wouldn't discount her. But listen, I can speculate about how almost everyone who was at that surprise party might have had a motive for doing away with the guest of honor. Until I figure out Belle's clues, though, I won't actually *know* anything. She's already provided me with the first clue, and when—and if—I decipher it, I'll receive the second one."

"So?" Jackie demanded excitedly. "What was the clue?"

"That in order to solve the mystery, it would be necessary to think the way the French do."

"That's all?"

"Pretty much."

"Those were her exact words?" Jackie persisted.

"Maybe not her *exact* words. But that's the gist of it."

"What do they *mean,* though?"

I shook my head dejectedly. "If I could answer that question, Jackie, I'd probably be halfway home."

Chapter 21

When Jackie and I got back to the office, I made up my mind to do . . . well, not much of anything. While I'd been in no mood to read Belle's manuscript earlier that day, I was in no *condition* to read it now. I mean, one glass of wine tends to render me almost totally useless.

I tried to conjure up some really simple make-work projects. Like straightening up my desk or maybe sharpening a few pencils. For all of about six seconds I even entertained the idea of purging some of my file folders of the unrelated papers I'd stuff into them whenever I didn't know what else to do with said papers. (This being a stupid—although temporarily expedient—little habit I'd acquired years ago and hated to abandon.)

But in the end, I had to admit that the pencil-sharpening idea was probably my best bet. So I saw to it that six of my pencils got the point of their lives. And then I went home.

It was still early when I walked into the apartment, and I wasn't the least bit hungry yet, especially since the portions at lunch had been surprisingly generous. Besides, by then I was anxious to read more of Belle's mystery. The effects of that one glass of wine hadn't completely worn off yet, though (I know; I'm a real wuss), so I put up a pot of coffee. I figured I might be able to focus better after a cup or two.

Have I mentioned before that my coffee has been called everything from nauseating to vile? Luckily, however, I myself don't have a problem with it. Which is proof, I suppose, that I have a surprisingly tolerant palate. Anyhow, I actually drank *three* cups before deciding to get down to business.

As soon as I removed the manuscript from my attaché case and flipped it open to the appropriate page, the phone rang. It was Ellen.

"Hey, I've missed you. Do you realize we haven't spoken in ages?" she said, her tone just a shade accusatory.

I thought for a couple of seconds. "Not that you're one to exaggerate, of course, but as a matter of fact, it was five days ago. You called last Thursday to let me know you'd straightened things out with your mother."

Ellen giggled—as only Ellen *can* giggle. "Sounds familiar. But it *feels* like it's been longer than that. See how much I miss talking to you? What's been happening, Aunt Dez? How's Nick?"

Well, I was still upset about last night's conversation with him, so I wanted to avoid even thinking about Nick (and, consequently, Derek) for a while. And Ellen didn't interrogate me about our miniweekend together, because— fortunately—she didn't know anything about it. Once Nick and I had made our plans, my subsequent conversations with her had revolved around Margot and her outrageous demand. At any rate, I responded with, "Oh, Nick's fine." Then I quickly inserted, "Is your mom still behaving herself?"

Ellen laughed. "So far, so good. Oh, I almost forgot. How are you doing with that million-dollar mystery of yours?"

"*Million*-dollar mystery? Like I said before, you're not one to exaggerate. To answer your question, though, I'm doing poorly. *Very* poorly." Then, before she had a chance to reassure me—which I didn't doubt for a moment she was about to do—I hastily steered her to her favorite subject. "But tell me, how is Mike?"

"Great. *Really* great." And she went on to enthuse about how well respected he was at the hospital and how she'd recently met some of the nurses there, and they were all simply *crazy* about him. She paused for a moment. "Oh," she clarified hastily—and unnecessarily—"I didn't mean that in a sexual way."

I tried to keep the smile out of my voice. "It never occurred to me that you did."

Ellen then proceeded to acquaint me with any number of quotes about Mike from some of his coworkers. And there was no way to turn her off without hurting her feelings. So I didn't try. Besides, hearing my niece so happy always made me feel extremely pleased with myself, in view of my having been responsible for pushing the two of them into a blind date in the first place.

What happened was, some years back, I had a frightening, almost deadly encounter with a killer in the hallway of an old apartment building downtown. From which little skirmish, incidentally, I eventually emerged victorious (in other words, alive). And the instant my attacker—that scum—fled the scene, I was lucky enough to pass out cold. I call it lucky because guess who lived in that building—and wound up ministering to me?

It didn't take me long to determine that Mike Lynton would be perfect for Ellen. I mean, he was kind, personable, attractive—and single. Plus, needless to say, I didn't deduct any points for his being a doctor. Of course, while it failed to occur to me at the time, this was hardly a guarantee that he wouldn't also turn out to be serial killer. (Ever hear of Dr. Harold Shipman? That estimable British physician has been credited with more than two hundred murders!) Anyway, being an incurable fixer-upper, I nagged them both until, practically kicking and screaming (especially Ellen), they agreed to meet. And all I can say is that if my matchmaking never produces any positive results again, well, I'm willing to rest on my laurels.

At any rate, Ellen was presently winding up her homage to her husband when she stopped short. "I'm going on and on, aren't I?"

"If you are, I hadn't noticed," I lied.

"Listen, you're coming to dinner Thursday, right?"

"You bet."

"Is Chinese okay?"

For a second or two, I was thrown by the question. When my niece invites you over for a meal, you take it for granted the cuisine will be courtesy of her neighborhood Chinese restaurant. (In Ellen-speak, "preparing dinner" refers to taking those little microwave-safe plastic dishes from Mandarin Joy and transferring the contents to some pretty platters.) Fortunately, Mike's fine with Chinese food; otherwise, he'd no doubt be emaciated by now. Assuming, that is, he remained among the living.

"Uh, Chinese is good. And I'll bring the ice cream. What time do you want me there?"

"Sevenish okay?"

"It's fine."

"We'll order after we've looked over the menu."

I had to suppress a laugh. There was no need to look over that menu. Even I knew it by heart!

After my chat with Ellen, I took the manuscript out of my attaché case. I was about to open it when Jackie's question leapt to mind. I mean, about whether the clue I was repeating to her was in the exact language it had been told to me. Now, while I'd abbreviated it a bit from the start, I did feel I'd extrapolated its meaning. Nevertheless, maybe I *should* try to recall the precise wording.

I plopped down on the sofa and began to rummage through my head for the clue as Belle had recited it to me. Almost immediately, though, I remembered that Belle hadn't actually *recited* that clue. Gary, at her instruction, had handed me a folder, and inside the folder was a single sheet of paper with the first clue to the mystery typed in the middle of the page. I could even picture that damn paper! The only trouble was, I couldn't manage to dredge up what it said—not verbatim, anyhow.

Well, I supposed that in the morning I should get in touch with Belle—or better yet, Gary—and ask to have a copy faxed to me. But, naturally, this wasn't something I was particularly anxious to do. After all, by this time, I should have memorized this crucial information—exactly as it was written.

Then it dawned on me that it was unlikely I'd tossed out that paper. The thing is, I'm kind of a pack rat. Why else would I have crammed all those folders with papers that didn't belong there?

But which folder contains the clue? I put to myself.

It occurred to me that instead of digging through every file I had, it might not be a bad idea to check the likeliest place first: the folder containing my contract with Belle. There was a good chance it was here at the apartment, too—sitting in one of the desk drawers.

I located the file marked, BELLE SIMONE CONTRACT, although, to be honest, even before I opened it, I was attempting to decide where to look next. But surprise! The paper I was searching for was exactly where it belonged, right there with the contract.

"To solve this mystery, you must first recognize the key," I read. "And to accomplish this, it's essential that you think the way the French do."

I have no idea how long I remained there, staring mindlessly at that piece of paper. Then one word leapt out at me, and my eyebrows shot up to my hairline.

Oh, my God! I shouted silently. *It's for real!*

Chapter 22

For a few seconds, I was barely able to breathe. After which I could feel this enormous grin spreading across my face. It was as if I'd reached the end of an interminable, totally frustrating, but ultimately very satisfying journey.

I wanted to shout at the top of my lungs, *I did it!* Instead, I just stood there, grinning and feeling inordinately pleased with myself.

Only moments later, however, the exhilaration—and the grin—were gone. The truth had gotten through to me: The toughest part of this "journey" still lay ahead.

I thought I'd wait until morning to phone Belle. I mean, if I called her now and told her I'd just grasped the meaning of the first clue, she might decide to lay clue number two on me right away—tonight. And my poor, overtaxed brain sorely needed a vacation until tomorrow. Still, I had to tell *someone*.

Ellen? She and Mike would have been the most likely candidates—along with Nick, that is. But I hadn't gone into any detail about the case when I'd spoken to Ellen, so they didn't have any idea I'd been wrestling with a specific clue. (I had planned to fill them in on Thursday, over our General Tso's Delight—or whatever.) As for Nick, on Saturday evening when he'd asked me if it would help to talk about Belle's mystery, I hadn't wanted anything to intrude on our special weekend together. So I said that maybe we could do it some other time. And "some other time" hadn't happened yet. Which put Nick's familiarity with the manuscript on a par with Ellen's and Mike's.

It occurred to me then that, anyway, I should be sharing my news with the person who'd finally pointed me in the right direction.

"What's up?" Jackie said in response to my hello. I could hear her chewing.

I looked at my watch then. It was ten minutes after seven. "Are you having dinner?"

"Uh-uh, not yet. I figured I'd just grab a cookie while I tried to decide which TV dinner to shove in the microwave tonight." (As you can gather, Martha Stewart has nothing to worry about from Jackie.) "What do you think, Dez—the beef Stroganoff or the Southern-fried chicken?"

"I'd go with the Stroganoff."

"Good choice. I was leaning in that direction."

"Do you want to get back to me after you've eaten?"

"Uh-uh. I'm in no rush. After today's lunch, I'm not really that hungry. So tell me, to what do I owe the pleasure of this phone call?"

"I wanted to thank you."

"For what?"

"You helped me decipher that clue I talked to you about at lunch."

"I *did*?"

"Yep. Remember my saying that the clue was: 'To solve the mystery, it's necessary to think the way the French do'? Something like that, anyway."

"Sure, I remember."

"You asked me then if those were the exact words, and I said no, but that this was the gist of it. Well, when I got home, I thought about your question. And it occurred to me that it was possible I'd missed something. And the fact is, I did." I paused here for dramatic effect.

"Well, go on," Jackie demanded.

"I dug up the paper Belle had given me when I met with her here in New York. And I saw that the *entire* clue reads, 'To solve this mystery, you must first recognize the key. And to accomplish this, it's essential that you think the way the French do.' Well, I stared and stared at those two sentences, and all of a sudden, it struck me! The key to the first clue, Jackie, is actually the *word* 'key'—which I'd been completely ignoring. And even with my limited knowledge of the language, I'm aware that *in French* 'key' is *clef,* as in roman à clef. You know, a novel in which actual people and events are disguised as fictional."

"*Ho*-ly shit," Jackie said softy. And a moment later: "Congratulations! I'm *very* impressed."

"Don't be. It certainly took me long enough. And without that prompt from you, who knows when I'd have looked at the entire clue."

"Um, just one thing, Desiree . . ."

Uh-oh, she called me Desiree. "What's that?"

"It wasn't necessary for you to define roman à clef for me. As it happens, I'm quite familiar with the term. In fact, I've even read a couple."

There was no mistaking that Jackie was miffed. And I couldn't have felt worse. The last thing I'd intended was to talk down to her. "God! You're one of the brightest people I know, Jackie. The definition just came out automatically. I would probably have said the same thing if I'd been having this conversation with Einstein."

"Well, that's a first."

"What is?"

"I've never been mentioned in the same breath as Einstein before."

"Honestly, Jackie, I—"

"Okay, okay," she said good-humoredly. "Apology accepted. I guess I *was* being a little oversensitive. So tell me, what happens next?"

"Tomorrow I call Belle to let her know I've solved clue number one, and she'll provide me with clue number two. And following that, I anticipate going crazy all over again."

After Jackie and I hung up, I made myself a peanut butter sandwich. (Okay, it was a sandwich and a half.) Then I had a cup of coffee and a scoop of Häagen-Dazs macadamia brittle (which, for years, I've been trying to convince myself is brain food). And a short while afterward, newly invigorated, I was ready for the next installment of the manuscript: chapter six.

Late Monday afternoon, driving back to the city from the Whites', Gabe commented that he could go for a thick, juicy steak. It didn't take much persuading for his partner to warm up to the idea and in less than twenty minutes, the two were occupying a table at the Palm Restaurant, an upscale but unpretentious steakhouse, where you didn't merely eat—you *dined*.

They began the meal with jumbo shrimp cocktails. Then, for the main course, both men opted for prime, aged rib-eye steaks, accompanied by mashed potatoes and string beans. They were close to polishing off the entrées when the conversation switched from basketball and baseball to murder.

"Do you realize that after speaking to almost everyone who was at that party, we've still got the same list of suspects we started with?" Gabe observed none too happily.

"We've only been on this case a couple of days, for crying out loud!" Ray pointed out. Then, thoughtfully: "Hey, you're not getting discouraged, are you? You're the one who started off with such a positive attitude."

"No, of course I'm not discouraged. I'm just a little impatient, that's all."

"Uh, listen, Gabe, I'm not sure I agree with you about the suspect list. You don't actually think that cousin of the vic's—Elaine—had anything to do with his death, do you?"

"Not really," Gabe answered as soon as he'd swallowed his last spoonful of mashed potato. "But I'm not willing to write her off yet, either. You?"

"I guess not," the younger man conceded reluctantly, "although I have a hard time picturing that loony lady as a murderer. What would have been her motive?"

Gabe shrugged. "Who knows? Maybe she's in Harwood's will. But probably not," he added quickly. "I would assume he left the bulk of his money—and I've got the impression

he had quite a lot of it—to his wife. Besides, I still think
he was iced because he screwed around with the wrong
woman." Then, with a smile that bordered on the lascivi-
ous: "And somehow I don't see Cousin Elaine as part of
that picture."

The detectives went on to speculate about the possible
motives of the rest of the suspects they'd met with. And
since their assessments were so close to my own—which
I've already mentioned—I'm not reprinting that portion
of the manuscript here. I should mention the one major
difference, though: Gabe was practically willing to bet
his pension that, sooner or later, Philip White would be
proven Rob Harwood's killer.

The waiter approached the table now, the book continued. "You gentlemen care for anything else?" he asked.
"Another beer, maybe?"

"I'll pass on the beer, thanks," Gabe told him. "Just
bring me a piece of cheesecake and a cup of coffee."

"Ditto."

"Hey," Gabe joked after the waiter had left them, "do
you always have to order the same things I do?"

"Funny. I was about to ask *you* that when you ordered
the rib eye."

"Listen, I had the rib eye in mind before you said a
word."

Ray rolled his eyes in response.

It was while they were waiting for the check that Ray
commented, "We keep talking as if Harwood was definitely poisoned. And I have to keep reminding myself that
without the autopsy report, we really don't know anything for sure."

Cocking his head to the side, his partner gave him a
penetrating look. "Don't we?"

Ray nodded slowly. "I suppose we do."

The Rileys had agreed to see them at eight a.m. on
Tuesday, so Ray pulled up in front of Gabe's building at

seven thirty. The weather that morning was miserable, the rain frequently coming down in sheets.

"I'm soaked already; I hate this kind of weather," Gabe muttered, as he jumped into the car.

"You think I like it? I left a nice, soft bed to come out in this."

"Never mind that. Who'd you leave *in* the bed?" Gabe teased.

"None of your goddam business."

"By the way, maybe you can help me out. My wife's birthday's coming up soon, and I promised we'd go and see that new movie *Flashdance*—Lily used to be a dancer herself, once upon a time. Anyhow, I'd like to take her someplace special for dinner afterward. I figured that, being such a swinging bachelor, you might have a suggestion."

"Being a *what*?"

"Well, a bachelor, anyway."

"Now, let me think. . . ." And after several seconds: "I've always found the cuisine at McDonald's to be quite pleasing to the palate."

"Cute."

"Seriously, Gabe, when I have a date, we usually go to a nice little neighborhood restaurant for Italian or Chinese—nothing fancy. But, listen, if something occurs to me, I'll let you know."

"Thanks, anyway, Mr. Sophisticate—and no offense; but I think I might be better off checking with my brother-in-law."

The pair had driven in silence for a few minutes when the senior officer mused, "Well, anyhow, today should be interesting. We'll be meeting the femme fatale, who—according to the widow's sister, at least—was caught in flagrante with the dead man by their mutual cleaning woman. I'd say that would make both Mr. and Mrs. Riley pretty decent suspects, wouldn't you? After all, we've got a rejected lover . . ."

"Who knows who rejected who?" Ray reminded him.

". . . and a jealous husband," Gabe continued, disregarding the interruption.

"It's very possible the husband wasn't even aware of the affair."

"It's just as possible that he was," Gabe insisted stubbornly.

Slightly exasperated now, Ray countered with, "Even if that's true, it's equally conceivable the perp was one of the other ladies our Romeo took up with. Or maybe it was the main man in *her* life who added a little something extra to Harwood's champagne."

Gabe sighed. "Maybe," he conceded. "Still, I have this feeling that today we'll finally be getting somewhere."

As it turned out, Gabe was right. Only not in the way he anticipated. Because today, instead of zeroing in on a suspect, they would be crossing three of them off their list.

My eyelids were drooping by now, so I put down the manuscript. The Rileys would have to wait until tomorrow.

I took a quick shower, then crawled into bed. It wasn't until I was dropping off to sleep that it suddenly hit me: *three* of them?

Chapter 23

My watch read ten thirty. She should be up by now, shouldn't she? I lifted the receiver. I could hardly wait to talk to her!

"Belle Simone's residence," a cheerful voice announced.

"Hi, Gary, it's Desiree."

"How *are* you, Dez? How's everything going?"

"Not too bad, actually." It was impossible to keep the smile out of my voice.

"You've deciphered the clue!" he said excitedly.

"I hope so."

"How wonderful! Wait till Belle hears this! I'll put her on."

The author picked up only a few seconds later. "Congratulations, sweetie! Gary tells me you've figured out the first clue."

Leave it to Gary! I wouldn't have thought he'd had enough time to preempt me. "I think I have. But I imagine you want to be sure I've got it right."

"You bet I do! So go on; I'm listening."

I told her the conclusion I'd reached.

"You're right, of course. I knew you'd figure it out. Well, are you ready for your next clue?"

"I suppose I am."

"Good. Why don't we meet for drinks later—around five thirty, six?"

"I can't make it this evening, Belle. I'll be tied up with this case I'm working on."

"Okay. How's lunch then?"

"Fine, only I'd have to leave the restaurant by two. That same case," I added quickly.

"No problem. Let's get together at twelve, then. There's a place in my neighborhood called the Purple Stallion. It's nice and quiet, so we won't have to yell at each other to have a conversation. And the food is *very* tasty—that is, if you like Italian." She paused for a response.

"I love Italian."

"*And* they make the most *outrageous* frozen margaritas."

The margaritas weren't exactly a selling point. Not only had I never tasted one in my life, I had no intention of rectifying the omission. I wasn't the least bit interested in a drink that had, for its main ingredient, something that came bottled with a worm. If I wanted a cocktail, a piña colada would do me just fine, thank you. Nevertheless I murmured, "Really?" just to be polite.

"Well, see you at twelve," Belle said. She sounded let down. No doubt due to my obvious lack of enthusiasm about the margaritas.

Less than five minutes after my conversation with Belle, Nick phoned.

"Hi, Dez, how are you?" The instant I heard the voice, my mouth went dry. (I have to stop reacting so viscerally to this man.)

"Pretty good, thanks. No, wait—I take that back. *Better* than pretty good. At long last, I've made a little progress with Belle's manuscript."

"That's great!" he enthused.

"I wouldn't call it *great*. I said I made a *little* progress, remember? But it's a start."

"I still don't know what's going on. When do you plan on filling me in on this weird case of yours, anyway?"

"The next time I see you—I promise."

There was a slight pause. "I'm afraid it won't be this weekend, Dez. Tiffany is dropping Derek off on Friday morning, so that she and boyfriend number two thousand nine hundred and ninety-one can get an early start on their getaway to wherever. I'll take the day off from work, and maybe Derek and I can go see a movie. Uh, you wouldn't happen to be available, say, this evening, would you? I was hoping we might be able to have dinner."

"I wish. I'll be on a stakeout then."

"You're kidding, right?"

"That's the kind of thing we PIs do, you know."

"Yeah? When was your *last* stakeout?"

"Um, I'm not sure."

"I thought so. Seriously, Dez, I hope you're not involved in anything dangerous."

Touched by the concern that had crept into his voice, I managed not to laugh. "I tend to doubt it, Nick. My client's about eighty years old, and he suspects that his wife, who isn't all that much younger, has been cheating on him."

"That's a relief, anyway." A moment later, he teased, "But tell me you're not going to be running around snapping dirty pictures tonight."

"*Yecch!* I assure you that I definitely will not. Fortunately, my client hasn't requested any pictures of his wife and her new *friend* doing the nasty. And if he did, I'd have a colleague do the snapping. But there's another, more important reason I'm relieved about my client's willingness to go by my findings. Believe me, if I wind up having to confirm his suspicions about the person he's been married to all these years, just hearing me say the words will be devastating enough for him."

"I shouldn't have been treating this so lightly," Nick apologized. "Does he have good reason for mistrusting her?"

"I'd say so. He *has* caught her in a few obvious lies about her whereabouts while he's at work."

"Well, I hope you'll be able to report back to the poor guy that his wife's been out taking fencing lessons or studying Swahili or something."

"Thanks, Nick. I hope so, too."

"Listen, how's tomorrow night?"

Being that I have such an agile brain, I responded with, "Huh?"

"Are you free for dinner tomorrow?" he spelled out patiently.

"I wish I could make it, but my niece, Ellen, invited me over there last week."

"Well, I suppose we'll have to wait until next week to get together, unless—"

"Unless *what*?" I pounced.

"Unless Tiffany and her latest decide to come home a day early."

I strongly suspected that Nick had been about to suggest that I join him and TKFH sometime over the weekend—but that my tone of voice had warned him off.

I had to give him credit, though. Even when he's sitting down, the man's pretty fast on his feet.

The conversation ended with Nick saying, "I'll miss you," and me echoing the words.

I was freshening up for my lunch with Belle when I started to get really uneasy. What if, after struggling so hard to unravel the first clue, I wasn't able to solve the second one?

But I immediately decided it wouldn't bother me. Not after I'd slit my throat, anyway.

Chapter 24

At five minutes before noon, I walked into the Purple Stallion.

It was a small place, dimly lit and homey—somewhere between a restaurant and a pub—with purple-and-white-checked tablecloths and purple candles in lavender ashtrays on every table.

I spotted Belle seated in a booth toward the rear, sipping a drink. She was wearing a floral-print dress again today, something that seemed to be her trademark.

When I reached the booth, she appeared to be caught up in her own private thoughts and was apparently a bit startled by my, "Hi." But she recovered instantly.

"Hi, yourself, lady." And putting down her now empty glass, she smiled. (Have I ever mentioned Belle's smile? I swear, I'd kill for those perfect white teeth!) As soon as I was seated, she remarked, "It's hot as Hades today, isn't it?" Then, before I had a chance to agree, she asked what I'd like to drink. "I have a feeling it won't be a margarita," she teased.

"Um, I think I'd prefer a piña colada today, thanks."

She signaled the waiter, a short, round fellow, who came waddling over to us. "My friend here would like a piña colada, Harry. And I'll have another margarita."

"You got it, baby."

"I gather you come here often," I remarked.

"I do. But Harry addresses all the female customers with endearing little terms—whether they like it or not. And evidently, quite a few of them aren't exactly crazy about it. In fact, a number of women have complained to the owner. He promised to speak to Harry, and I understand that he did. But Harry goes right on doing his thing."

"I'm surprised he hasn't been fired."

"Jake's wife—Jake's the fellow who owns the place— would kill him if he got rid of Harry."

"She's fond of the man?"

"I couldn't swear to *that,* but he *is* her brother. By the way, I thought we'd have our lunch before I hit you with the second clue—if it's all right with you."

"It's fine with me."

"Why don't you take a look at the menu now? I know it by heart."

I picked up the menu in front of me and was about to open it when I realized that something was missing— that "something" being Gary. "Uh, Gary wasn't able to join us today?"

"The poor guy's at the dentist's; he's been walking around with a terrible toothache for days now, and it finally got to the point where he couldn't take it anymore. Oh, by the way, in case he neglected to mention it, Gary finally got around to telling me he'd lied about your not wanting to go to that Eskimo restaurant. I forgave him, although I did dock him a week's salary—just to teach him a lesson."

On seeing my expression (I must have looked horrified), Belle chuckled. "I'm *joking,* Desiree," she clarified, eyes twinkling.

"Oh, I figured you were," I said, but not very convincingly, I'm afraid.

The food at the Purple Stallion was as good as Belle had proclaimed it to be. We both began with the fried zucchini. After that, on Belle's recommendation, I joined her in ordering the veal scaloppine with lemon sauce. Which was a terrific dish! And following this, we gorged ourselves on chocolate-covered strawberries lavished with whipped cream.

I'm not sure how it came about, but that afternoon we spoke briefly about our personal lives for the first time. I told Belle I'd lost my husband many years ago. "Ed was

a former police officer who'd left the force and become a
PI, too. We were only married five years when he died.
Looking back," I said sadly, "I wish we'd done at least
a few of the things *then* that we'd promised each other
we would do together 'someday.' We always used to talk
about buying a little weekend retreat in the Poconos and
taking piano lessons and traveling to India—things like
that."

Belle nodded. "I know exactly what you mean. I'm a
widow, too. And so much of what my husband and I
were planning to do 'later' never came to pass, either.
Have you any idea why I began to write, Desiree?" she
asked rhetorically. "It was to keep from just sitting
around, stuffing my mouth with potato chips, and feeling
sorry for myself." Then changing the subject abruptly:
"But let's talk about something more cheerful. Like your
making me $24,940 poorer. Don't worry," she put in
quickly, on noting my expression. "Listen, I'm spending
that money exactly the way I want to. And I'll tell you
a secret, Desiree: I can afford it."

It was when we were having our second cup of coffee,
the last vestige of strawberry having vanished from both
our plates, that Belle said, "Well, shall we?"

Suddenly, I was nervous. "I guess so," I answered,
almost reluctantly.

Reaching into the large beige tote bag sitting next to
her on the seat, Belle removed a folder and handed it
to me. As before, inside the folder was a sheet of paper
with the clue typed in the center of the page: "It is now
necessary," I read, "for you to identify each of the suspects *and* the victim by their true given names. This requires that you concentrate on where the individuals are
from. And here's a hint: In order to succeed, you must
think *multinationally*."

I looked up, stunned. "I'm not sure I understand this.
You want me to somehow figure out the *real* first names
of all the characters in the manuscript, right?"

"Not *all* the characters, Desiree. Only those of the
victim and the actual suspects."

"What about the last names of these people?"

She waved her hand. "Don't worry about last names. I simply made them up."

I left Belle at ten of two after a brief argument about the check. She'd taken care of it the last time, and I wanted to reciprocate. Only she wouldn't hear of it. "This is my party," she had insisted. "It'll be your turn once you've gotten that money out of me." And to my astonishment, she'd leaned over and kissed my cheek.

Five minutes later, I picked up my car—which I'd moved from the garage near my office to one near the restaurant—and headed for Felix's address in the West Nineties.

A teenager with spiky green hair and a gold stud decorating one nostril had just parked in the one available space on the block. And it happened to be diagonally across the street from the old but well-kept apartment house where Felix Lugash made his home.

I pulled up parallel to the car, a snazzy, late-model tan convertible, no less. (And while it was pretty small-minded of me, and I'm a little ashamed to admit this, it crossed my mind—although only for an instant, I swear!—that there was a good possibility I was looking at stolen property.)

"Listen," I called out to the teen, "I'll give you five dollars if you'll let me have that space."

"Five bucks don't buy you spit, lady," he informed me, smirking.

"All right, ten."

"You're a real sport, you are. Now, let's cut the shit, huh? What's it *really* worth to you if I move my car?"

"I'll go to fifteen," I told him firmly.

Evidently, it wasn't firmly enough. "Stop yankin' my chain. You're pretty damn anxious for this space, from what I can see. So we both know you'll go higher than fifteen."

"Okay, twenty-five. But that's my absolute limit."

The teen's eyes became mere slits now, as he apparently tried to determine whether or not I was bluffing. "Make it thirty, and I'm outta here," he declared a few seconds later.

"Make it twenty-five, and you're twenty-five dollars richer than when you drove in here."

He continued to look at me through narrowed eyes for a good ten seconds before throwing in the towel. "Okay, but the money first."

"You've got to be kidding! The space first, the money after *that*."

"Tell you what. Since you want this spot so bad, I'll let you have it. But if you don't come across with that twenty-five, I'm gonna make an accordion outta that piece a junk you got for wheels."

Well, the kid finally vacated the space, then pulled up alongside me and grabbed the bills I held out to him through the open window. After which I parked my poor, maligned Chevy and sat there, my binoculars trained on that building across the street, as I waited anxiously for Felix's cheating (but maybe not) spouse to put in an appearance.

Chapter 25

As I waited for Shirley Lugash to show, I mulled over Belle's second clue.

Just how was I supposed to figure out where these people were from, anyway? As far as I could remember, the one hometown that was even mentioned in the manuscript was Huckleby—Huckleby, Pennsylvania—where both Tess and her close friend Ellie White had grown up. But according to Belle's instructions, I was to think multinationally. And somehow, I didn't feel Huckleby filled the bill.

So what could that clue possibly mean?

After about five minutes of fruitless ruminating, I turned my thoughts to something a lot more pleasant: Nick. And later, to something a lot *less* pleasant: Derek. But while my mind was on my personal life, my binoculars were focused on that building across the street. And three times, a likely Shirley walked out: blond, no longer young, of medium height, medium build. But, of course, this could apply to a good portion of the female population of Manhattan. So in each instance, I examined the ancient photograph Felix had provided, only to conclude that whoever the lady was, she almost certainly wasn't Mrs. Lugash.

Finally, at three sixteen, yet another Shirley candidate emerged from the apartment house. This time, however, when I checked out that photo, I actually saw a resemblance. A resemblance that, in spite of the age of the picture, was close enough for me to proceed under the assumption that the lady in question was Felix's wandering spouse.

I hurriedly started my engine, all set to take off in hot pursuit of the taxi I expected the woman to hail. I soon realized, however, that she was traveling on foot.

Damn!

I practically threw myself out of the car and rushed after her. But keeping that lady in sight was no easy task. I had to mobilize my underutilized lower limbs like they hadn't been mobilized in years (and, hopefully, would never be again). The thing is, Shirley didn't walk; she *strode*. And I needed to take two or three steps to every one of hers, while at the same time maintaining a decent space between us. I comforted myself with the thought that at seventy-four years of age, she couldn't keep up this pace much longer. But four blocks later, Shirley Lugash was still going strong. Finally, she turned into a subway station. And now I had to forget about being cautious. I almost broke my neck scurrying down the stairs after her.

Shirley quickly swiped her MetroCard in the turnstile slot and, barreling through, made a run for the train that was stopped at the station. She got there just in time.

I managed to stay close behind her (well, pretty close, anyway). I followed her through the turnstile; then, huffing and puffing, I, too, made a run for that train. I got there just in time for the doors to shut in my face.

Well, wherever Shirley was headed in such a hurry, it didn't figure she'd be back anytime soon. And I needed to catch my breath. So when I passed a diner on the way back to my car, I felt this was as good a place as any to stop and relax for a few minutes. Which shows you how much *I* know.

I sat down at the counter, and right away, the counterman took my order. After which, I glanced around me. At this moment, it occurred to me that I could have found a better place to reenergize myself. The customers here—all two of them—were both men in their late fifties or early sixties who looked as if they hadn't bathed in months. What's more, they were obviously—and soon very noisily—drunk. Then, when I took a sip of my coffee, I could hardly believe my taste buds! The coffee here was even inferior to my own god-awful brew! But it was the saucer that finally convinced me to vacate the premises. That dark speck I noticed on the rim when I'd picked up my cup? Well, all of a sudden it started to move!

I tossed two dollars on the counter and got out of there so fast Mrs. L. would have had a tough job tailing *me*.

After walking only half a block, I noticed Sam's Café, a small coffee shop on the opposite side of the street. Well, I wasn't about to make a second mistake this soon after the first. So I peered in the window. There were about a dozen people inside, all of whom looked to be decently dressed and sober—outwardly, at least.

I went inside and plopped down at one of the smaller tables. And almost at once, I began berating myself. If only I'd managed to put on a little more speed, I'd have made it onto that train and then followed Shirley to wherever she was headed. As it stood now, though, unless the individual she was meeting took her home later—and I certainly couldn't count on that—the best I could do for Felix was to tell him what time his wife had left the house and when she returned. Which was definitely not what he'd hired me for.

The thought could hardly escape me at this point that it would certainly have helped if I'd been in better physical condition. I mean, it's not as if I'd been chasing some marathon runner; this was a senior citizen, for crying out loud! And now, it actually crossed my mind that it might not be such a terrible idea to enroll in a gym. *Hey, let's not go crazy!* an inner voice protested. Well, there was always the option of jogging. *God, no!* Okay. At least I could stop with all those taxis and do a little *walking,* for a change.

I'd eat healthier, too—beginning tomorrow. Right now, though, I planned on having a slice of coconut cream pie with my coffee—that is, until I recalled that it would be my second rich indulgence of the day. So very reluctantly, I settled on the fruit cup.

Hold it a minute. Who knows how many pounds I'd
already shed this afternoon as a result of that failed attempt to keep up with Mrs. Felix? Besides, what was I
trying to do to myself, anyway? Listen, I couldn't even
remember the last time it had been necessary for me to
follow someone on foot. And believe me, I didn't intend
to repeat the experience anytime in this century.

That did it. I ate my coconut cream pie, guilt free.
(And enjoyed every last crumb of it, too.) Afterward, I
ordered a chicken salad sandwich and a Coke to-go (for
tonight's dinner). Then, just before leaving, I discovered
another reason to be pleased that I'd stopped at Sam's
Café. You should have seen the nice, clean ladies'
room there!

Back at my car a few minutes later, I settled in for
what I expected would be a very long wait.

I took out Belle's manuscript, figuring it would be a
good time to get a little more reading done. But I kept
sneaking peeks at the building across the street. What if
the woman came home early for some reason—a lover's
quarrel, maybe—and I messed up on that, too? I'd have
absolutely nothing to report to my poor client.

So I put away the manuscript and kept my eyes glued
to Felix's apartment house. Twice within the space of
ten minutes, I spotted women who might conceivably be
Shirley Lugash, about to enter the building, and I
grabbed my binoculars. But one of the "women" turned
out to be a man with hair almost to his shoulders, and
the second had to be at least thirty years Shirley's junior.
Much later on, there would be yet another false alarm
before I finally set eyes on the real thing again.

In the meantime, at one point during my vigil, I got a
leg cramp. So I jumped out of the car and walked back
and forth for a couple of minutes.

Around seven thirty, I ate my dinner—without even
tasting the food. I was too intent on keeping an eye out
for Mrs. L.

Fifteen minutes after this, my foot fell asleep. I
stamped it on the floor of my Chevy a half dozen times,

but that didn't help. So I got out of the car again and took another short back-and-forth walk.

At about eight o'clock, it began to get dark. But this, at least, didn't present a problem. There was a street lamp almost directly in front of the entrance to Felix's building.

It had been a hectic day, and by eight thirty, my eyes were at half-mast. I was afraid that before long I'd need toothpicks to keep them open. Also, my bottom was sore. I may be well padded, but you couldn't say the same for my Chevy—not anymore.

Then, at eight fifty-three, a big black sedan pulled up in front of the Lugash residence. The driver, a tall man with silver hair (I only saw the back of his head), got out and ran around to the passenger's side of the car to open the door. The woman who exited looked very much like Shirley Lugash. No doubt because, as it turned out, she *was* Shirley Lugash.

The two of them stood on the sidewalk, talking, for about a minute, after which the man kissed Shirley on the cheek. Then he waited for her to enter the building before getting back in his car and driving off.

Well, this didn't appear to bode well for Felix. But at least he'd soon know the identify of his wife's mystery friend, since—thanks to that street lamp—I'd been able to make out the license plate number of the sedan.

See? You never know, I informed myself. *Somehow, this wound up being a successful stakeout after all!*

Chapter 26

Well, while technically the stakeout might have been a success, I was afraid that the end result would be anything but. Nevertheless, I knew Felix had to be close to bursting by this time, so as soon as Shirley's friend sped away, I called the poor man from my car—although very reluctantly.

"Jerome's," a woman informed me. She sounded terribly put-upon.

"I'd like to speak to Felix, please."

Her, "Okay," was punctuated with a sigh. "Hold on."

I didn't have long to wait before Felix was on the line. "Hello?" he said tentatively, making the word sound like a question.

"It's Desiree, Felix."

"Thank God! I been so nervous waiting to hear something from you that a half hour ago, you know what I did? I dropped a blintz in some lady's chicken soup! She carried on plenty, too. But who can blame her? 'Specially since she got a little wet—from the soup splashing on her. Believe me, Desiree, never before did I do such a clumsy thing. Not in the forty-seven years I been a waiter." Then, hesitantly: "So? You . . . uh . . . maybe got some news for me?"

"Nothing definite yet. I followed your wife to the subway this afternoon. But right after she got on the train, the doors closed, and I lost her. Well, I waited across the street from your building until she was dropped off there at around nine o'clock, and—"

" 'Dropped off,' you said? Somebody was with her?"

"Yes. But listen, Felix, it's quite possible this isn't what you think. He could be an old friend or—"

"He?"

"Uh, that's right. But it doesn't mean there's anything going on between them. He might be just a casual acquaintance of Shirley's." Before Felix could interrupt again, I hurried on. "The man had his back to me, so I didn't see his face. But he was tall, and he had silver hair. Can you think of anyone who fits that description?"

Felix evidently gave the question some thought, because it took him a few seconds to respond. "No," he answered firmly. Then, a little less certainly: "At least, I don't think so."

"He was driving a late-model car—a big black one," I prompted.

"What make?"

"I'm afraid I couldn't tell you. I'm . . . um . . . I'm not very up on cars."

"It's okay. I haven't got no idea why I asked. What does it matter the kind of car he's got? The only important thing is that after all these years, my Shirley's not my Shirley no more. She's got herself a lover." I was racking my brain for an encouraging response when Felix muttered an exasperated, "Just a minute, Desiree." Evidently, he had his hand over the mouthpiece, but I heard him say something that sounded like, "Hold your horses," to somebody. And after a few words I didn't catch, he informed whoever it was that he'd be right there. Then he was back on the line.

"Try not to assume the worst, Felix," I pleaded. "I have the license plate number, and I'll check with Motor Vehicles tomorrow. They'll be able to supply the name of the car owner, and it could very well be an individual you know—perhaps an old friend of both Shirley's *and* yours. In the meantime, *please* don't jump to any conclusions."

"Jumping, I'm not. But you tell me, Desiree, if Shirley hasn't got herself a . . . a lover, then what could it mean—all the lies and now some man driving her home late at night in a fancy automobile?"

I didn't point out that nine o'clock was hardly the dead of night. "There could be a very simple explanation, Felix. At any rate, I hope to be able to answer your questions very soon. So promise me you'll keep an open mind."

"Promising, I'm not. But I'll do my best, Desiree, that much I'll tell to you."

I hung up the phone and started for home. It wasn't long before I found something new to worry about.

Maybe I shouldn't have given Felix any false hope. I mean, if there was no hanky-panky between Shirley and Mr. Big Black Sedan, then why all the secrecy?

The first thing I did when I got to the office on Thursday was to phone my contact at Motor Vehicles.

"Hi, Beth, it's Desiree. How are—"

"If you want me to check something for you, Desiree, you've called on the wrong day. Two people are out, and I'm up to my cute little rump in paperwork."

"This won't take long, Beth, I swear. And it's important, honestly."

"You say that every time you call."

"Listen, my client is this poor guy around eighty years old who suspects that his wife of many years is running around on him."

"Eighty years old, did you say?"

"That's what I said."

"I suppose she's also up there in age."

"She's just a few years younger than he is."

"Good for her, then!"

My feathers were ruffled. I had to remind myself that I was calling to ask for a favor, and reaming the woman out would hardly work to my advantage. "Not in this case," I maintained. "My client is *such* a decent person. And this suspicion that the wife he loves so dearly might have found someone else is eating away at him."

"Oh."

"He's driving himself crazy, Beth. He has to find out what's going on—one way or the other."

There was a two- or three-second lapse before Beth

muttered, "Oh, hell, I'll get back to you as soon as I can. It'll be in the afternoon, though."

"Today?"

"Yeah, today," she grumbled. "Well? Give me the lousy number already."

I recited the number I'd copied off the license plate, and Beth recited it back to me to ensure there was no mistake. "Thanks, Beth," I said then. "I can't tell you how much I appreciate this."

"Never mind the 'thanks, Beth.' You owe me a nice lunch for this one."

"A *very* nice lunch. And that's a promise."

After my conversation with Beth, I began thinking about the second clue to the manuscript, which I considered much more challenging than the first. But possibly this was because I'd already figured out the earlier clue.

I had no intention of repeating the same mistake I'd made with clue number one, however. I assure you, I wasn't about to ignore so much as a single syllable of the wording. I took that all-important piece of paper from my attaché case and studied it again. "It is now necessary," I read, "for you to identify each of the suspects *and* the victim by their true given names. This requires that you concentrate on where the individuals are *from*. And here's a hint: In order to succeed, you must think *multinationally*."

Huh?

Forget the clue for a while, I advised myself. And I was happy to oblige. At the moment, I was anxious to read more of the manuscript.

A couple of nights ago, I had been in the middle of chapter six when my eyes shut down on me. And since then, Felix's Shirley had been keeping me busy. I recalled, though, that on my last visit with the two detectives, they were driving over to the Rileys'—during what was a very rainy morning.

"We need to get Mrs. Riley alone somehow," Ray said in the elevator on their way up to the apartment. "I can't see the woman admitting to an affair with Harwood if her husband's in the room."

"Hardly," his partner agreed. "Well, we'll just have to talk to her when he's not around—even if it means making a return visit. What I'm worried about, though, is whether she'll own up to the affair at all."

"Maybe she won't," Ray countered. "Still, it's worth a shot."

Megan Riley opened the door. She was a tall woman—fortyish, Gabe assessed—with platinum hair and an engaging smile. And although it's true that some might have considered her slightly overweight, others (Ray among them) would no doubt have argued that she was built the way a woman *should* be built: full-figured and voluptuous.

"You're both soaked!" she cried out, immediately relieving them of their dripping umbrella and equally waterlogged raincoats. "Wait here a minute!" she ordered, hurrying away. "I'll bring you some towels."

In no time, Megan returned with two thick, oversize Turkish towels and pointed the men to the powder room, where they dried off as well as they could as quickly as possible. A few minutes later, they rejoined her in the foyer, and she led them into the study and pulled the door closed ("for privacy"). "Make yourselves comfortable, Officers," she directed.

Her husband was seated in one of the club chairs here, drinking coffee and smoking a cigar. He stood up to shake hands with the detectives, and it was apparent that, insofar as height, Megan Riley topped her spouse by a good two or three inches. Poor Walt fell short in the hair department, as well, obviously missing more than he'd retained. But what he lacked in those areas, he made up for in girth, his considerable poundage having provided him with three chins, while depriving him of a waistline. "Would you gentlemen care for a truly excellent cigar?" he offered when they were seated on the sofa opposite him.

"Uh, no, thank you, sir," Gabe responded. "Neither of us smokes."

Walt looked at his wife, who'd taken the chair next to his. "I don't suppose you've asked our visitors if they'd care for some coffee," he said, his tone somehow managing to straddle the line between teasing and snide.

But if his attitude offended her, Megan wasn't about to allow it to show. "Henny will be bringing in some hot coffee and tea any moment now."

As if on cue, there was a knock on the door. Megan rushed to open it, and a formidable-looking, gray-haired woman in an ill-fitting black dress entered the room. She was carrying—effortlessly, it seemed—a very large tray, which held a carafe of coffee, a pot of tea, a good-size coffee cake, plates, and flatware.

"Here, let me take that, Henny," Walt offered, quickly resting his cigar in an ashtray. Then, scrambling to his feet, he relieved her of the tray and set it on the cock-tail table.

Henny, whose cheeks had turned crimson, looked at him with something akin to adoration. "Thank you, sir," she murmured—and fled.

"Henny has *such* a crush on you, Walt," Megan commented.

"Don't be silly," her husband snapped.

"The woman thinks Walt can walk on water, but she's only been with us for two months," Megan said with a little laugh. "She'll learn." Her spouse shot her an exasperated look.

Gabe and Ray had been planning on having breakfast once they were through here, but they were getting hungrier by the minute. So they allowed themselves to be persuaded to have some cake and a cup of coffee as they set about questioning the couple.

Gabe opened with, "I assume you're already aware of the possibility that Mr. Harwood was poisoned."

Megan nodded. "Tess mentioned it to me."

"You were friendly with both the deceased and his wife?"

It was Walt who responded now. "Yes, Rob and I were business associates. But the four of us were good friends, as well."

You don't know the half of it, mister, Ray thought. After which he quickly amended this with, *But then again, maybe you do.*

"As a matter of fact," Megan put in, "I spoke to Tess last night."

"We have to proceed on the assumption there was foul play here, in the event this should turn out to be the case," Gabe explained. "If we were to wait for the autopsy report—which might take weeks—it's less likely the folks at the party would be able to recall much of what occurred that evening."

"I'm sure this is true," Megan told him. "But I'm afraid we can't be of any help to you. You see, I became ill right after drinking a glass of champagne, and—"

"What Meg means is, she felt sick after polishing off her *second* glass of champagne—which in my wife's case is almost invariably one glass too many. At any rate, we went downstairs so she could get some air."

"What time was this?" Ray inquired.

"I didn't look at my watch, but it was very soon after Rob's arrival. I'd say it was about twenty to seven, or possibly a few minutes earlier."

"Rob hadn't even gone upstairs to change yet. He wanted to freshen up before partying," Megan elaborated.

"And when did you rejoin the others, Mrs. Riley?"

"When everyone was heading into the dining room. And, please, it's Megan."

"That would be at around seven fifteen, correct, Megan?" Gabe put to her, remembering the notes he'd been given by Jack Gray, the homicide detective originally called in on the case.

"I believe so."

"Listen," her husband interjected, "you can check with the doorman—Barney's his name. He was there when we came downstairs, and he was there when we got back, too. He'll no doubt remember us, since on our return he asked Megan if she was feeling any better. So you see, neither of us was around to witness anything, and we couldn't have done away with poor Rob ourselves, either— even if we wanted to. Which, I assure you, we did not."

Both detectives sat there mutely for a few seconds. But while Ray was extremely pleased—close to elated, in fact—to hear that their damned suspect list would now be a bit more manageable, Gabe had mixed feelings about this revelation. True, there'd be a couple less perp possibilities to be concerned with. But, on the other hand, they'd be losing two of their most promising contenders for that very dubious honor.

"You were downstairs for quite some time," Gabe observed.

"We went for a little walk, but then Meg required access to a ladies' room—*frequent* access. So we parked ourselves in a diner on the next block. I was even able to persuade her to have a cup of tea."

Gabe nodded. "Perhaps you can help us with something else, though. There's been talk that the deceased was a playboy, a real love-'em-and-leave-'em kind of guy. Are you aware of that?"

"No, I'm not," Walt answered. "But chances are, he fooled around a little. A great many men do."

"Megan?"

"I did hear some gossip to that effect. However, whether it was true or not is anybody's guess."

"Well, for the purpose of this investigation," Gabe informed the couple, "Detective Carson and I feel that it's advisable for us to presume that Rob Harwood failed to honor his marriage vows. So tell me, do either of you have any idea whether *Mrs.* Harwood knew about this?"

"I couldn't say," Megan answered promptly.

"I'd guess," her husband offered, "that if Rob did have other women in his life, Tess had to be completely in the dark about it. My impression of this lady, for what it's worth, is that if she thought he was cheating on her, she'd have packed up and left him."

Ray jumped in at this point. "To your knowledge," he

inquired of the pair, looking from one to the other, "is there anyone at all who hated Mr. Harwood enough to kill him?"

Megan's, "No, no one," and Walt's, "I can't think of a soul," were almost simultaneous.

"One thing more. Can either of you tell us how to get in touch with a woman named Francesca? I believe she once worked for the Harwoods, and I understand she also worked here for a time."

"I'm afraid I can't help you," Megan answered, looking properly apologetic. "Francesca used to fill in on the days that Dinah—Henny's predecessor—was off. And occasionally, she'd also come in to give Dinah a hand. But a couple of years ago, she went back to Honduras—that's where she's from—to see her family. She was gone for months, so eventually, I had to find someone else. Anyway, since then Francesca's gotten married, and I haven't a clue where she's living now. Why would you want to talk to her, though?—if you don't mind my asking."

"No, we don't mind," Ray told her. "The reason we're interested in locating the woman is that it's conceivable she might have learned something about Mr. Harwood's extracurricular activities during the period she was employed there."

"Hold it a minute, Meg. Didn't Francesca send you a birth announcement last year?" Walt asked.

His wife colored. "Yes, she did, but—"

"As I recall, you even sent a gift."

"That's right."

"And unless I'm mistaken, you also jotted down her information in our address book."

"Oh, I don't think so," Megan countered. Then hurriedly: "Actually, I'm *sure* you're wrong about that."

"Well, why don't I take a quick look, anyway—just in case." And with this, he rose and crossed over to the desk. Then, opening one of the drawers, he promptly extracted a small black leather book. "What's her married name, anyway, Meg?" he called out.

"I can't remember. It was an American name, though—or maybe Irish."

Still standing at the desk, Walt began leafing through the book. Then, about ten seconds later, he announced triumphantly, "Ah, here it is! Francesca Gonzalez. You had it listed under *F*, Meg. And, incidentally, you've got 'Kirkpatrick' in parentheses. I suppose that's her married name."

"I suppose," Megan agreed, most of the color having drained from her cheeks by now.

"The woman doesn't live far from the city, either," a self-satisfied Walt reported. "I'll write down the address for you, Officers."

"I was *sure* I hadn't made a note of that address. I mean, why would I?" Megan murmured lamely.

Walt shrugged. "Who can figure out why you do the things you do, my love?" And turning to the detectives: "If you have no more questions for me, I'd like to get over to the office."

"No problem," Gabe responded. "I think that about does it."

"Good. I've gotta make a living," Walt said with a wink, "so I can keep this high-maintenance wife of mine in chinchilla coats and outrageously expensive little baubles." Then he shook hands with the two policemen, who told him how much they appreciated his cooperation. "I only wish I could have been more helpful to you. I'd like nothing better than to see the bastard who poisoned my friend rot in jail," he muttered.

And now, he walked over to his wife and, bending down, brushed her cheek with a perfunctory kiss. After which he strode purposefully from the room, closing the door behind him.

"Uh, was there anything else you wanted to ask me?" Megan inquired nervously.

"As a matter of fact, there are a couple of things we'd like to talk to you about. But it shouldn't take very long," Gabe assured her.

"Oh. Well, all right. Go on."

"We're aware that you had a romantic involvement with Ron Harwood at one point."

Megan looked stricken. "How . . . how did you find out?"

"That's not important. What concerns us is whether his wife suspected that there was another woman—or women—in his life. Were you leveling with us before when you said you didn't have any idea if this was the case?"

"Yes, I was."

"Your own relationship with Mr. Harwood—was it serious at any point?"

"*Serious?* God no! I have better sense than that. Besides—and this will no doubt strike you as strange—I *love* my husband. And in spite of his doing an excellent job of hiding it, he loves me, too. Walt's no Cary Grant, of course, but neither was Rob. It's just that, well—this is rather awkward—Rob was better . . . he was a better lover. Besides, Walt did his share of bed-hopping, too—although, as far as I can tell, that's in the past."

"Do you think your husband had any inkling that something was going on between you and his good friend?" Ray interjected.

"I'm *positive* he didn't. If he ever found out about Rob and me, he would've been outta here. Either that, or I'd be a dead woman by now." There was a pause. "Uh, if there's nothing else . . ."

Ray glanced at Gabe, who shrugged. "No, that's about it. And we thank you for giving us so much of your time."

"You're welcome. I only hope you find out who did this awful thing."

Gabe was the one to respond. "So do we, Megan," he said softly. "So do we."

Chapter 27

Reluctantly, I put away the manuscript. It was the end of that particular section, so it seemed as good a time as any to give it up for a while. Especially when you consider that for the last ten minutes, my stomach had—excuse the expression—been bellyaching like crazy.

The ringing of the phone drowned it out a little. It was Felix. "You got maybe a minute to talk now?"

"Of course."

"I knew you wouldn't be able to call to my house, on account of Shirley being there. So I'm using the telephone on the corner—in case you already heard something. Which, most likely, you didn't," he added hastily.

"My contact at the Department of Motor Vehicles hasn't gotten back to me yet; that's why I haven't phoned you. She—my contact—said she'd speak to me this afternoon, and I've been waiting for the call. I'll get in touch with you at work the minute I know anything. I promise. Uh, are you holding up okay?" I asked now. "I mean, how are you doing?"

"How I'm doing? I'm doing not so wonderful, is how."

"I realize this is very hard on you. But we still have no idea as to what's actually going on. So, please, Felix, hang in there a little while longer, and let's hope for the best."

"Okay, Desiree." I could just picture him shrugging his shoulders. "I'm hanging—and I'm hoping."

Well, it was about noon by now, and it was a beautiful day. I'd have liked to go out for a burger and then maybe taken a walk over to this little whatnot shop a couple of blocks away. There's been a GOING OUT OF BUSINESS! EVERYTHING 60% OFF! sign in the window of that place almost from the day it opened around two years ago. But along with the chintzy vinyl tablecloths, the melamine dinnerware, and the world's ugliest lamps, the store occasionally gets in some fairly good-looking earrings. (And in case I haven't mentioned it, earrings are one of my many major weaknesses.)

Naturally, you won't find anything in sterling silver or fourteen-karat gold—or even ten-karat gold—at Annie's Home, Office, and Gift Shop. And, also naturally, the red stones in the earrings aren't genuine rubies and the green ones aren't emeralds. Nevertheless, I often check out Annie's jewelry section when I need a bit of a lift and can't afford the real thing. I mean, so what if, every once in a while, my ears turn green? It's not as if it's a permanent condition or anything.

Unfortunately, though, I had to forget about even sticking my nose outside this afternoon—not until I talked to Beth. The thing is, I'd neglected to give her my cell phone number. And suppose she called here while I was out—and then I wasn't able to reach her when I tried returning the call?

At any rate, I wound up eating a sandwich at my desk and casting malevolent glances at the telephone between every bite. Finally, at three twenty (by which time I'd become pretty discouraged), the phone rang.

"Guess who," Beth said when I picked up.

"Bless you," I told her.

"You have a pencil and a piece of paper handy?"

"You bet."

"Okay, the car's registered to a Stanley Kholl—that's K-h-o-l-l—and he lives on the Upper East Side. By the way, his date of birth puts him at sixty-two. Looks like your client's cheating wife has a thing for younger men." She cackled at her little witticism before providing the address, which, as it happened, wasn't that far from my own. "Got it?" she asked.

"Got it. But, uh, you did say the first name was Stanley, right?"

"Yeah, that's right. Why?"

"I thought his first name might be Tony, that's all."

"Well, you thought wrong."

"Apparently. Anyhow, Beth, thanks a million. As soon as things quiet down around here, I'll phone you about lunch, and we'll go somewhere special." I gulped before saying the next words: "I was thinking of the Four Seasons—if that's all right with you."

"I suppose it'll have to do," she quipped.

We hung up then, and I told myself that sometimes it's worthwhile in the long run to spring for something you really can't afford. (I had no intention of billing Felix for this little extravagance, since I regarded it as not only a gesture of appreciation, but a down payment on future goodwill.)

At any rate, it was too late for me to do anything today about Beth's report, particularly since I was due at Ellen's at seven, and checking out something like that often winds up being very time-consuming. But I vowed that tomorrow I'd find out who this Stanley Kholl was—along with precisely *what he was* to Shirley Lugash.

I didn't waste any time in passing Beth's information on to Felix, spelling out the name of his wife's mystery man.

"I never heard of no one by that name," he told me.

"You're sure?"

"Better than sure. I'm *positive*."

Jackie walked in right after my brief conversation with Felix.

"Hi, Dez, how are things going?" And with this, she plopped down in the chair across from my desk—the only available seating in my cigar box of an office.

"Ask me that when you've got a few hours to spare."

Jackie's brow wrinkled. "What's wrong?"

"Nothing, really. I'm just kidding."

"Everything all right with Nick?" she persisted.

"So far, anyway. In other words, we're still status quo." I quickly came back with, "What about Derwin? Everything okay there?"

Jackie smiled happily. "*Very* okay. He took me to kind of a pricey restaurant the other night, and he didn't bat an eye when the check came. For once, he even left a decent tip." She lowered her voice to a whisper before confessing, "I peeked." And almost in the same breath: "What's happening with the mystery? Have you figured out the second clue yet?"

"You've gotta be kidding!"

"Well, tell me what it says. Maybe I can save your little keister again."

(Did I hear my *little* keister?)

I reached for my attaché case, took out the typewritten sheet, and handed it to her. After close to a minute (she must have reread the thing a dozen times), she raised her eyes and shook her head. "Je-*sus*! You need a clue to decipher the clue!"

"I was hoping you'd help me figure it out," I told her, straight-faced.

"Don't be such a wise guy. Besides, you've already had your happy accident there. Don't count on its happening again."

We chatted for a few minutes longer; then Jackie went back to her desk. Me? Like an idiot, I sat there staring at that piece of paper as if transfixed—and got more discouraged by the second.

I decided then to check the Internet for the little Pennsylvania town where, according to the manuscript, Tess and Ellie grew up. I mean, forget that "think multinationally" business. I needed to do *something*, and this was the only something to occur to me.

I went online and Googled the word "Huckleby." No town by that name was listed in Pennsylvania—or anywhere else. And I ask you: If you can't believe Google, who *can* you believe?

Well, it was what I'd expected; nevertheless, I was even more dejected than I'd been a few minutes earlier. So I called it a day.

I felt a little better as soon as I got into the taxi, having evidently managed to leave some of my negative feelings behind me at the office—at least for now. Then, once I was back in my apartment, it didn't take long before I was actually in good spirits.

There may not have been a smile on my face, but there was certainly one inside me as I showered and changed. Tonight, I'd be having dinner with two of my very favorite people.

Chapter 28

I got to Ellen and Mike's promptly at seven. Mike was the one to open the door, and, bending his six-foot-plus frame practically in half, he planted a kiss on my cheek. Then he smiled at me warmly—Mike has a great smile—and I handed him my usual modest contribution to one of our Chinese dinners. This being two quarts of Häagen-Dazs: Belgian chocolate—Ellen's favorite—and, of course, macadamia brittle, which, from my perspective, no Chinese meal is complete without. (Ditto the cuisines of Italy, France, Spain, Germany . . .) Anyhow, I'd have brought along Mike's favorite, too, only he's always insisted that he has no preference at all—as long as it's ice cream.

Ellen put in an appearance almost at once. She was wearing formfitting white jeans paired with a black and white striped polo shirt, and, in my humble, unbiased opinion, she looked incredible. Ellen's five-six, and about the width of a matchstick. Plus, she has these large, liquid brown eyes; silky, shoulder-length dark brown hair; and a dynamite smile. Now, while I've always maintained that she resembles the late Audrey Hepburn, for some reason, this was especially true just then. In fact, I challenge anyone to find me someone who looks more like Audrey than Ellen did that night! Anyhow, she enveloped me in one of her usual affectionate hugs, almost squeezing the breath out of me before I managed to wriggle out of her grasp.

I sat down on the living room sofa, while Mike poured the Cabernet Sauvignon and his recently acquired wife busied herself with rearranging the cheeses that occupied a large serving dish sitting on the coffee table—right alongside a very nice selection of crackers. After this—and turning down the helping hand I'd volunteered—Ellen dashed into the kitchen. She emerged only a minute or two later with a plate of bacon rollups, a really delicious hors d'oeuvre that Mike (who else?) had learned to prepare since their marriage. And soon the three of us were eating a little and drinking a little and talking a lot.

We covered a variety of topics, including the new, improved Margot (she was still holding to her promise about letting up on that baby business). This was followed by a monologue from Ellen concerning her job. (A couple of weeks ago, a new assistant had been foisted on her, and the woman was driving her crazy!) A short while later, I asked Mike about the trip his parents had taken to London about a month back. (Mike's mother is every bit as nice as Ellen's mother *isn't*.) "They had a wonderful time; they still rave about it," he told me, obviously pleased that I'd remembered.

He'd barely gotten the words out when Ellen brought up the subject of Nick, as I expected that, sooner or later, she would. I told her he was fine. Following this, she remarked—as she had on a couple of earlier occasions—that the four of us should go out together some evening. And I gave her the same response I'd given her before. "Yes, we really should," I agreed—before quickly changing the subject. The thing is, I just didn't know how much longer Nick would be in my life, and the last thing I wanted was for my family and friends to have any expectations of our whatever-you-want-to-call-it evolving into something permanent.

After a while, Mike phoned Mandarin Joy with our order. There hadn't been any need to check the menu first (as Ellen had suggested to me on the phone the other night). I mean, maybe I wasn't as familiar with the fare as she and Mike were. But then, I doubt if anyone except the restaurant's chef could compete with them for this honor. Nevertheless, I was still able to name just about every Mandarin Joy dish I'd ever eaten—mostly because our selections seldom varied. At any rate, about a half hour after Mike's call, the deliveryman was at the door.

The folding table had already been set up in the living room, covered with an elegant damask cloth and set with sterling flatware, crystal stemware, and Limoges china, all of which had been part of Ellen's engagement/shower/ wedding bounty. She quickly transferred the contents of the plastic microwave-safe containers to her Limoges serving platters. And soon we were feasting on spareribs, egg rolls, fried rice, moo shu pork, sweet and sour chicken, and shrimp with black bean sauce. All of which, unless I'm very much mistaken, we'd had the last time I was here—and any number of times prior to that.

Over the spareribs (or maybe it was the egg rolls), Ellen asked if I'd made any progress yet with regard to my make-believe murder.

"As a matter of fact, I have. And what I've learned is that there's nothing make-believe about it."

Ellen's eyes opened wide. "I don't understand."

"I've solved the first clue, and it reveals that what Belle Simone wrote about was for real."

"Are you saying that the book is about a murder that . . . that actually *occurred*?" And before I could respond: "You're kidding," she gasped.

"That's great—your solving the clue," Mike broke in. "Congratulations, Dez! Listen, I'd love to hear about the case—if you don't mind talking about it, that is. All I was able to get from Ellen is that you're being paid close to twenty-five thousand dollars to come up with the solution to some romance author's mystery."

Smiling, I shrugged my shoulders. "Do you *believe* it? I have no idea why she'd want to hand over that kind of money. Anyway, I haven't finished the manuscript yet, but I can give you a brief synopsis of what I've read so far, if you like."

"I'd like very much."

"Same here," Ellen piped up.

So from my last bite of fried rice until my first mouthful of macadamia brittle, I proceeded to acquaint them with Belle's mystery. After this, I explained that I'd now have to figure out the meaning of two more clues in order to arrive at the solution to the murder. "I just got the second one yesterday. And if I thought clue number one was a challenge, well, it was before I had a look at *this* doozy."

"Can I be of any help to you, Dez? Not that I expect to be able to decipher the clue on my own, but I'd be happy to serve as a sounding board when and if you need one."

"I'd feel as though I were cheating if I involved you or anyone else. At this point, at any rate," I added hastily. "But if I don't get anywhere after a reasonable amount of time, I'll probably relax my standards a little. So may I reserve the right to pick your brain if it should become necessary?"

"Be my guest anytime," Mike responded genially.

"Uh, maybe you'd care to see what you can do with that first clue, though—just for fun. By the way, even if you knew absolutely nothing about the plot, it would still be possible to figure out the clue."

"Really? Well, it sounds like an interesting challenge. I wouldn't mind giving it a try . . . if you're sure it's all right with you."

"It's fine. When we finish eating, I'll write out the clue for you—precisely as I received it."

"Thanks." Then, grinning like a little boy: "Hey, this is exciting!"

After dinner, we sat around the table, talking some more and sipping coffee. (Listen, where is it written that a person has to drink tea with Chinese food?) Then, all of a sudden, one of us (me, I think) noticed that it was close to twelve.

So I provided Mike with the promised clue and got ready to leave. At the door, I gave them both a peck on the cheek and a quick hug, managing to avoid Ellen's clutches before she had the chance to wrap those harmless-looking—but deadly—matchstick arms around me.

*   *   *

The light on the answering machine was blinking when I got back to my apartment. The call was from Mike.

"I thought you might be home by now. I just wanted to let you know that I'm reasonably certain I have the answer to clue number one," he announced. "The book's a roman à clef."

He went on to talk about how great it was to see me again, but I tuned him out. This man—my own nephew— had just told me precisely what I needed to hear—right? I mean, it had taken me what seemed like an eternity to decipher that damn clue, and then Mike did it in . . . what? Five minutes? Ten minutes?

I tuned him back in, just in time to hear, "Of course, I prefer not to admit, even to myself, that you gave the whole thing away."

I gave the whole thing away?

Mike answered my unspoken question. "In case you've forgotten, you'd already let us know that this was a true story."

That's right! I did, didn't I?

"Plus, the clue itself reads that it's necessary to think the way the French do."

That's right! It does, doesn't it?

I felt a whole lot better than I had only moments earlier. Okay, maybe I was no Hercule Poirot. But—as yet, at least—Mike hadn't proved himself to be any Desiree Shapiro, either.

Chapter 29

The first thing I thought when I woke up Friday morning was, *My God! I forgot to tell Jackie!*

How could I have let this happen? I mean, in Jackie's mind, there was no excuse for failing to let her know you wouldn't be in on a particular day. Listen, I once heard her liken it to wearing socks with high heels. (I swear!) And while I've never been able to figure out the logic of that comparison, it isn't important. What mattered was that I still had time to rectify the oversight. I reached for the phone.

"Uh, I just found out I have to be somewhere this morning, and there's a good chance I won't make it to the office at all today."

"What's going on?" Jackie asked—as I knew she would.

"I have to check out the wife of a client," I admitted reluctantly.

"She's cheating on him, huh?" Jackie pounced. She seemed to relish the idea.

"I'm not sure." I didn't give her a chance to utter another syllable. "Listen, Jackie, I'm running late; I've really gotta leave now. Have a good weekend, okay?" And with this, I put the phone back in its cradle.

Breaking a personal speed record then, I dressed and ate in a little over an hour. After which I took a taxi to Stanley Kholl's address.

The apartment building was fairly large and quite old but looked to be well kept. It had a kind of faded charm, I decided. I also decided that the tenants here had to be paying a pretty hefty rent.

A young uniformed doorman stood at the entrance, holding the door open for an elderly lady.

"Uh, I wonder if you could help me," I said, when the woman had gone inside. "A friend from Belgium asked me to look up her cousins—she's planning on coming to New York. I'm not sure I have the right address, though. Does a Stanley Kholl live here?"

"Apartment twelve-C," he answered promptly.

"You wouldn't know if he has a brother, would you?" I put to him. I was figuring that maybe the brother's car was out of commission—or possibly the brother didn't even *have* a car. But in either event, he (Tony) borrowed Stanley's. Of course, this could also be true of a close friend, I realized. But I preferred not to think about that now.

"I'm afraid not, ma'am."

"You're afraid he doesn't have a brother, or you're afraid you don't know?"

The boyish-looking doorman grinned, and I couldn't help noticing that he was kind of cute. (Listen, I was well aware that he was too young for me, but cute's cute.) "I have no idea whether or not Mr. Kholl has a brother. All I can tell you is that it's only him and his wife in the apartment."

"Mr. Kholl's married?"

"Yep. He's not in right now, but maybe you'd want to talk to Mrs. Kholl—only her name isn't Kholl; it's Pierce. Antoinette Pierce. She kept her maiden name, I suppose. Anyway, I'm sure she could tell you if her husband has a brother."

"I really needed to speak to Mr. Kholl. But thanks very much for your time."

I was discouraged, but I wasn't ready to call it quits. I stopped at a nearby coffee shop to refuel and come up with some kind of plan on how to proceed with this thing. Two cups of coffee and half a blueberry muffin later, it hit me: Toni—with an *i*—is a nickname for Antoinette! At that moment, I would have bet the $24,940 I hoped was in my future that Shirley Lugash's "mystery man" was a woman!

I walked quickly (for me) back to Stanley Kholl's building. I had one last question for the young doorman.

He was standing just where I'd left him. "Well, look who's back," he said, smiling broadly.

"I have another question for you."

"How come I'm not surprised?"

"Mrs. Pierce. Can you tell me if she goes by the nickname of Toni?"

"I'm afraid I couldn't say. I hardly ever see the woman—she rarely leaves the apartment. The poor lady's an invalid."

"Thank you, thank you, thank you!" And, reaching into my pocket, I handed over the twenty dollars I'd prepared for him.

I could hardly wait to talk to my client. But, unfortunately, it was too early to reach him at Jerome's. So I stopped off at D'Agostino's and practically bought out the store. Then, once my order was delivered—about an hour later—I proceeded to make a lasagna, which kept me occupied while I waited for Felix to arrive at work.

I called the restaurant at a few minutes after three. And today it was Felix who answered the telephone. (You couldn't mistake his, "Jerome's.")

"Felix? It's Desiree. Good news!"

"Good news?" He sounded skeptical.

"Toni is a nickname for Antoinette," I explained. "And this particular Toni—the one Shirley's been hanging around with on Wednesdays—is an invalid. You've never heard your wife mention a woman named Antoinette Pierce?"

"I don't recall nobody by that name. But, uh, Desiree? What about that man Kholl?"

"He's Toni's husband, and no doubt he just gave Shirley a lift home from their apartment Wednesday night."

"This Toni you're speaking about, you're *sure* she is the individual—the same Toni—my Shirley goes to see?"

"I'm sure. It all fits. I'm still checking out a couple of things, though. And hopefully, I'll be able to fill you in on everything later this evening. But, listen, Felix, this is wonderful—we couldn't have asked for anything better. So, please, believe the truth, and be happy."

"I'm happy, Desiree, I'm happy. It's just . . ."

"What?"

"This being the case—that her friend is a woman—why wouldn't she just tell me she's been visiting her all these weeks?"

" 'Why' is right. I'll talk to you later, and I should have the answer by then."

"Desiree?"

"Yes, Felix?"

"God bless you."

Felix's words had me close to tears. I couldn't remember the last time anyone had blessed me. (Other than after I sneezed, I mean.) I crossed my fingers that this whole thing would be cleared up tonight. In the meantime, however, even if not all the i's were dotted and the t's were crossed yet, I was still extremely pleased with how the investigation was turning out.

A couple of hours later I stuck the now fully baked lasagna in the freezer and zapped my supper—some leftover meat loaf—in the twentieth century's greatest invention. Then at around eight o'clock, I headed back to Antoinette/Toni's building.

The doorman presently on duty was middle-aged and huge—in both directions. I got a crick in my neck just looking up at him. And his measurements from east to west were every bit as formidable.

"Uh, excuse me," I said.

Yes?" I noticed that he wasn't smiling.

"I'm with the Manhattan Society of Disabled Women, and we're gathering some statistics on the living arrangements and quality of life of our local disabled. I wonder if you'd mind giving me a few minutes of your time."

He actually smirked. "Do I look disabled?"

"No, of course not. I—"

"Well, I must look like a woman, then."

I swear I would have punched him in the nose—that

is, if I could have reached that high. "Listen, I just want to find out if there are any disabled tenants in this building."

"You don't fool me," he retorted, glaring. "You want me to give you the names of these people so you can hit 'em up for money or something."

"You couldn't be more wrong. I'm only interested in the sort of lives they lead. This is strictly for research purposes, I assure you; you don't have to mention names at all." He didn't respond, so I removed ten dollars from my wallet and held it out to him. He glanced at the denomination and made a face. He was about to say something when a woman carrying a couple of large, bulky packages came up the walkway.

"Can you give me a hand with this stuff, Rick?" she called out. "Just to the elevator will be fine."

"Certainly, Ms. Ryan. Be glad to." He relieved the woman of her burden, then followed her into the building without so much as a glance in my direction.

When he returned, the ten in my hand had been joined by its twin, along with a five. "I really need all the help I can get with this survey," I murmured, holding out this increased inducement and looking up at him with what I hoped were sorrowful eyes. "It won't take more than five or ten minutes," I assured him.

"Make it five, and you got yourself a deal," he said firmly, relieving me of the bills and shoving them in a pocket.

"Okay, five," I reluctantly agreed. Immediately after which I fished around in my humongous handbag for a pen and a pad. (I felt that making notations—along with posing some questions I had no real interest in having answered—would lend some authenticity to my performance.) "To start with, how many disabled tenants are there in this building?" I inquired, my pen poised.

"You talkin' completely disabled or partly?"

"The survey also includes the partially disabled."

"There's only two," he responded immediately, then quickly corrected himself. "No, three." I began jotting down his answers now.

"Can you tell me their approximate ages and who they live with?"

"Christ! I'm no judge of age!"

"All right. Are any of the three teenagers?"

"One of 'em looks like a kid, but she could be in her early twenties. Like I said, as far as age, you can't go by me. Anyhow, that young lady lives with her mother."

"On what floor is her apartment?"

Rick peered at me through narrowed eyes.

"An important section of the survey is devoted to living accommodations," I was quick to inform him.

"First floor," he grumbled.

"Any of the other women live on the first floor?"

He shook his head. "One's on twelve. She must be near seventy, and she's got a husband. The other's prob'ly around forty. Her apartment's on eight—or maybe seven. No, I'm pretty sure it's eight. Anyhow, I don't know much about her—she just moved here a couple weeks ago. All's I can tell you is she lives alone, although Dave—he's the doorman comes on at seven in the a.m.—says some health care worker goes up there every morning."

"What do these women do in the way of outside activities—both day and evening? Are they able to get around? Do they have many visitors? That sort of thing."

"The girl on the first floor, she's in a wheelchair. Sometimes in the afternoon, her and her mom do some shopping, or her mom takes her for a walk—maybe over to Central Park. But Central Park's only a guess. And once in a while, they'll have company. Occasionally, they go out for a few hours in the evening, too—maybe to dinner or a movie, maybe to both. Who can say?"

"And the other two women?"

"This guy comes over two or three nights a week, right around suppertime, to visit that new lady. He's always carryin' food, too—mostly Eyetalian, my nose informs me. I don't know if he's her brother or her boyfriend, or what. So don't bother askin'. During the day, it's possible that health care woman she's got comin' in takes her for walks, and maybe she gets visitors, too. Only not during my shift, which is from three to eleven p.m. The fact is, I only saw the lady herself this one time, and that was when she was movin' in."

"She's in a wheelchair, too?"

Rick shook his head. "She walks with two canes—one in each hand."

"And the woman on twelve?" My mouth immediately went dry in anticipation.

Before he could respond, however, a middle-aged man was about to leave the building, and Rick hurriedly opened the door for him. "How's your son doing, Rick?" the man inquired, pausing in the open doorway.

"He's comin' along fine, Mr. Deitz. Doctor says he should be out of that cast by next week."

"Good for him!"

By now, my heart was thumping so loudly I was afraid Rick could hear it. "You were about to say something with regard to the tenant on twelve."

"Oh, yeah. All's I can tell you is she's not real steady on her feet. She was going out with her husband one evening, and after they walked away, I did hear one ten-ant tellin' the other that this lady we're discussin' had MS—multiple sclerosis. Considering your line of work, you know what that is, right?"

"Yes, I do."

"Of course, who can say if that tenant knew what she was talkin' about? Anyways, sometimes this lady—the one on twelve—and her husband go out to dinner, but not real often. And at least once a week her daughter comes to visit."

"Uh, that's it?" I was so afraid this was all he was going to tell me about Toni that the words just pushed their way out.

Rick frowned. "No, as a matter of fact that's *not* it. Every Wednesday, Mr.—" He caught himself and broke off. "What I meant to say," he began again, "is that every Wednesday night, her husband walks outta here sometime after eight with three ladies, and a while later he comes back alone. Well, this one night I kidded him about havin' a harem, and he had himself a good laugh. Seems that on Wednesdays his wife plays canasta with these ladies, and he always drives 'em home. And this, missy, is all I can tell you."

I could have kissed him! (And I might very well have, too—if he'd been the doorman I'd talked to this morning.) "Thanks, Rick, you've been a very big help. May I call you Rick?"

"Suit yourself," he answered, shrugging. Then he checked his watch. "I thought so. Listen, Ms. . . . ."

"Ames," I supplied. (It was as good a name as any.)

"Well, Ms. Ames," he groused, "this took a lot longer than five minutes. You prob'ly know it, too." And he held out his hand, palm up.

"Yes, it certainly did," I agreed, ignoring the unspoken demand. (I mean, this was, in effect, Felix's money I was paying out.) "You really should learn to talk a little faster." And so saying, I shook the outstretched hand.

As soon as I was back in my apartment I dialed Felix. And for the second time that day, I could hardly contain myself.

Of course, I was still in the dark as to the reason for Shirley's secrecy. But maybe Felix would have some idea of why she'd chosen to conceal from him the fact that she participated in these harmless little canasta games.

And, to my astonishment, he did.

"I have an update for you, Felix. Listen, if your wife does any cheating on Wednesdays, it's at cards."

I couldn't have been more surprised by his response. "She promised she wouldn't!"

"Wouldn't what?"

"Play cards no more. I don't like Shirley should gamble, and she knows it."

"I'm not even certain the women play for money. And if they do, it's probably just for pennies."

"Today it's pennies; tomorrow it's dollars. Maybe a lotta dollars." He clicked his tongue. "Gambling's a terrible thing, Desiree."

I'm aware that it wasn't very professional of me, but I was more than disappointed by his reaction; I was actually angry. "Listen, Felix," I snapped, "would you rather Shirley had found herself a lover?"

There was a long silence before he admitted softly, "God forbid."

"And as I told you, the woman who hosts the canasta games at her apartment—this Toni—is an invalid. Cards give her an opportunity to socialize, something that I understand she doesn't otherwise get to do very often."

My client let out a long sigh. "Listen, Desiree, my brother Aaron? He started out small, too. But he kept betting a little more, and a little more after that. Craps, he played." Then, with tears in his voice, Felix said softly, "One morning—it will be thirteen years next week—they found Aaron in an alley. He had a bullet in his head." There was a long pause before he added, "He was the baby in the family."

The fog in my brain had just lifted. "I'm so sorry . . . so *very* sorry for your loss, Felix. But I'm sure these ladies don't play cards to gamble; it's mostly the idea of getting together for a few hours. And I believe this is especially true in Toni's case; I understand she's pretty much homebound."

There were two or three seconds of silence before a contrite Felix murmured, "I got to apologize to you, Desiree. I'm an old fool; that's what I am. I should thank God every single day that I got such a wonderful wife like my Shirley."

"I'm so glad to hear you say that. Uh, one more thing. Would you like to do yourself a favor, Felix?"

"I imagine so."

"Don't ever let on to Shirley that you know about the card games. Because if she should ever learn that you didn't trust her, that you hired someone to poke around in her life, it's likely you'll be in big trouble. *Really* big trouble."

"That much I could figure out. Hey, maybe now she'll be able to add to the family fortune," he joked. Then very soberly: "I realize now how foolish I acted a couple minutes ago. You know what I should have said to you right away?"

"I'm afraid not."

"Well, I'll tell to you what. It was, 'Thanks, Desiree. For giving me back my life.'"

Chapter 30

I slept late on Saturday. (Listen, with the kind of day—and night—I'd put in yesterday, I figured I'd earned it.)

When I opened my eyes, the first thing that came to mind was Felix's words to me just before we hung up: *Thanks, Desiree. For giving me back my life.*

Well, I've been a PI for a long time, and believe it or not, I've had quite a number of grateful clients. But what Felix said—and the way he said it—really touched me. Recalling those words now, for a few brief moments I felt pretty damn good about myself all over again. So good, in fact, that even before I crawled out of bed, I mentally slashed—by another ten percent—the already low fee I'd intended charging him.

After breakfast, I spent what little was left of the morning and a good chunk of the afternoon cleaning my apartment—and trying not to think about Nick. I wound up doing a better job on the apartment than I did on censoring my thoughts.

As much as he cared for me—and I was sure that Nick *did* care for me—there was no way his only child would allow me to remain in his life. I had little doubt that, one way or another, TKFH would sabotage my relationship with his father.

I looked down at my hand. I was beating the bejesus out of the sofa cushions.

At shortly after three, I was through playing Mrs. Clean, and I picked up the manuscript again. The detectives, I reminded myself, had just been to see Walt and Megan Riley, where they'd obtained the address of the

cleaning woman Rob Harwood had allegedly bribed to
keep his affair with Megan secret.

Part two, chapter seven opened with:

On leaving the Rileys' building, the detectives were
pleasantly surprised to see that the sun was actually shining now.

"I think it's about time we had a talk with the neighbors, don't you? Gabe said, as he was about to open the
car door.

Ray stopped alongside him. "*Whose* neighbors?"

"The Harwoods', of course."

"You think it might have been the widow who made
that little contribution to ol' Robbie's champagne?"

"You're still wet behind the ears, aren't you?" Gabe
cracked, grinning. "Listen, the spouse is invariably the primary suspect in homicides of this sort—so it's something
we need to do. Not that I'm optimistic about the results,
but you never can tell, right?"

Ray frowned. "Thanks for the lesson, Dad," he muttered.
"But I'm aware of that. I was just wondering about *your*
thoughts on Mrs. Harwood."

"At this moment, I don't really have any. All I know is that
she's a woman whose husband has just been murdered."

That morning, the two policemen spoke to the doorman
presently on duty at the Harwoods' residence, as well as
to a number of their neighbors. (They would be returning
this evening to question Barney, who was on duty from
three to eleven p.m. And at a later date, they'd be back
to talk to the doorman on the eleven-p.m.-to-seven-a.m.
shift, along with several more of the building's tenants.)
Everyone appeared to be in agreement: The Harwoods
were a normal, happy family—as far as they knew, that is.

"Surprise, surprise," Gabe muttered after that first fruitless visit.

At a little past noon, Gabe and Ray returned to the
precinct to attend to some long-overdue paperwork. Af-

terward, Gabe obtained the phone number of Francesca (Gonzalez) Kirkpatrick and called to arrange a meeting with her. He could hear a baby wailing in the background.

"Something ees wrong, Officer?" Francesca asked nervously after he'd identified himself.

"Nothing for you to worry about," Gabe assured her. "But we're looking into the death of a former employer of yours: Rob Harwood."

"Oh, my." She said it almost casually.

"We believe he may have been murdered."

"Madre de Dios!" the woman exclaimed. "How he die?"

"We're reasonably certain he was poisoned, that someone slipped something into his drink the night of his sixtieth birthday party."

"Who could 'ave did thees terrible thing?"

"That's what we hope to find out. My partner and I would appreciate it if you could spare us a little of your time."

"Why? I don' know nothing about a murder."

"No, no, of course not," Gabe put in quickly. "But you may be able to tell us something about Mr. Harwood himself that would be of help." And before she could respond, he supplied the usual, often hollow promise: "We won't keep you long."

"I take Steven—my baby—to pediatrician for checkup two o'clock," Francesca told him. "But ees okay if you come around four."

"Thank you, Mrs. Kirkpatrick. We'll be there at four."

The conversation had no sooner concluded than the officers placed a call to Chicago, to the offices of Shaw and Carlisle, Financial Consultants. Gabe informed the woman who answered the phone that he was with the New York City Police Department and wanted to speak to Mr. Michael Carlisle, heretofore known as Rebecca's friend Mickey.

The man was on the line less than a minute later.

"This is Sergeant Wilson, Mr. Carlisle," Gabe said. "My partner, Detective Carson, and I have a couple of questions we'd like to ask you regarding the party you attended at the Harwoods' on Friday evening."

"No problem. As a matter of fact, I've been expecting to hear from you, Sergeant."

"I gather you've spoken to Mrs. McMartin, then."

"Yesterday afternoon. She telephoned to let me know you suspect that Rob—Mr. Harwood—was poisoned."

"Unfortunately, this could be the case. But we'll have to wait for the autopsy report to know for certain. In the meantime, though, we're proceeding under that assumption. I suppose Mrs. McMartin mentioned that the deceased left his drink unattended at one point, while he went upstairs to change his clothes."

"Yes, she did."

"We're hoping you noticed something that could help us identify who might have doctored that drink. Possibly someone acting in a suspicious manner or behaving a little unusually?"

"I'm afraid not." He sounded sincerely regretful. "Rebecca said you'd probably also be interested in finding out whether I saw anyone go in or out of the dining room prior to dinner. And, unfortunately, I can't help you there, either."

"Tell me," Gabe put to the man now, "did you get to speak to Mr. Harwood at all that evening?"

"Just for a minute—if that. Rebecca went over to him—with me in tow—and introduced us. This was quite soon after he walked in. He seemed like a pretty nice guy."

"Mrs. McMartin was apparently very fond of him."

"Rebecca was *crazy* about him." Then, almost the instant the words were spoken: "But don't get the wrong impression. There was nothing romantic about her feelings for Rob Harwood. She's a widow and still deeply in love with her deceased husband."

"He died years ago, I understand."

"True, but she's not over him yet. And it's quite probable she never will be. They were devoted to each other."

"This is Detective Carson," Ray interjected now. "I gather, then, that you'd met Mr. McMartin."

"Once—years back."

"So you've been to our fair city before," Ray commented in an attempt to put the lie to Rebecca's contention that this was her friend's first visit here.

"Nope. The one and only time I was ever in Warren's company was at our ten-year college reunion. And that took place in Columbus, Ohio—Rebecca and I had both attended Ohio State, which, in case she didn't mention it, is where our friendship began. Anyhow, he was a great guy, Warren. My wife said he was one of the most charming men she'd ever met."

"You're married?" Ray blurted out, somewhat surprised at this mention of a wife.

"A widower. Sally died last year."

"Oh, I'm sorry," Ray murmured. "Uh, my deepest . . . our deepest sympathies, Mr. Carlisle."

"Thank you, Detective."

"Incidentally, how did you like it here in our bustling metropolis?" Gabe inquired a moment later in an attempt to lighten the mood.

"It's a pretty nice place. But, of course, it's not Chicago."

And amen to that, Gabe responded silently.

I suddenly recalled that when I was reading the mystery the other day, there was a mention in the narration that *three* names were about to be deleted from the list of suspects. Well, I'd figured that, in all likelihood, Meg and Walt Riley would wind up being two of the three, since the officers had been on their way to question the couple at this point in the story. However, I wasn't able to put my finger on who else would soon be scratched. Now I didn't have much doubt.

"So," I read on, "where do you come out on this?" Ray asked his partner almost as soon as the conversation was over.

"I don't see this Michael or Mickey or whatever you want to call him as having a viable motive; that's where

I come out," Gabe answered. "Of course, I may be over-looking something. But I don't think so."

"Same here. You ready to remove him from the suspect list?"

"I suppose I am," Gabe said somewhat tentatively.

Ray grinned. "You know, we should probably celebrate; we've just exed out our first suspect."

"Not really. Technically, that bunch from the caterer were our first scratches. Plus, if the doorman backs up the Rileys' alibi—as I'm almost certain he will—they'll go, too. And an argument could be made for their also having preceded Mickey." Then, dryly: "At any rate, that'll mean we've got a mere nine possibilities left."

"If you weren't so hardheaded, we could make it eight," Ray shot back.

"You still harping on Cousin Elaine?"

"That's right. I have a real tough time picturing her doing the murder. Besides, I ask you again, why would she?"

"Okay, okay, you wore me down. And to tell the truth, I can't picture it, either. But if we find out the victim left her a bundle, Cousin Elaine is back on the list."

Francesca Gonzalez Kirkpatrick lived in a pleasant little suburb only twenty miles from Manhattan. Her home, which was a kind of cotton-candy pink, was on a quiet, tree-lined street, along with fifteen very similar residences, most of them also painted in food colors: cream, lemon yellow, pistachio . . . There was even a milk chocolate house at the end of the block.

The doorbell was answered by a short, thin, Hispanic woman in her late thirties or early forties. She wore a black T-shirt and black toreador pants, both of which emphasized the fact of her less than voluptuous figure.

"Mrs. Kirkpatrick?"

"Yes. And you are Sergeant . . . Sergeant . . ."

"Sergeant Wilson, ma'am. And this is my partner, Detective Carson."

"Come een, please." And, smiling shyly, Francesca motioned the detectives inside. She preceded them into a good-size living room furnished with only a sofa and two end tables. "Please," she murmured, gesturing toward the sofa. "You would like coffee, maybe?"

"No, thank you," Gabe responded. "We had some only a little while ago."

"A Coca-Cola? Ees very warm day."

"No, no, we're fine. But thank you."

"I come right back." Less than two minutes later, she was in the doorway, struggling under the weight of the kitchen chair she was carrying.

Ray was the first to jump up. "Wait a minute, Mrs. Kirkpatrick! Let me have that!"

Francesca shook her head. "Ees not heavy," she protested.

"It sure looks it." And after inducing her—with some difficulty—to relinquish the chair, he placed it opposite the sofa.

Francesca positioned herself on the edge of the seat, hands folded in her lap, her legs crossed at the ankles. "We 'ave order more furnitures months ago," she explained, obviously embarrassed. "But nothing ees deliver."

"I know exactly what you mean," Ray empathized. "It took over six months for me to get this bedroom set I ordered."

Gabe's eyes widened, and he had to swallow a grin. He'd been to his partner's apartment a couple of times, and the bedroom was furnished with a creaky, dilapidated bed, a bureau with drawers so warped they didn't even close properly, and a night table that was in the same sorry state as the banged-up brass lamp standing on it. But Francesca now seemed to feel a kind of camaraderie with the young detective and smiled at him warmly.

"We've got just a few questions for you, Mrs. Kirkpatrick," Gabe told her.

She nodded, then tilted her head expectantly.

"What sort of person was Mr. Harwood?"

"He was okay."

"And Mrs. Harwood?"

"She ees nice lady. *Very* nice lady."

"Did Mr. and Mrs. Harwood get along?"

Francesca looked blank. "Get along?"

"I mean, did they seem to like each other?"

"I suppose so."

"You never heard them argue?"

"I never hear *nothing* like that."

"Let me ask you this, then. Do you regard him as having been a good husband?"

Two deep red spots suddenly appeared on Francesca's cheeks. "I dunno. He was not very much at house when I come there."

Ray stepped in now. "According to someone who knew the Harwoods pretty well, Mr. Harwood cheated on his wife."

"You think *she* keel him? And for *that*? Never!" Francesca protested, eyes blazing. "Maybe she would 'ave leave him—but *keel* him?" She shook her head emphatically. "No. I don' believe."

"You seem to be extremely fond of Mrs. Harwood."

"She ees kindest lady I ever work for."

"We understand you worked for her sister, too."

"Meesus Feller?" She wrinkled her nose. "Yes, I work for her." It was obvious by her tone—and her nose—that Francesca didn't hold Catherine Feller in the same high regard as she did the widow.

"What's your opinion of Mrs. Feller?" the young detective probed.

Francesca shrugged. "She ees okay."

"How about Mrs. Riley?"

"I like her. I don' always like what Meesus Riley, she ees *doing*," the woman confided, "but I like her anyway; I cannot help it."

"What sort of things did Mrs. Riley do?"

"I don' remember. It was nothing very bad, though."

Ray could tell from the set of Francesca's chin that this was all she intended to say on the subject of Megan Riley's wrongdoing. So for his follow-up, he settled for, "And *Mr.* Riley, how did you feel about him?"

"I never see heem hardly. He work, work, work. All the time, he working."

"Catherine Feller claims you once told her you walked in on Mrs. Riley and Mr. Harwood when they were . . . uh . . . in bed together. Is this true, Mrs. Kirkpatrick?"

Francesca swallowed hard. Then, contemplating her toes, she whispered, "Ees true."

"He gave you money—two hundred dollars, I believe—to persuade you not to say anything to his wife," Gabe threw out.

"No, no! This ees lie!" she declared angrily, her face flushed, her small hands clenched into fists. "He *want* to give me two hundred dollars for not to tell Meesus Harwood what I see. But I don' take. I don' say nothing to Meesus Harwood, because I don' want to make pain for such a good lady."

"So Mrs. Feller lied?" Ray asked.

"Yes, she lie. But you know *why* I tell her about Meester Harwood and Meesus Riley? Was because I don' like what *her* and Meester Harwood, they are doing."

Gabe's eyebrows shot up almost to his forehead. "Are you saying there was also something between Mr. Harwood and his sister-in-law?"

"*Si*—uh, yes."

"How do you know this? Did you walk in on them, too?"

"No. I smell heem in her bedroom."

"You *smelled* him?"

"Yes. He wear strong cologne. And two, three times I smell thees cologne on Meesus Feller's peellowcases."

"But he isn't the only man who wears that scent," Ray pointed out.

"I know thees. So, at first, that ees what I say to myself. But I change my mind one day when I take shirts of Meester Harwood to Chinese laundry—and on collar of shirt, I see leepsteek."

"Uh, I'm sorry," Gabe broke in, "there was what on his shirt collar?"

Ray translated for his partner. "Lipstick, Gabe."

Francesca nodded in agreement. "And ees exac' same color Meesus Feller use."

"What I said about the cologne applies to the lipstick,

too, Mrs. Kirkpatrick. Millions of women wear that same shade," Gabe pointed out.

"But—" Francesca began, before a piercing scream interrupted her. Gabe stiffened at the sound, while Ray dropped his notepad. Francesca, however, smiled proudly. "Ees Steven, my baby," she informed them. "He got strong lungs, no?"

"Well, what do you think?" Gabe asked his partner as soon as they left the house, their exit following a brief—and noisy—get-together with the youngest Kirkpatrick.

"That she's right."

"You think the vic was screwing his sister-in-law?"

"I was talking about Steven—her kid. He *does* have a great pair of lungs."

"Very funny."

"Okay, to answer your question, let's put it this way: I wouldn't be the least bit surprised."

"I wouldn't, either."

"Still," Ray mused, "as far as her being our perp . . . Look, let's say Harwood and his sister-in-law *were* playing house. And let's assume that when Francesca dropped that little bomb on her about Megan Riley, Catherine was mad as hell. Well, don't forget that was around two years ago. Would she have waited this long to whack the guy?"

"Could be that something set her off recently. Or she might just have been biding her time until the perfect opportunity came along. And what could be closer to perfect than poisoning Harwood when there were all those other people around who had their own grievances against him?"

"I suppose that's possible," Ray said uncertainly. "Still, Catherine Feller didn't strike me as being a very patient woman. But, as you say, not long ago, Rob may have pulled something that really got to her. And here's another thing I'm wondering about. You see, I believe Francesca *refused* that bribe."

"I'm pretty sure she did, too."

"So what did Catherine have to gain by claiming she'd accepted it?"

"Damned if I know. It's conceivable she was trying to undermine the woman's credibility in the event we ever got around to questioning her. Or maybe she was aware at the time that Francesca was deriving some pleasure out of tattling to her about Harwood's involvement with another woman. And she said what she did out of pure spite."

These were the last words either of them spoke for some time. As usual, Ray was at the wheel on the drive home, and Gabe, who'd spent his third sleepless night in a row agonizing over the case, had closed his eyes for a moment. . . .

"Wake up, Gabe," Ray said softly about a half hour later, accompanying the words with a gentle poke in the ribs.

The response was brief: "Huh?"

"We're about five minutes from Burgers 'n' Stuff," his partner informed him, referring to a coffee shop not far from the precinct. "Feel like stopping off there?"

Gabe rubbed his eyes for a couple of seconds. Then he sat bolt upright, fully awake. "Geez, I didn't mean to conk out on you like that."

"No problem. You're better company when you're sleeping, anyway."

"You sound like my wife."

After a quick bite, the pair headed for the Harwoods' address. A round little man in a doorman's uniform was standing just outside the entrance, smoking a cigarette, when the officers approached him. He answered to the name of Barney.

In light of its outcome, he had no problem recalling the evening of the party—and Mr. and Mrs. Riley, as well.

"I remember buzzing the two of 'em upstairs. She's a good-looking woman, you know," he added by way of explanation. "And right after Mr. Harwood comes in, they're back in the lobby. That really surprised me—them leaving right after the guest of honor shows up. But then I saw that the lady was kind of under the weather. And her husband says to me she's not feeling too good and that they're gonna take a little walk so's she can get some fresh air. 'We'll see you in a few minutes,' he tells me. A few minutes, my foot!"

"Why do you say that, Barney?" Gabe asked.

"I looked at my watch just before they got back, because it seemed to me they'd been gone quite a while, and I was hoping everything was okay, you know? Anyhow, it was around quarter after seven when they showed up." He shook his head. "*A few minutes,* my foot!" he repeated.

"Only one more question," Ray said now. "Mr. and Mrs. Harwood, how did they appear to get along?"

"Fine, far's I know. It's a shame, what happened." And scowling, he shook his head again. "A goddam shame."

They were walking toward the car when Gabe stopped short. "I'd like to check out something else."

"What's that?"

"The diner Riley claims they went to."

"Why? You think they bribed the doorman?"

"No, I don't. But we can't be sure, can we? So let's take a little stroll, huh? Riley said it was on the next block."

The detectives walked east for slightly more than a block. There was nothing in sight that even resembled a diner. They retraced their steps, then covered the same distance in the opposite direction. Once again, no luck. But when they headed south—voilà!

Diagonally across the street, and just a block from the Harwoods' building, a neon sign was blinking at them. THE COZY NOOK, it said.

As the name indicated, the diner was small and . . . well, relatively cozy, anyway. Less than a dozen customers were there tonight, most of them eating at the counter. Doing the honors behind the counter were a stocky, middle-aged man and a tall, gaunt-looking woman, who appeared to be deep in conversation. The detectives headed straight for the counter and sat down directly in front of them. Gabe took out his wallet, opened it, and, clearing his throat, flashed the shield inside.

Now that he had their attention, he described the Rileys in some detail, then asked the pair if they recalled the couple's being there on Friday evening at about seven.

"Fancy clothes, huh?" (Gabe had felt it was safe to assume the Rileys had been elegantly turned out for the occasion.) "Doesn't sound like anyone who was sittin' at the counter that night," the man said.

"They were most likely at a table."

The man shook his head. "'Fraid I can't help you then. Fridays and Saturdays are our big nights, and I'm too busy back here to pay much attention to who's occupyin' the tables. The exception being if it was Marilyn Monroe."

"Fat chance," the woman told him. "She's been dead for years."

He glared at her. "Do you have to remind me?"

She turned to the officers. "I usually wait on the tables—me and Georgette over there." She inclined her head in the direction of a slender blonde, who was standing next to one of the tables, taking an order. "Now, I don't remember seeing a couple who fits that description. Could be, though, it's because they were at Georgette's station. I'll call her over."

But Georgette was already hurrying toward the counter to put in the order. Gabe wasted no time in flashing his shield again and repeating his request for information. Only this time, his description of the Rileys produced immediate results.

"*Her*, I'm not likely to forget. She kept running to the ladies' room every other minute—and all she had here was a cup of tea, too! At one point," the blonde confided, "I had to use the facilities myself. And I was in there the same time she was—we've got two stalls. Anyhow, I got so sick hearing her retch that I came close to losing my supper."

"Satisfied?" Ray asked his partner as they were leaving the Cozy Nook. "It looks like we're down to eight suspects now."

Gabe raised an eyebrow. "Satisfied? As far as I'm concerned, that's seven too many."

Chapter 31

I took a break for supper; then, over coffee, I went back to Belle's mystery. Only tonight, I didn't do any more reading. Instead, I gritted my teeth and wrestled with that damn clue again.

In order to identify the *real-life* suspects, I'd have to figure out where they were from, it said. (I'm paraphrasing.) By this, I could only assume that Belle was referring to where the *fictional* characters were from. All I knew for sure was that Huckleby, Pennsylvania, was out. And that I was to think multinationally . . .

For the longest while, my mind was totally blank. Then, suddenly, something occurred to me. But it was definitely not something I'd be able to tackle alone. I needed help, and I knew where to find it.

I went online, and as soon as I was connected to Google, I typed in the words "name origins." In seconds, there were a number of sites I could check out.

I began by looking up "Catherine," since it was the first name to pop into my head. (The reason for this might well have been because, subconsciously, I was rooting for that sweet lady to wind up being the killer.) Anyhow, I found out that "Catherine" was of Greek origin. Then I typed in "Helen." That turned out to be Greek, too. Anyhow, I was hoping that the *real* names of the fictional Catherine and Helen could be anagrams of "Greece."

And now I attempted to rearrange the letters in "Greece" to form a feminine name. It didn't work. Not as an anagram, that is, since I wasn't able to get anywhere by utilizing all of the letters. Still, it was possible my basic premise might not be that far off, after all.

I proceeded to fiddle with the letters in "Greece" to see if I could find a feminine name by using just *some* of those letters. Well, you try coming up with *one* feminine name in "Greece," let alone two!

But being a desperate woman, I was only ninety-nine percent discouraged at this point. So I went online again, this time to see if I could do anything with "Rebecca" and "Anne." These, I learned, were both Hebrew in origin. And, of course, no one can be *from* Hebrew.

Frustrated, I gave up—for the time being, at least. I reminded myself that I *was* a little tired. So I held out hope that I'd be smarter after a good night's sleep.

This didn't mean I was ready to trot right off to bed, though. In fact, a few minutes later, I turned on the TV and channel surfed. I lucked out, too. I happened on a Joan Crawford movie—*Humoresque*. (Have I mentioned that I *love* Joan Crawford movies?) It made no difference that I'd seen it a couple of months ago—and for the third or fourth time, too. In the end, when poor Joan walked into the ocean and drowned herself, I still sobbed so loudly I was afraid that Barbara—my friend and next-door neighbor (we share a common wall)—would think there'd been a major tragedy in my life.

At any rate, I seemed to have worn myself out with all that bawling, because that night I fell asleep almost the instant my head touched the pillow.

On Sunday morning, a shrill and persistent sound intruded on this very nice dream I was having. Not yet fully awake, I fumbled for the phone—and promptly knocked it to the floor. I picked up the receiver just as a dear, familiar voice was saying, "Is anything wrong, Dez?"

Now I was fully awake. "Nick?"

"What happened? Is everything okay?"

"I dropped the telephone, that's all."

"I hope I didn't drag you out of a sound sleep."

I looked at the clock: ten thirty-three. "No, of course not."

"I was wondering if you might be free for brunch today."

"Uh . . . I'd really like to, honestly. But . . . well, I'm not sure that's such a good idea."

There were a couple of seconds of silence before Nick responded with, "Oh, you mean because of Derek. I'm sorry, Dez, I should have mentioned this to begin with: Tiffany and Toby—the boyfriend—were at the Jersey shore for the weekend. But, apparently, Toby got a little too much sun yesterday, and they're heading back to the city this morning. Tiffany just called to ask if I'd mind if they came for Derek a little earlier than we'd arranged, and I told her it was okay. In fact, they should be picking him up around noon. So . . . brunch?"

"Brunch. And we'll be having it at my apartment."

"Uh-uh. I don't want you to bother," Nick argued. "Especially when you're so busy with that mystery. Which, incidentally, I'm still waiting to hear about."

"You will. I'll fill you in later. Listen, I'd *enjoy* fixing brunch for us. How's one o'clock?"

"It's fine. But are you sure you want to do this?"

"Positive."

A pause. "Well, okay. What can I bring? And 'nothing' isn't an acceptable answer."

"For your information, that's *not* what I was going to say. I was about to tell you that pastries would be nice."

"Good. See you at one."

I bolted out of bed, threw on some clothes, smeared on some lipstick, and—praying I wouldn't run into anyone I knew—headed for D'Agostino's. Fifteen minutes later, I was back in the kitchen, having a quick cup of coffee and a slice of burned toast. Then I went to work.

First, I mixed a pitcher of mimosas. Well, not exactly, I suppose. The thing is, instead of the traditional orange juice and champagne, I combined the juice with Toffoli Prosecco, which is an Italian wine that tastes like champagne, only better. In my opinion, anyhow. (And I'd have felt that way even if there *had* been a bottle of champagne lying around the house.) I stuck the pitcher in the refrigerator, along with a couple of champagne flutes. After this, I made a fresh pot of coffee (Nick,

along with Ellen and Mike, being among the elite few
who have never said unkind things about my brew).

And now, turning my attention to the food, I prepared
whatever I could in advance. Then I cleaned up the mess
I'd just made of the kitchen. Fortunately, I'd done a
decent job on the rest of the apartment yesterday. So
once I'd set up the folding table in the living room, I was
ready to concentrate on the one thing that still needed to
be whipped into shape: me.

I probably took the quickest shower I've ever had in
all my not-so-tender years. The fact is, I needed every
second of whatever time was available to make myself
look devastatingly attractive. Well, presentable, anyway.

I put on my makeup with only one minor mishap—
which, for me, was something of a rarity. What happened
was, I dropped my mascara wand and couldn't find it.
(And God forbid I should greet Nick with naked eye-
lashes!) When I finally convinced myself to get down on
all fours, there it was—hiding behind the sink. A short
while later, following a minor skirmish with my glorious
hennaed hair, I got into the outfit I'd (hurriedly) decided
on in the shower: a white cotton tunic and a dark brown
cotton A-line skirt. In my humble opinion, I looked pretty
good, too—especially after I slipped on a pair of strappy
bronze high-heeled sandals. And so what if they pinched
a little. They're the sexiest shoes I've ever owned!

Nick was exactly on time. And, as always, he looked
great. Today, he had on a navy and white striped polo
shirt and navy slacks. In his right hand was a small, nicely
wrapped package and, in his left, a white box that I (correctly) assumed to be the pastries.

He planted a kiss on my cheek. Then, cocking his head
to the side: "You're even prettier today than usual—or
am I imagining it because I've missed you so much?"

My heart started to race, and I could feel myself blushing. "I like the sound of both of those."

He grinned that irresistible gap-toothed grin of his.
"My meager contribution to our brunch," he said, handing me the box of pastries. "Uh, I have something else

for you, too." He held out the smaller package. "I, well, I thought you might like this."

"Why, thank you, Nick. I'm sure I will," I murmured, practically melting at this gesture. "I want to get us something to drink, though. So I'll leave it in your care until I join you in the living room—which should be in about five minutes."

"Is there anything *I* can do? I'd like to help, Dez."

"There's nothing, honestly. So relax for a little while—turn on the TV, if you want." And with this, I headed for the kitchen.

Out of the freezer and into the microwave went the leftover mushroom hors d'oeuvres I'd made a couple of months ago, when Ellen and Mike were coming over for dinner. (I'd prepared enough of those things to feed a battalion!) After this, the three cheeses I'd just bought at D'Agostino's went on a tray, accompanied by a variety of crackers. Then I retrieved the mimosas and chilled flutes from the refrigerator, and after not much longer than the aforementioned five minutes, Nick and I were seated side by side on the sofa, and he was making a toast. "To us," he said softly.

I was more than happy to drink to that.

"Hey, this is delicious," Nick commented after a few sips of his bogus mimosa. (But I have no doubt he'd have said the same thing if I'd given him castor oil.) "Well, aren't you going to open your present?" he asked, placing the gift in my lap.

"Try and stop me." I hurriedly tore away the wrapping. Underneath was a bottle of Ivoire, my favorite—and very hard to come by—cologne. I looked at the bottle again. This wasn't cologne; it was the perfume!

"Oh, Nick," I murmured, touched that he was even aware of the fragrance I wore. "Where did you find it?"

"On the Internet—where else?"

I threw my arms around his neck—almost causing him to spill his drink—and planted a big smooch on his cheek. "Thank you *so* much," I whispered. Then I prodded myself to ask—because I knew I should, "How was your weekend with Derek?"

"Really nice." He reached for his second mushroom hors d'oeuvre. "We went to two movies and had dinner at Serendipity on Friday, and on Saturday I took him to this new, very kid-oriented restaurant in the Village. He seemed to enjoy himself, too." There was a pause. "Listen, Dez, I want to talk to you about Derek."

Uh-oh, here it comes. "Go ahead," I said, steeling myself for what would follow.

"You know, it wouldn't surprise me if Tiffany and this new boyfriend of hers were serious. Derek told me they used to go out together a long time ago—whatever 'a long time ago' means to a child—but then, for some reason, it ended. Well, evidently it's on again."

"Derek doesn't resent his mother's involvement with this man?"

"I understand from Tiffany that he did at first. Quite a bit, in fact. But Toby manages a couple of rock bands, and through his connections in the music business, he's been able to present Derek with the autographs of some fairly well-known performers. And naturally, Derek was pretty impressed. Now Toby tells him he's friendly with a buddy of Kelly Clarkson's—you know, that *American Idol* winner—and Derek's absolutely smitten with her!"

"He stays up to watch the show?"

"Occasionally. But more often than not, Tiffany tapes it for him. At any rate, Toby promised Derek he'd have this mutual friend get Kelly Clarkson's autograph for him. And my son's been on cloud nine ever since."

"I can't get over Derek's being that accepting of this man. I mean, he was absolutely committed to seeing you and Tiffany get back together."

"True. But this was before his mother began seeing someone who can provide him with the autographs of famous people, including that of the singer he's so enamored with. And by the way, Tiffany swears the fellow doesn't do drugs—in spite of his profession. She also says he never has more than one or two drinks and that when he's driving, he forgoes liquor completely."

"What's your impression of this Toby?"

"Look, to be honest, I'm not crazy about Derek's having another father figure in his life, but it's something that I've always known would come about, sooner or later. And while I haven't had much contact with Toby, from what little I've seen, he appears to be intelligent and down-to-earth and . . . I don't know, a pretty decent person. Besides, the one thing I can say for Tiffany is that she cares deeply about our son. And in spite of all the creeps that have been marching in and out of her life since we split up, I don't really see her winding up with someone who wouldn't be good to him—or good *for* him." Nick smiled now. "What I started to say before, though—and it seems like an hour ago—is that suddenly Derek doesn't appear to be so adamant about the three of us being a family again one day. And you know what that means, don't you?"

"It *does not* necessarily mean he'll be more favorably disposed toward me, if this is what you're thinking."

"Listen, if things should work out between Tiffany and Toby, well, Derek will have to acknowledge—I'm talking about to himself—that his mother and I will never remarry. And this is bound to affect how he feels about my relationship with you."

"I hope you're right," I said. I didn't add the rest of what was on my mind: *But don't count on it.*

Soon after this, I went into the kitchen—which is so tiny it makes that shoe box I call an office seem positively spacious. And while I prepared the food, Nick stood in the doorway, and we chatted.

Finally, we sat down to brunch, which consisted of an omelet with chopped ham, cheese, and sautéed onions, served with what Nick very graciously referred to as "the best home fries I've ever eaten." There was also toast with blackberry jam, plus the miniature cheese and apricot Danish that Nick had brought to our little repast. Naturally, all of this was accompanied by my coffee, which that wonderful man swore was really very good—and with a straight face, too! Then, when I gave him the fish-eye, he amended the words with, "Well, it's not half-bad, Dez. Honestly."

Anyhow, at the end of the meal, I filled Nick in on

Belle's mystery. When I got around to reciting the second clue, this bewildered look appeared on his face. "I have absolutely no idea what that means," he said flatly. And after I described my recent, failed attempt to work it out, he shook his head from side to side to commiserate. "I'm drawing a blank, Dez. And I'm very sorry; I only wish I could help you."

"I know. I wish you could, too."

"You'll figure it out on your own, though; I'm sure of it. In the meantime, I'll give it some more thought. I may even come up with something." He grinned. "Hey, miracles *do* happen."

We cleared away the dishes, then played a couple of games of Scrabble. (Nick won them both.) At around ten o'clock, we were hungry again. A new pizzeria had opened up only a block from our mutual building, so we decided to go over and give their pepperoni pizza a try. It was pretty good, too. But, of course, it didn't hold a candle to the pepperoni pizza at Little Angie's (a place near my office), Little Angie's pepperoni pizza being nothing short of divine.

Nick stayed over that night (I'd have curled up in a ball and died if he hadn't). And I pleaded with him to wake me when he got up, so we could have breakfast together. But, as usual, he was gone when I opened my eyes. On the pillow next to me, however, was a note:

Thank you, Dez, for a wonderful day. Is it me, or do things just keep getting better and better with us?

Nick

P.S.: You were sleeping so peacefully, I'd have felt like a lowlife if I woke you.

Chapter 32

Sunday couldn't have been more perfect.

And when I woke up Monday morning and read Nick's note, I was euphoric. For a short while, I allowed myself to daydream about a decent relationship between Derek and me. I mean, it could happen (couldn't it?) that this Tiffany/Toby thing would pave the way for the boy to start regarding me with a little less antagonism. But soon, my past experience with TKFH began to intrude on my optimism. And by the time I got to work, the euphoria had completely evaporated.

A few minutes after I sat down at my desk, I took out the folder containing Belle's manuscript. But even before I opened it, I began thinking about that damn clue again. I was just about positive that I wouldn't find any help in the manuscript itself. So I promptly closed the folder.

And now I jotted down the first names of all the suspects and stared at them until my eyes burned. It could be that the clue had nothing to do with the origin of the names, I informed myself. But eventually I gave that notion short shrift. I couldn't afford not to. After all, this was the only possibility to occur to me.

Anyhow, I decided to pay another visit to the Internet, only this time to check out a couple of the male names. I can't explain why I repeated the same failed approach I'd taken on Saturday. But that's what I did—and with a predictable outcome.

The origin of the name "Simon" (he was Tess's cousin, remember?) turned out to be Hebrew. And "Philip" (the husband of what's-her-name—that model) was derived from the Greek. I mean, these were the exact results I'd gotten on Saturday with the feminine names I'd posted! Well, if I'd needed any further convincing that I was on the wrong track, this was it. The only trouble was, I had no idea how to arrive at the *right* track.

Grasping at straws, I picked up the manuscript. Maybe I was mistaken. Maybe something in there *would* give me a shove in the right direction.

Chapter eight began with Gabe's phoning the widow. She had vacated her sister's apartment and moved back into her own home by this time. The two spoke briefly, and the detective was pleased to note that she sounded relatively together now. Then, at his request, Tess provided the name of the family attorney—the one who'd drawn up her husband's will.

Later that same day, Gabe and Ray paid a visit to Herman Doyle, Esq., who informed them that the deceased had designated his widow as the sole heir to what was a very substantial estate.

Now, if I'd really expected this chapter to provide any insight into that damn clue, I would have been disappointed. But I hadn't. So I wasn't. Still, I cautioned myself, I couldn't be sure there wasn't a hint of some sort in the remainder of the manuscript. Only I wasn't about to do any more reading just then. In fact, I decided to hold off trying to figure the thing out for a while. Maybe—just maybe—if I stopped agonizing over the problem, sooner or later the solution would come to me.

I was pretty much at loose ends for the rest of the morning. I would have paid a couple of overdue bills, but according to my calculations, there was just $84.32 in my checking account. What's more, my math is extremely questionable, so who knows if I was even in the black?

At that moment, I could think of only one thing to do: put on fresh nail polish. But when I took out the polish remover, it had evaporated!

I sat there, my chin in my hands, trying to come up with some way to occupy myself. I had narrowed down the options to either a very early lunch or suicide when Jackie popped her head in the doorway. "Busy?"

"Why? Do I look it?" I grumbled.

"Pretty touchy this morning, aren't we?"

"Sorry. I've been having a rough time—an *impossible* time—with Belle's new clue. But never mind that. How was your weekend?"

"Good. Very good, in fact. Derwin and I spent Saturday and Sunday at his sister's place in Connecticut. We relaxed, we swam—she and her husband have their own pool—and we barbecued. Plus, on Saturday night—get this—we went to a karaoke bar after dinner, something neither Derwin or I had ever done before."

"Sounds like you really enjoyed yourselves."

"We did. How was *your* weekend?"

"Wonderful. At least, that's how it ended up. But I'll tell you about it at lunch. Assuming, of course, you're free."

"Free as a bird."

"And let's make it someplace nice, too. My treat."

"Why, for heaven's sake?"

"Listen, if it weren't for you, I might not be driving myself crazy with clue number two. There's a good chance I'd still be driving myself crazy with clue number one."

"I deserve very little credit for your coming up with that answer. So let's go Dutch. I'd feel more comfortable, honestly."

"Hey, with any luck, I'll be getting a bundle of money in the not so distant future, remember? So don't argue. I'm treating. Where would you like to go? And keep in mind that coffee shops aren't an option."

"There's that French restaurant about two blocks down—right off Second Avenue. La Vie, it's called. Ever hear of it?" I shook my head. "I ate there once, and it wasn't bad, but nothing special. I passed by the other day, though, and this sign outside says they've got a new chef—some guy from Paris. So it sounds promising—kind of, anyway."

"I'm game if you are."

"Hey, you only die once. I'll make the reservation for noon."

* * *

La Vie turned out to be a cheerful place, with check-ered tablecloths, a nice selection of recorded French songs, and colorful prints of Parisian street scenes on the walls. It was fairly crowded, too. No doubt our fellow diners had been lured—as Jackie was—by the announce-ment in the window proclaiming that the kitchen was now under the supervision of Chef Jean-Claude Dubois of Paris. (Whoever *he* was.)

I ordered a bottle of Merlot, although judging from my many past lunches with Jackie, neither of us was likely to finish even a glass. (Being the host, though, I didn't want to give the impression I was penny-pinching.) Anyhow, after briefly studying the menu, Jackie decided to start with the onion soup, while I went with the Co-quille St. Jacques. For her entrée, Jackie chose the filet mignon. As for me, when I saw duck à l'orange on that menu, I didn't look any further.

We chattered pretty constantly throughout the meal, Jackie kick-starting the conversation over our wine with, "Well?"

"Well, what?"

"You were going to fill me in on your weekend."

"Oh, right. Let's see . . . On Friday, I discovered that my client's wife wasn't cheating on him at all—this is the case I mentioned to you on the phone that morning, if you recall. At any rate, the client wound up happy, and so did I. Saturday, however, was another story. I kept trying and trying to decipher Belle's second clue—and getting nowhere. It was unbelievably frustrating. I was—"

"Look, Dez," Jackie interrupted, "if you think it might help to bounce that clue off me, go ahead. In fact, I'd really like to hear it. But it's extremely doubtful I'll be able to come up with the same sort of nothing question that led—although *very indirectly*—to your figuring out the first clue."

"Thanks, Jackie. I'm sure I'll be taking you up on that—only not today. Today, I'd just like to sit here and enjoy our lunch."

"Okay. Remember, though, I'm available anytime. But

you were telling me about how agitated you were on Saturday night when you couldn't make sense of the clue."

" 'Agitated' isn't the word for it. I might have drowned myself in the bathtub this weekend if Nick hadn't come over for brunch yesterday."

Jackie smiled. "I gather everything's good between the two of you."

I wasn't able to keep the insipid grin off my face. "It couldn't be better."

"So? Tell me!"

Well, the grin had been inspired by that note of Nick's on my pillow this morning—the contents of which I had no intention of sharing. Instead, I talked about Tiffany's acquiring a new boyfriend and the possibility that the two might be getting serious.

"Nick's pride and joy hasn't tried to assassinate the guy yet?"

"Apparently, Derek doesn't have a problem with him. Toby's in the music business and seems to know a number of famous people. He's been bringing Derek all these autographs, and the kid's thrilled. So it's conceivable that he wouldn't object to Toby's becoming his stepfather."

"And if this Toby and Nick's ex *should* make it legal, Derek will have to stop obsessing about Mommy and Daddy's remarrying," Jackie observed. "For all we know," she added, "he may have done it already."

"True. But he and I have a pretty lousy track record. Listen, even if Tiffany does march down the aisle again, it doesn't mean that it'll be okay with Derek if I remain in his father's life."

"You could be right, of course. But you could be wrong. I believe his mother's remarriage might very well work in your favor." And then, to reassure me further, Jackie tagged on, "I honestly do." And reaching across the table, she clasped my hand for a moment.

I asked her then how things were going with Derwin. "In general, I mean."

"So far, so good. I'm always afraid he'll slip back and start squeezing the life out of a quarter again. But—and

I have my fingers crossed—that hasn't happened. Right now, I'm *completely* happy, Dez. Probably for the first time in my life, too."

I was so delighted to hear her say this that tears sprang to my eyes. (In case you haven't noticed, I'm ninety-nine percent mush.) On purpose, I began to cough, which enabled me to take out a handkerchief and cover my mouth, while at the same time surreptitiously mopping up the tears.

At any rate, leaving Nick and Derwin behind us after this, we nevertheless managed to keep right on talking straight through coffee and dessert (Peach Melba for us both).

All in all, it was a lovely meal, I thought. And Jackie certainly appeared to agree. Little did I know that as a result of today's lunch, I'd soon be cursing the restaurant and its chef.

And if I'd been a little smarter, I'd have recognized, too, that this same lunch contained the key to Belle's elusive second clue.

Chapter 33

That night, I would have welcomed death.

Everything was fine when I got home from work. I wasn't at all hungry, thanks to today's lunch. But I figured I should fix myself something to eat, anyway. Otherwise, as sure as the sun rises in the east, by about ten o'clock my stomach would be giving me what-for. So I smeared some peanut butter on two slices of white toast, had a cup of coffee—and that was it. (I swear.)

After supper—if you can call it that—true to my vow not to try figuring out that clue for a while, I stretched out on the sofa, turned on the TV, and relaxed. At a few minutes past nine, the phone rang.

It was Nick.

"Hi, Dez," he said. "Listen, I want to thank you for yesterday."

"You're welcome. And I thank you, too."

"It was the best brunch I've ever had, bar none. Of course, as good as everything was, the main reason I enjoyed it so much was because you were sitting across the table from me." Hearing those words, I felt almost giddy. "Anyhow . . . uh, I was hoping we could spend a nice, long weekend together, starting Friday. Emil said that if I wanted the time off, he'd cover for me and maybe get his nephew to come in and lend a hand. I was even thinking it might be nice to revisit that little bed-and-breakfast in New Jersey—provided you were agreeable, naturally. Or else, if you'd rather, we could try someplace new."

"I'd love to go back to that B-and-B in New Jersey—if you would."

"Damn! I have a feeling I'm doing a lousy job of communicating, Dez. What I'm trying to say is, this is what I had in *mind*—until Tiffany called a little while ago."

"Is something wrong?"

"Not really. But it did put the kibosh on our weekend—yours and mine. I promise I'll make it up to you, though."

"What happened?"

"Apparently, Toby has to fly out to L.A. on Friday, and he's anxious for Tiffany to accompany him. She even said something that led me to believe they may be making it permanent soon. I can't remember her exact words, but this was the impression I got. Well, I don't want to do anything that could put a crimp in their relationship. That's why, when she asked if I'd take Derek from Friday through Sunday, I didn't feel I should turn her down. I hope you understand."

"Of course I do. Don't worry about it. There'll be other weekends."

"We can drive out to Wheeler again in a couple of weeks, okay?"

"Very okay."

"In the meantime, are you free for dinner some evening during the week? I can try to pick up a couple of theater tickets, too. Is there anything in particular you'd like to see?"

"Nothing I can think of. Why don't we just have a nice, long, relaxing dinner?"

"That's fine with me. What night would be good for you?"

"Is Wednesday okay?" I asked, thinking that maybe I should do a little more reading tomorrow night—or at least leave myself with that option.

"Wednesday's fine. Er, by the way, have you gotten anywhere with the new clue yet?"

"I'm afraid not."

"Don't worry, I haven't the slightest doubt that you'll dope it out. I mean it, Dez. And I expect you to call me as soon as you do. But in the meantime, about Wednesday . . . is eight o'clock all right?"

"Eight's fine."

"See you then." He actually made the words sound sexy.

I went back to the TV for a while. But I couldn't find anything worth seeing. I kept changing channels until about eleven thirty, when I decided I might as well shower and go to bed.

I'd just lathered up, when *wham!* It hit me. I turned off the water. Then, doubled up, I scrambled out of the tub, almost every inch of me still covered with soap.

Never before had my stomach pained me so much. And never before had I felt this nauseous. It was as if my whole body had suddenly betrayed me!

I was immediately certain it was food poisoning, simply because there was nothing else it *could* be. Now, if you've ever had food poisoning yourself, you know I wasn't exaggerating when I said before that I'd have welcomed death. And if you've *never* had this delightful experience, all I can say is, think the worst. And let me assure you, it's even more awful than that.

When I finally left the bathroom, I dragged myself into the bedroom and crept into bed. I lay there in agony, spewing silent invectives at La Vie. Then I vented my anger on the food itself. And since I had no idea just what it was I'd consumed that had put me in the shape I was in, I covered all the bases, cursing everything to pass my lips at lunch, even the Merlot. I didn't neglect the restaurant's new chef, either, this Jean-Claude Dubois of Paris. Could be *he* was to blame. I mean, they had to import the guy? Why hadn't that damn Monsieur Dubois remained in France and inflicted his culinary artistry on his own countrymen?

Suddenly, it struck me that Jackie might be in the same deplorable condition I was in. What's more, at this moment, she could be aiming a few choice words at *me*. True, she'd mentioned La Vie. But I'd been the one who'd suggested lunch in the first place.

Anyhow, I finally fell asleep after a horrendous night of getting into and jumping out of bed close to a dozen times. When I last looked at the clock, it read six eighteen a.m.

I heard the phone ring, so I realized that at least I was still alive.

I was able to pick up the receiver without lifting my head, which I wasn't prepared to chance just yet. I managed a muffled, "Hello?" and was rewarded for that monumental effort with a shrill: "Do you know what *time* it is, Desiree?"

Well, I needn't have worried about Jackie's having suffered my same fate, and I was momentarily relieved. "Uh, no."

"It's past eleven. I would have phoned you earlier, but I was in Elliot's office taking dictation for most of the morning. I just this minute returned to my desk, and Edna informed me that you hadn't come in yet. I was worried that you might be sick or something," she scolded.

"Jackie?"

"What?"

"Do I sound okay to you?"

She hesitated for a moment. "I, um . . . why? *Are* you sick?"

"You might say that. I have food poisoning. I was up most of the night, and I didn't call you because it was after six this morning before I finally got some sleep."

"Oh, you poor thing!" Jackie commiserated. "And I had to wake you up, too. I am *so* sorry. How are you feeling now?"

"I can't tell. I'm not really awake yet."

"What did you have for supper, anyway?"

"A couple of slices of toast with peanut butter. But, believe me, my supper had nothing to do with this. It was something I ate at lunch. In fact, I was afraid you might have come down with food poisoning, too."

"No, I'm okay. You're *positive* it was the lunch?"

"Yes."

"Well, if that's the case, my money's on the Coquille

St. Jacques. But anyhow, what do you need? I can be over in about an hour and—"

"Thanks very much, Jackie. You're a doll, but the only thing I need now is sleep."

"Are you *sure* I can't do anything for you?"

"I'm sure, but I really appreciate the offer."

"All right. Call me when you wake up, though, and let me know how you are. Okay?"

"Okay."

I fell back to sleep for a couple of hours before being awakened by stomach pains. But I crawled back into bed a short time afterward and phoned Jackie as instructed. Then, almost immediately, I dropped off again. When I opened my eyes about an hour later, I had this feeling that the worst was over.

I made myself some tea and toast then, and there were no repercussions.

With any luck, I told myself, by tomorrow I could even rejoin the living.

Chapter 34

Happily, I slept through the night.

When I opened my eyes, I had a vague recollection of hearing my alarm clock go off sometime earlier. I couldn't believe I'd been stupid enough to set it last night! Anyhow, I remembered fumbling around on my bedside table to shut the thing up, while my eyes remained tightly closed.

I glanced at the clock now: almost one! I reached for the phone.

"Oh, Dez, I'm *so* glad you called! Three times, I stopped myself from calling *you*; I held off in case you were still asleep."

"I was, Jackie. I just this minute woke up."

"How do you feel?"

"A whole lot better than I did yesterday. I guess you could say I'm a work in progress, though."

"Never mind the cute stuff. Do you need anything?"

"Nothing, honestly."

"Are you sure?"

"Positive."

"Well, holler if something occurs to you."

"I will, Jackie. And thanks."

I had tea and toast for breakfast—or maybe you'd consider it lunch. Then I showered and stretched out on the sofa to read more of Belle's manuscript. I hadn't even opened it when I remembered: This was Wednesday! And Nick and I had made plans for tonight!

I phoned him at the shop to cancel our date. But, as

it turned out, this wasn't so easy. I got only as far as telling him I was recovering from food poisoning.

"Why don't I stop off for some stuff on my way home, and we'll stay in tonight."

"I really appreciate the offer, but I'm not up to eating much of anything, Nick. Honestly."

"Not even something light? Like chicken soup?"

"Tea and toast is as far as I go. Besides, I'm not exactly anxious to have you see me looking like this."

"I'll wear a blindfold."

"Seriously, I—"

"Okay, okay, I can take a hint—eventually. But listen, call me if you change your mind, all right?"

"All right."

"And if you should think of anything you need—or something you might like—pick up the phone and I'll drop off whatever it is at your door."

"Thanks a lot, Nick; I'll do that. And I'm really sorry about tonight."

"So am I. But just feel better, Dez. I'll talk to you later."

Right after my conversation with Nick, I opened the manuscript. I had come to the final chapter, part three: "The Investigation Concludes."

The two detectives were becoming increasingly discouraged. Neither had a leaning toward a particular suspect. Even the fact that the victim's widow would soon be coming into a considerable amount of money failed to influence them. After all, why resort to murder when, given Rob's proclivity for fun and frolic, a good divorce lawyer could no doubt have obtained a hefty settlement for her. The motive for the homicide, both men agreed, was much more likely to be intertwined with the dead man's character than with his finances.

A few days after the officers had paid a visit to Tess and to the family attorney, Gabe Wilson decided to look through his partner's notes. True, Gabe himself had frequently jotted down what he regarded as pertinent information. But Ray's notes, now neatly typed, were much more complete—voluminous, actually.

The sergeant read slowly and carefully. And for the first time, one small and, Gabe cautioned himself, very likely meaningless bit of information impacted on him. And he couldn't seem to dismiss it from his mind. Even in view of having learned of this particular occurrence from the very person who risked being placed under suspicion by bringing it to light.

On the other hand, he countered, the disclosure could have been prompted by this individual's fear that someone else might—perhaps even innocently—call it to the attention of the police. Rob Harwood's killer could simply have been exercising a form of damage control.

Exasperated at this point, Gabe bit his lip—hard. This . . . this *thing* that was troubling him was hardly proof of guilt. The truth was, after mulling it over a while longer, he began to feel he was exaggerating its importance. Nevertheless, he decided to share his concerns with his partner.

Ray listened attentively. "What you're telling me *does* make sense. Only if the two of *us* aren't so sure how significant it is, how can we expect to convince anyone else?" Then, shrugging his shoulders: "Besides, as you say, it's definitely not enough to act on."

Ray was right, of course. Still, over the years, whenever he'd think about the case, Gabe would recall this one small fact. And he'd wonder. . . .

It had now been almost two weeks since the death of Rob Harwood. In the very beginning, all of the New York newspapers had played up the story of the sudden death of this prominent Manhattan Realtor on the night of his sixtieth birthday celebration. And although the papers stated that the cause of the man's demise was yet to be determined, in each instance, mention was made of the fact that the NYPD hadn't ruled out the possibility of foul play.

The articles had generated a number of calls to the

detectives working the case from people claiming to have important information. And some of these continued to trickle in.

Not as atypical of these as you might think was a conversation Ray had with a woman who phoned to report that her husband had been cheating on her with Tess Harwood. "I seen that widow's pitcher in the papers," she said, "and I'm *sure*—well, almost sure—she's the one I caught him with in that motel." She hadn't wanted to get George in trouble, she explained. "But now that he's moved in with that bimbo, screw 'em both."

In spite of juggling a heavy caseload (which at this point included another high-profile homicide), and ignoring the instinct that told them it was unlikely this "lead" would lead anywhere at all, Ray checked out the caller's story. Not surprisingly, while George *was* cheating on his wife, the lady in question wasn't Tess Harwood. Or even a reasonable facsimile. Nevertheless, the detectives would continue following up on all but the most bizarre information they received. As Gabe put it, he and his partner had no intention of "packing this case away in mothballs."

Not long after this, Ray spotted a brief item in the *New York Times* announcing that a memorial service was being held for the victim the following morning. He handed the paper to his partner. "Well?" he said as soon as the other had read it.

"Well, why not?"

So the next morning, at ten a.m., Gabe and Ray were standing at the rear of the chapel, while a young priest droned on about the virtues of "our dear, departed brother, Robin Harwood" to a crowd of about seventy-five people.

Now, almost instantly, the two had become aware of the chapel's obviously defective air-conditioning system. But while Ray appeared to be taking the heat in stride, Gabe was visibly uncomfortable, continually running a finger under his collar. Soon, he loosened his tie, and soon after *that,* he felt obliged to undo the top button of his shirt—which was as far as he dared go. "It's hot as hell in here," he muttered.

"Maybe old Rob could tell you otherwise now," Ray whispered, grinning.

"Funny."

After delivering his eulogy, the priest—Father Morgan—asked if anyone in attendance would care to come forward and share his or her thoughts about the deceased. Among those who spoke eloquently of the murdered man were three of the guests at his sixtieth birthday party.

Now, Belle's manuscript quoted this trio, which consisted of the forever-loyal Rebecca McMartin; Rob's tennis buddy (and Tess's cousin), Simon Cooper; and the dead man's good friend, Walt Riley (whose wife had been an even better friend to the victim). I've decided not to reprint any of this here, however. It's sufficient, I think, to tell you that all three practically canonized the far-from-saintly Robin Harwood. And it made me gag.

"That was what I'd call a gold-plated waste of time," Gabe remarked. The pair had ducked out of the chapel after listening to the last of the eulogizers and were now driving away—and cooling off—in an air-conditioned car.

"We *both* figured it was worth a shot," Ray reminded him.

"When you're right, well, those are the few times you're not wrong," Gabe quipped. "Actually, though, this thing might have been marginally tolerable if it hadn't been so damn hot in there." He chuckled. "Then again, probably not. Anyhow, the truth is, I'd have bet on our getting nowhere today. But there's always one chance in a million that someone will say something revealing. And considering the shape we're in on this . . ." There was no need to say more.

"Let me ask you something, Gabe. Do you still feel there's a possibility we can wrap this one up?"

"All I can say is that I'm not ready to throw in the

towel. Hey, we haven't even gotten the results of the autopsy yet."

Almost four weeks to the day after that fateful birthday party, the long-awaited autopsy report came in. It confirmed what the detectives had been virtually certain of from the beginning: Rob Harwood had been murdered. Ray, however, was somewhat puzzled when he learned that the cause of death was a lethal dose of cyanide. "I'm surprised no one in close proximity to the vic noticed the smell," he remarked, referring to cyanide's characteristic odor of bitter almonds.

Gabe, who'd investigated two previous cases involving cyanide, explained that not everyone's sense of smell is acute enough to detect it.

"At least being partnered with an older guy has *some* advantages," Ray joked.

"Very funny," the "older guy" grumbled. But he was attempting to conceal a smile.

At any rate, as a result of the autopsy report, Rob Harwood's death made headlines again, only this time, they all screamed, "MURDER!"

The public's dormant interest in the investigation was suddenly reawakened, and the homicide detectives received a rash of phone calls, along with several visits. None of which advanced the investigation one iota. By far the strangest of these visits occurred two days after the newspapers hit the stands trumpeting this latest development.

It was late afternoon when a small, dark-haired, middle-aged woman in an outsize black straw hat flounced into the station. She informed the desk sergeant it was imperative that she speak to the officer in charge of the Harwood murder. "I have vital information for him," she announced. The sergeant directed her to Gabe.

Moments later, she plunked herself down, uninvited, on the chair alongside the detective's desk, declaring that she was here to talk about Robin Harwood's poisoning.

Gabe wasted no time in buzzing his partner, who quickly dragged over another chair and joined them.

The woman removed her hat and placed it on the desk, almost knocking over Gabe's coffee in the process. "I am Madam Rosa. And I am a psychic," she announced with a faint foreign accent neither of the men could identify.

"I see," Gabe responded, suppressing a smile and avoiding his partner's eyes. "And you have information concerning the murder of Robin Harwood?"

"I have *vital* information," she corrected.

"Just what is it you know about the murder?"

"Last evening, I had a vision. And in this vision, I saw a celebration of some kind—a party. Then I saw the hand of the murderer."

"You saw *what*?" Ray put to her. But he, too, managed to keep the smile inside from materializing on his face.

"A hand. And on that hand was a ring with a blue stone—a sapphire. The hand was holding a small vial. And then, as I watched, the hand emptied the contents of the vial into a glass of champagne—Robin Harwood's glass."

"This hand—was it a man or a woman's, ma'am?" Ray asked, humoring her.

"I cannot be certain; it was in shadow. Even the ring itself I was unable to see very clearly. Only that sparkling sapphire jewel was plainly visible."

"And, uh, how do you know this was Mr. Harwood's champagne glass?"

"Tell me, Officers, was there anyone else at this party who was poisoned?" the psychic posed, smiling coyly.

"Well, no," Ray admitted, not quite able to conceal his amusement now. He was about to question how she was even able to determine this was Harwood's party, but he was preempted.

"You do not believe what I am saying—either of you," the woman accused, looking from one to the other.

"It isn't that, Ms. . . . ?"

"*Madam* Rosa," she reminded the young officer testily. "Let me explain something to you. In my vision, I could see that room—the room where this occurred—as clearly as I see this one." And closing her eyes, she put a hand to her forehead and slowly, as if in a trance, described, in minute detail, what she represented to be the living room of the Harwood penthouse. When she opened her eyes again, Madam Rosa raised her left eyebrow. "*Now*, do you believe me?" she demanded, smirking.

Gabe—who, by this point, had difficulty recalling much of what he had seen of the penthouse—chose his words carefully. "Perhaps you *are* familiar with the room, but it's conceivable that you were there at some time."

"I assure you, this is not so. I had never *heard* of these people. Until this moment, I saw that room only once— and that was last night, in my vision."

"Then how do you know whose home you were seeing?"

"I have no idea *how* I know," Madam Rosa responded testily. "I just know."

"Would you mind leaving us your telephone number," Gabe asked, "in case we should want to contact you about this?" He wasn't certain, but he got the impression the woman was hesitant. So he put in hastily, "It's also very possible we'll want to call on you for assistance on other matters at some future time."

Madam Rosa reached into her small handbag and instantly produced a card. She handed it to Gabe. "Madam Rosa, Psychic Reader. By appointment only," he read. There was a telephone number on the card.

"I must go now," she suddenly announced. "But remember: Look for some person at that party who wore a sapphire ring, and you will have the killer of Robin Harwood." And, springing to her feet, she slapped the hat back on her head and hurried from the room.

"Well, what do you make of *that*?" a bewildered Ray asked.

"There has to be a logical explanation."

"Yeah, I know. But what is it?"

"That's what we're going to find out."

Minutes after Madam Rosa's departure, Gabe contacted Tess Harwood and asked if he and Ray could stop by to see her the next morning.

"Yes, of course. Do you have some news for me?"

"Nothing I've got any faith in, I'm afraid. Nevertheless, I think we should talk."

"I appreciate your not giving up on us, Sergeant Wilson. What time can I expect you?"

According to his appointment book, tomorrow promised to be hectic. "Uh, would eight a.m. be too early for you?"

"Not at all; I'm an early riser. Well, see you at eight," she confirmed.

The following day, promptly at eight, Gabe and Ray rang the bell to the Harwood apartment. The woman who opened the door bore little resemblance to the person they'd glimpsed at the memorial service. And she was a far, *far* cry from the individual they had questioned on the Sunday following the murder. Today, Tess was dressed in jeans and a T-shirt, both of which showed off her slender but curvy figure. What was more, this was the first time either detective had ever seen her smile.

Gabe declined her offer of coffee. "I wish we could, but we have a tight schedule today." Tess nodded and ushered them into the living room.

"Do you mind if we just look around the room for a couple minutes?" Gabe asked once they were seated on the beige sectional sofa Madam Rosa had spoken of. It was decorated with the silk turquoise throw pillows the self-proclaimed psychic had also mentioned.

"No, of course not," Tess said, obviously perplexed.

And now both detectives took note of many of the other items around them: the handsome brown velvet chairs, the huge glass coffee table, the fireplace on the wall opposite the sofa—even the five tiny figurines sitting on its mantle. All of which—and more—Madam Rosa had so accurately "divined."

"A woman came to the station house yesterday. She calls herself Madam Rosa," Gabe said at last. "And she insists she had a vision in which she saw someone with a sapphire ring holding a vial and emptying whatever it contained into a glass of champagne."

"And you connected her so-called vision to Rob's

death? After all, the fact that it was his champagne that had been laced with the cyanide"—she shuddered when she said the word—"was just in all the newspapers."

"The thing is, though, she also claims she saw this room—*your* living room—in that vision, and she described it to a T."

"She *did*? What does the woman look like?"

Gabe was able to portray Madam Rosa fairly accurately. When he was finished, the frown lines on either side of Tess's nose became more pronounced. And for close to a minute, it was apparent that she was deep in thought. Then she shook her head slowly. "I have no idea who this could be," she said softly.

"Well, if you should think of anyone who fits that description, give us a call," Gabe told her.

"Uh, by the way," Ray asked then, "and this is just to satisfy my curiosity—would you happen to know anyone with a sapphire ring?"

"I'm afraid not. At any rate, not that I can recall off-hand. Oh, no pun intended," she added, laughing. "But seriously, I'll get in touch with you if something should occur to me."

It was almost a week later that Tess phoned. Gabe was away from his desk at the time, so she spoke to Ray, who left a note for his partner. "Stop in to see me," it said. Well, nothing had gone right that day, and Gabe was tired and grouchy and anxious to head home. But he hunched his shoulders and reluctantly made the trip to Ray's desk a few yards away.

"What's up?" he asked, standing over him.

"Tess Harwood phoned. She tried to reach you, but since you weren't available, she settled for me. Anyhow, she's solved the mystery for us—regarding Madam Rosa's 'special gift,' I mean."

"Go on," Gabe directed.

"Pull up a chair and sit down for a minute, for crying out loud. I hate having to look up to you!" And once Gabe reluctantly complied: "It suddenly occurred to her that six years ago, this magazine—*Beautiful American*

Homes, she said it's called—had featured her penthouse in one of their issues. They did a big spread on the place, with *lots* of pictures. She also informed me that she hasn't replaced so much as an ashtray since those photos were taken."

"So *that's* how our 'psychic' did it! I'm glad Mrs. Harwood finally remembered. This thing's really been bugging me! Clever lady," Gabe murmured, mostly to himself, following the words with a chuckle.

"I wouldn't exactly say that," Ray countered. "It took her long enough to recall that photo shoot."

"I'm not talking about Mrs. Harwood, you jerk! I'm referring to that kook, Madam Rosa!"

As the months wore on, the Harwood investigation faded almost completely from the news. Then, in August, on the anniversary of Rob's death, one of the papers (no doubt due to a dearth of more current items to report on that day) ran a short article. The headline read, "Who Killed Robin?" Under this was a photograph of the victim and the caption: "Wealthy Manhattan businessman Robin Harwood, murdered one year ago today."

Very likely, it was this story that precipitated a response the following afternoon that, in its own way, was even more outrageous than Madam Rosa's. And this time, it was the widow herself who was contacted.

The woman on the telephone—she introduced herself as Sherry Tyler—claimed, in a thin, high-pitched voice, to have met the dead man thirteen months earlier at a charity fund-raiser that she herself had helped to organize. She provided the name of the charity, and Tess vaguely remembered Rob's mentioning at the time that he planned on attending it. (Tess had opted to pass on that one.)

Sherry contended that their meeting—hers and Rob's— had led to a short-lived affair, which ended in early August—about two weeks before he was killed. Brief as it was, however, this liaison produced a child—a beautiful baby boy, according to his mother. "Rob Junior was born in April," Sherry continued. After which she added (no doubt in the event Tess had flunked math), "He's four months old now."

Then the woman got down to business. "You can't imagine how difficult it was for me to get in touch with you like this, Tess. Oh, I hope it's all right to call you Tess." And when there was no response: "But tell me, what kind of a mother would I be if I hadn't picked up this telephone? After all, Rob Junior is *entitled* to share in his father's estate; it's his legacy."

She hoped, she said, that Tess would "do the right thing" and that this matter could be settled amicably. The conversation ended with Sherry's magnanimously offering to give Tess an opportunity to think things over. "I'll talk to you again in a few days," she said pleasantly.

Tess didn't buy the woman's story. *Sherry Tyler sounds like Minnie Mouse, for heaven's sake!* she fumed. *Rob would never have been able to tolerate that squeaky little voice of hers. Not in a million years!*

The widow wasted no time in contacting Gabe. He asked the name of the charity that had sponsored the fund-raiser and where it had been held. "I'll check into this," he promised. "And in the meantime, try not to worry. Hopefully, it'll all work out."

Gabe got back to Tess three days later. "Good news." Sherry Tyler, he informed her, lived in a small town upstate, and he'd canvassed the hospitals in that area, finally locating the one where her baby was delivered. The records confirmed that she'd had a son who was born this past April, all right. Only he was three months premature. "I guess I don't have to tell you that this means he was conceived in October. Your husband couldn't possibly have fathered this child, Mrs. Harwood. Not unless he impregnated that woman from the grave."

That latest newspaper story on the Harwood homicide produced only a handful of other responses. And eventually, the dwindling number of phone calls dwindled down to none, the mystery of the affluent Realtor's death all but forgotten by the press and public alike.

*   *   *

Robin Harwood's murder remains an open case to this day.

Detective Ray Carson left the NYPD a number of years ago for a partnership in a private security firm.

Gabe Wilson is still with the city's police department—as a lieutenant now. In spite of an enviable record of accomplishments, however, there are times—although increasingly rare—when he thinks back with frustration to this still-unsolved crime and to that one small, disturbing fact.

And, once again, he wonders. . . .

Chapter 35

I was at the kitchen table, reflecting on the manuscript over a cup of tea and *two* slices of toast. (Which I regarded as a dramatic improvement in the state of my health.) And, like Belle's detective, I was doing some wondering.

I mean, this wasn't fiction; it was fact—or, anyhow, *based* on fact. So assuming that the number of people remaining under suspicion at the mystery's conclusion was for real, there would be eight of them. And one of those eight (someone who might not even be alive today) was a murderer.

But which one?

Well, somewhere on the pages of Belle's manuscript was a clue to the identity of the individual who'd poisoned Rob Harwood. And Sergeant Gabe Wilson had a strong feeling that the perpetrator—perhaps exercising a little damage control—had actually brought that clue to the detectives' attention. But—

The downstairs buzzer sounded then. The voice over the intercom informed me that there was a delivery for a Ms. Desiree Shapiro, so I buzzed the man in. And when I opened the door to my apartment, I was bowled over! The bouquet Nick had sent (I didn't have to read the card to know this was from Nick) was the most glorious assortment of flowers I'd ever seen. And it was positively *huge,* besides!

The card said, "I don't feel well when you don't feel well. So get better fast." It was signed, "Nick." As if he had to identify himself!

Naturally, I immediately phoned to thank him. I suppose I gushed (but, honestly, you should have *seen* that arrangement!), because Nick joked, "It's not a diamond bracelet from Tiffany's, Dez."

"I'm not big on diamonds," I told him (which could be because I don't have any). "But I *love* flowers. And especially these."

"I'm glad. More important, though, how are you doing?"

"A lot better."

"Have you changed your mind about my picking up some soup or something for you?"

"Thanks, Nick, but I'm still in pre-soup condition."

"Okay, if you're sure . . . Remember, though, I'm here if you need me."

"I'll remember."

"Well, have a good day, and I'll talk to you tomorrow."

I was standing there, admiring my flowers, when, out of the blue, it occurred to me that I hadn't spoken to Ellen since Thursday's dinner. I dialed her office number, but someone picked up her extension and advised me that she wouldn't be in today. So I tried the apartment.

Mike answered the phone.

"Hi, Mike, it's your sweet ol' aunt."

"Well, hi, Dez."

I didn't give him an opportunity to get in another word. "Thursday night was great, and I've been meaning to call all week to thank the two of you. But, I don't know, things kind of got away from me. I wasted a good bit of time trying to decipher that new clue of Belle's, and then Nick came over for brunch, and after that I was preoccupied with the manuscript itself—which I just finished reading today—plus, I'm recovering from food poisoning. Still, I should have taken a few minutes to—"

"Wait. You did say food poisoning, didn't you?"

"I'm afraid so."

"How are you *feeling*?"

"Much better than I felt the other night, anyway."

"Thank God for that. Do you have any idea what caused it?"

"I certainly do. On Monday, I had lunch with Jackie—you know, my secretary—at a French restaurant near the office. It was very good, too—at least, this is what I thought until around eleven that night."

"Is Jackie okay?"

"She's fine. Except for the Peach Melba, we didn't order the same dishes."

"Lucky lady. I suppose you want to talk to Ellen."

"If she's available."

"She's out now. Today was her day off from Macy's, so what does she do? She goes *shopping* with Ginger—our upstairs neighbor. It's kind of like a busman's holiday."

"You have the day off, too, I gather."

"Nope. I'm working tonight. If I have to leave before Ellen comes in, though, I'll write her a note that you phoned. By the way, before you hang up—that second clue, how is it going?"

"Not too great. Not even good, actually."

"As I've said before, if I can be of any help, just holler."

Oh, what the hell! I certainly wasn't making any progress on my own. "Do you have a few minutes to talk now?"

"Sure. I'm not due at the hospital for a couple of hours."

"Hold on, and I'll read the clue to you, so you get the exact wording. I haven't been able to make any sense out of it myself."

Moments later, I was back on the line. " 'It is now necessary,' " I read aloud, " 'for you to identify each of the suspects *and* the victim by their true given names. This requires that you concentrate on where the individuals are *from*. And here's a hint: In order to succeed, you must think *multinationally*.' "

There was silence on the other end of the line. "Mike?"

"I'm still here. But I'll be damned if I know what that means, either. I gather the manuscript makes no mention of where the characters were born or grew up or anything."

"Only in a single instance. But it didn't get me anywhere. So I figured I'd look up the origins of the characters' given names. I went online, and two of the pseudonyms I checked out—Rebecca and Anne—were derived from the Hebrew. And 'Hebrew' is definitely not someplace you're *from*. The names of two other characters I looked up—Catherine and Helen—were from the Greek. But—"

"Was that Helen—as in Helen of Troy?"

"That's right." And suddenly, it hit me! "Helen *of* Troy! You're a genius, Mike!"

"I wish I knew what you're talking about. I wasn't sure if you'd said Helen or Ellen."

"Look, in my head, I kept thinking 'from.' But 'of' is often used in place of 'from,' right? I should have figured this whole thing out when I saw the sign in the window of that lousy restaurant that gave me my food poisoning. It announced that the new chef there was Jean-Claude Dubois *of* Paris. So thank you, Mike. Thank you, thank you, thank you!"

"I didn't do anything, Dez—except fail to catch what you said. But, listen, are you saying that you got a given name out of 'Troy'?"

"That's right. When you said Troy, something clicked. In my mind, I automatically reversed two letters—and came up with Tory."

"Tory is a *name*?"

"You betcha. There's even an actress named Tory— Tory Spelling. Sound familiar?"

"Well, now that that you mention it . . ." (Actually, I was wrong here. I later found out she spells her name "Tori." There's this fashion designer, though, Tory Burch, who spells it with a *y*. So I was still okay.) "But listen," Mike added, sounding concerned, "do you think this will work with all the other names?"

"I'm hoping. It *feels* right—do you know what I mean?

But I'm going to start making sure right now. Give Ellen my love, and tell her I'll call her tomorrow."

Only seconds after this conversation with Mike, I realized I was hungry. So I had another cup of tea and two *more* slices of toast. Then, ten minutes later, I put on the kettle again. I wondered idly if I'd ever before consumed this much tea in one day!

I finally set down my cup and just sat there at the table for a while, shaking my head with something akin to disbelief.

Was it possible that I'd actually come up with the key to clue number two?

Chapter 36

That afternoon, I faced the computer with a mixture of fear and expectation. I would have crossed my fingers, but I'm a lousy enough typist as it is. I began by making a list of the eight suspects (in no meaningful order):

1. Tess—the victim's widow
2. Anne—the victim's stepdaughter
3. Catherine—Tess's "sweet," "caring" sister
4. Eleanor, a.k.a. Ellie—Tess's very close friend
5. Philip, a.k.a. Phil—Ellie's husband
6. Simon, a.k.a. Sy—the victim's buddy (also Tess's cousin)
7. Helen—Simon's wife
8. Rebecca—the victim's former coworker and ardent champion

Then I added the victim himself, whose actual given name I'd also been instructed to supply: Rob, born Robin.

And now, mentally rolling up my sleeves, I got down to business. I assumed that the people and places I was dealing with were a mishmash of fact and fiction, because I figured it would have been too difficult for Belle to devise something like this if she'd restricted herself to one or the other. Anyhow, I concentrated on the men to begin with, since there were fewer of them.

I kicked off with Robin. The first—and only—possibility to occur to me was Sir Robin of Loxley (better known as Robin Hood). I realized instantly that, unlike Troy, there was no anagram in Loxley. (Which was to hold true in all of the other instances, as well.) But by utilizing some of the letters within the geographical location, I was able to form the given names Leo and Lex. Then I seemed to remember seeing the location spelled Loxlee, as well. So I included this variation, too, which, in addition to Leo and Lex, also contained the name Lee.

I tried Philip next. Now, there was a Philip of Macedonia (at least the name seemed to ring a bell). I went online and found out he was the father of Alexander the Great. Which earned him a spot on my list. I got quite a few names out of Macedonia, too: Mac, Don, Ian, Dan, Dean, Dane, Dana, Ned, Adam, and Aiden. (I wasn't about to exclude nicknames, since I couldn't be sure that Belle had.) I was ready to move on, but just then, another, much more current Philip came to mind: Prince Philip, Duke of Edinburgh. And I planned to submit him to Belle, as well—along with Ned, Herb, Bud, and the unlikely Bing.

With Simon, I drew a blank. I'd revisit him later, when I was a little fresher.

And now I considered the women.

Tess, like Simon, was a problem for me. The only Tess I could come up with was the heroine in the Thomas Hardy novel *Tess of the d'Urbervilles*. But unfortunately, "d'Urbervilles," if my memory still served me, didn't refer to a place, but to a family. Which meant I'd now struck out twice. After finally arriving at a valid premise, however, I wasn't about to junk it because of a couple of temporary (I hoped) setbacks. I'd revisit Tess later, too.

When I got to Anne, my first thought was of Anne of the Thousand Days, one of the wives of Henry VIII. (Which, I admit, was really dumb. I mean, "the thousand days" was no more someplace you could be *from* than "Hebrew" was.) Then I remembered Anne of Cleves—who, as I recalled, was also among Henry VIII's formidable collection of wives. I went online again and verified that *this* Anne was born in Cleves, Düsseldorf, Germany. My search for given names in Cleves produced Eve and Lee.

For Catherine, I thought of Catherine of Aragon—who was also once married to Henry VIII. (I was beginning to regard the man as a veritable gold mine!) Anyway, Aragon yielded Nora. And in playing around with the destination a little longer, I realized it was also an anagram for "angora," which, of course, had nothing to do with anything. (But I thought I'd share.)

I drew a third blank with Eleanor, although I kept thinking this one was just out of reach and that it would come to mind any minute now. Only it didn't.

I decided there were probably a couple of reasons I was having trouble today. First off, I was giving my brain a more strenuous workout than it had been accustomed to lately. Also, I was still feeling a little subpar physically. Nevertheless, I wasn't prepared to take a break yet.

Helen, of course, was like a freebie, since I'd already arrived at Helen of Troy—and Tory—yesterday.

Rebecca, blessedly, was a cinch, thanks to the classic children's novel *Rebecca of Sunnybrook Farm.* There was certainly no shortage of feminine names in Sunnybrook Farm, either: Mary, Brook, Bonny, Bunny, Fanny, Ronny, Sunny with a *u,* and Sonny with an *o.* Even Yoko!

Now that I'd reached the end of the list, I had a change of heart. A time-out might not be such a bad idea, after all.

It was close to eight o'clock, and I figured I'd have my last cup of tea for the evening *and*—in view of all those cups I'd consumed over the past couple of days—for the foreseeable future, as well. Plus I'd accompany the tea with a small (although not *tiny*) dish of Häagen-Dazs— a definite indication that I was no longer facing imminent death.

Well, although I refused to so much as *consider* that I might be totally on the wrong track, as I was sitting there trying to enjoy my macadamia brittle, I managed to drive myself a little crazy with regard to my progress.

What if I wasn't able to work out those three names I'd temporarily abandoned? And right on the heels of this, something else dawned on me. It was conceivable, I realized, that I'd already latched onto the wrong location with regard to one or more of the other names. For instance, suppose that in addition to Helen of Troy, there was a famous Helen of Atlantic City? I'm kidding about the Atlantic City, naturally, but you see my point, don't you? Fortunately, I'm not prone to migraines, because if I were, at this rate I'd soon be experiencing a doozy. Especially since another what-if quickly succeeded that one.

Even assuming I had all the correct locations, what if I failed to include the actual names of all the flesh-and-blood people represented in the manuscript? I mean, I might not have spotted every possibility—something that I had to admit was not that unlikely.

At this point, I finally convinced myself that all this angst was getting me nowhere. I'd simply have to wait and see. (And do a whole lot of hoping, besides.)

I had just reached the momentous decision to take a bubble bath before going back to the manuscript when the phone rang. *Ellen,* I thought. I was wrong.

"She's dead!" a voice I couldn't recognize sobbed into the phone.

My heart skipped a beat. "*Who's* dead?"

"B-B-Belle. She was . . . she was *murdered*! Can you come?"

"*Gary?*" I said incredulously.

"Y-yes."

"I'll be right over."

Chapter 37

I'd never before—or since—dressed as quickly as I did that evening. I just threw on an old skirt and an older sweater. I didn't even take the time to comb my hair or pull on a pair of panty hose or, most egregious of all, put on some lipstick.

Fortunately, as I left the building, what did I see heading down the street? An *available* taxi, that's what! En route to Belle's brownstone, I ran a comb through my hair and applied a little makeup. I mean, Gary had already been traumatized once tonight. And enough was enough. Besides, I was so upset myself that this gave me something to do.

Not even fifteen minutes later, the cab dropped me off in front of Belle's West Seventy-third Street home. Gary was sitting on the steps, a handkerchief pressed to his eyes. Seated next to him was a large, good-looking man who got to his feet when I approached. "You must be Desiree," he said in a deep, rich voice. Then, without waiting for a response, he stuck out his hand and reached for mine, clasping it gently. "I'm Kyle," he told me, "Gary's significant other."

Gary pulled the handkerchief from his eyes and scrambled to his feet. "Hi, Dez," he said in a barely audible voice.

"Oh, Gary," I murmured, hugging him. There was a lump in my throat the size of an apple.

"I just don't *understand* this. Who could have done such a . . . such a *monstrous* thing to my wonderful Belle!" he exclaimed. After which he burst into tears and sat back down again.

My own eyes were filling up quickly now. I reached

into my handbag and eventually located a packet of tissues, which I immediately put to use. When I was a little more together, I turned to Kyle. "What happened?"

"Look, why don't we go over to my place and talk? It's slightly more comfortable than a front stoop, I promise. And it's only a block away. We were just waiting for you to get here."

Gary looked up. "The police are inside going over everything in sight. They questioned us for a few minutes, and then they said we could leave if we wanted to. Anyhow, I'll fill you in on everything when we get to Kyle's, all right?"

"Would you care for some tea, Desiree?" Kyle asked. Gary and I were seated in the living room of Kyle's small, sparsely furnished apartment—Gary on a large tweed club chair, and me across from him, on the matching sofa.

The very thought of tea made me want to gag just then. "No, thanks, I just had some before I came over here."

"Well, how about coffee? Or better yet, a glass of wine? I have a nice pinot noir if you like red."

"I'd love some wine, Kyle, thanks."

"Three glasses of pinot noir, coming up," he said, leaving the room.

I turned to Gary. "Are you up to talking about what happened now?" I asked softly.

He nodded. Then, after a moment: "I had today off, you see, and Kyle and I went to a movie—we wanted to see *Pirates of the Caribbean*. Following this, we had dinner—Chinese food. Same restaurant you, Belle, and I met at for lunch that time, remember, Dez?" He smiled faintly, but his lower lip was trembling.

I returned the smile. "I remember. Are you normally off on Wednesdays, Gary?"

"No, it varies. Belle is always—*was* always," he corrected himself, "pretty flexible. And yesterday I said that if she didn't need me on Wednesday—today—I'd like to take in a flick with Kyle. She was fine with it."

Kyle returned with the wine now, and after handing a glass to Gary and me, he perched on the arm of Gary's chair, his wineglass in his right hand, his left resting comfortingly on the shoulder of his significant other.

"Anyhow," Gary resumed, "it was around seven thirty when I got back to the house—Kyle has an appointment first thing tomorrow morning, so we thought we'd make an early night of it. But it didn't quite turn out that way, did it, Kyle?" he asked rhetorically, looking up at the other man for a moment. "Well, I walked in kitchen, and—oh, God!—I found Belle. She was slumped over the table, an empty champagne flute in front of her. A bottle of Krystal was sitting in the middle of the table. And opposite Belle, on the other side of the table, was another flute, only this one still contained a little champagne. Like she'd had company, you know?

"I tried to see if there was a pulse, but I'm no expert. Besides, I was too upset to be much good at anything. So even though I was almost sure Belle was"—he ran his tongue over his lips—"uh, *dead,* I kept hoping I was wrong. Anyway, I called emergency services, and then, right after that, I called Kyle. He got here in around five minutes. He was just about to see if he could find a pulse when EMS came. This EMS guy checked Belle's vital signs; then he looks at me and shakes his head. 'I'm sorry,' he tells me.

"I really lost it, Desiree. Belle was so good to me and so interesting to work for, too. Plus, she was so much fun. She'd play little jokes on me sometimes, and she didn't mind my getting back at her, either. Not after she had her morning coffee, anyhow." And he smiled a small, forlorn smile.

Suddenly, he sat bolt upright in his chair. "I almost forgot the reason I asked you to come over tonight! Belle left a note for you on the table, Dez—it was right next to her glass. She must've realized she was dying, and she knew I'd be the one to . . . to find her. Anyhow, I put it in my pocket before the cops showed up, and, well, here it is."

I took the note from Gary with a shaky hand. A single,

barely legible sentence was scrawled on the paper: "Desiree, the person who killed Rob killed me." It was signed, "Belle."

"Oh, my God! Do you have any idea who she could be talking about, Gary?"

"I wish I did."

"How long had you worked for Belle?"

"Eight or nine months, I guess. I answered her ad in the *Times*. It actually said that an eccentric novelist was looking for a secretary."

"And was she?" I asked (although I already knew the answer). "Eccentric, I mean."

"Are you kidding? Would a person who wasn't eccentric pay someone $24,940 to solve a mystery she wrote?"

"You've got something there."

Gary smiled sadly. "The thing is, working for Belle, well, it wasn't like working for anyone else in the world. We used to play all kinds of games when she wasn't busy writing. And not only the usual things like Scrabble and Monopoly, either. She was also hooked on puzzles and all kinds of word games that I'd never even heard of. I think she must've made up some of them herself."

All this time, Kyle had been sitting there quietly on the arm of Gary's chair, listening. Now, he put in, "Gar?" And when the other man turned around: "Don't you think you should tell Desiree what you told me? About that novel of Belle's, I mean."

Gary's forehead crinkled up. "I'm not sure what you're referring to."

"Well, a while back, you said you didn't believe she ever really intended to publish that book. You thought she was just playing a game then, too, to see if anyone— and this turned out to be Desiree—could figure it out."

Gary nodded. "That's true, Kyle." And to me: "At least, this is the impression I got. But I may be wrong."

"Did Belle have any family you're aware of?" I asked then.

"She was a widow; I'm positive of that. And she once mentioned something about a child. But after that one time, she made it pretty obvious that she didn't want to talk about the past; I think it was very upsetting for her. Anyhow, neither of us ever went there again.

"But listen, what do you make of that note?" And before I could respond: "You'd think she would just come out and ID the person who . . . who did this, correct? But not my Belle." He shook his head in exasperation. "She even has to make a game of her own murder," he murmured, as a single tear slid down his cheek. Then, a moment later: "Have you been able to figure out who the killer is yet?"

I couldn't believe what I was hearing! "Are you kidding me?"

"I'm talking about the killer in the manuscript."

I could feel my face coloring. "Oh. Um, I haven't even been given all the clues yet, remember? Listen, you wouldn't happen to know what the third clue is, would you?"

"Uh-uh. Belle didn't hand me the second one to type until after you'd deciphered the first. I imagine this is also what she planned on doing with clue number three."

"Well, that's all changed, of course. As of today, it's apparent that Belle expected me to solve the mystery— *and,* hand in hand with that, her own murder—without that final clue."

"She *did*?"

"Why else would she have left me that note?"

Chapter 38

It was past midnight when I got home. I was surprised to find a message from Gary on my machine.

"It's me, Dez. Sometimes I can't *believe* myself. Two minutes after you left Kyle's, I remembered Belle had once told me that if anything should happen to her, I was to inform you that her attorney would be in touch with you about the manuscript. Well, just thought you'd want to know. Talk to you soon." I was about to walk away when I heard: "Oh, her attorney also has Belle's instructions concerning the funeral. I'll keep you posted. Talk to you soon," he repeated.

I took a quick shower, and twenty minutes later, I was in bed. Tomorrow, I'd reread the manuscript in the hope of identifying Rob's—and Belle's—killer. But after about fifteen minutes of tossing and turning, I got out of bed, picked up Belle's manuscript, and sat down at the kitchen table. Like my mother always told this procrastinating daughter of hers, "There's no time like the present."

I have to admit, though, that I didn't get very far that night. I mean, right after finishing the introduction, I began rubbing my eyes. And by the time I was through with the first chapter—the one about the surprise party—I couldn't keep my head up any longer. So I called it a night.

On Thursday morning at about nine, I opened one eye, looked at the clock, and fell back to sleep. Then, at a couple of minutes past ten, as I was attempting to drag myself out of bed, the phone rang. *Jackie,* I informed myself. It was Ellen.

"I didn't wake you, did I, Aunt Dez?"

"No, of course not."

"Mike told me! How *are* you?"

Not fully awake yet, I thought for a moment that she was referring to Belle's murder (which, of course, she knew nothing about). "I feel just awful about this. It came as such a shock, too."

"I understand it was a French restaurant."

"It . . . what?" Then the fog lifted. "Oh, you're talking about the food poisoning! I think I'm pretty well over that. I was referring to . . . to Belle Simone's being murdered last night."

"Oh, my God! How did it happen?"

"She was poisoned. She was able to leave a note for me before she died, though. In the note, Belle said that the person who did this to her is the same one who poisoned Rob—the victim in the manuscript."

"Uh, why didn't she just write down the killer's name?"

"Good question. The purpose of the note—as far as I can figure out, at least—was to let me know that she wanted me to discover the murderer's identity for myself. Um, Belle was kind of eccentric."

"You're telling me! This is pretty crazy, though."

"I suppose it is."

"You're not going to do it, are you?"

"Well, I'm certainly going to try."

"But why? This is what the police are for."

"I realize that. But they failed to solve the first murder—the one Belle wrote about. Besides, this is something she wanted *me* to do. And something *I* want me to do, too."

"Oh, God," Ellen murmured.

"What's wrong?"

"Your getting involved like this could be dangerous."

"I don't see how. The answer must be somewhere in that manuscript, so it's not as if I'll be out tailing the bad guy. Besides, if I learn anything, I'll go straight to the police."

"Promise?"

"I promise."

"I hope you really mean it."

A simple "I promise" is never enough for my niece. "I really do. But I have to go now, Ellen. I'll talk to you tomorrow."

As soon as the conversation with Ellen was over, I reported in to Jackie and told her I wouldn't be coming to the office today—and probably not on Friday, either. But I assured her I was feeling much better, that there was just something I had to take care of. I said I'd explain when I saw her.

Once I started working, I didn't want to be interrupted—not even by Nick. And I knew he'd be checking in later to see how I was feeling. So I did the checking in before he got around to it.

"I was waiting to call *you*," he said when he heard my voice. "I figured you might still be asleep. How are you?"

"Lousy."

"Oh, I'm sorry. Yesterday, you seemed to be doing so much better."

"It's not the food poisoning, Nick. Evidently, I've managed to survive that. It's something worse—a *lot* worse." And I told him about Belle. And about her note.

"That poor woman! How awful!" he exclaimed. "What do you intend doing?"

"I can't imagine her leaving that note for me unless there's a hint of some sort about Rob's murder in the manuscript. So I'm going to reread it and hope I can uncover the bad guy."

"Just as long as you don't put yourself in jeopardy."

"Count on it. Listen, I think I finally have a handle on that second clue of Belle's. And she was going to send me the final clue once I deciphered this one. Without it, though, I'm not too sure how far I can get. Still," I reasoned, speaking more to myself now than to Nick, "it's pretty obvious that she believes I'll be able to solve this thing, regardless. So I suppose it's possible."

"If anyone can do it you can," Nick said encouragingly.

"I'd *love* to believe that. But anyhow, if I *do* make some headway, I'll go to the police, tell them everything I know, and let them take it from there."

"That's my girl! Well, I wish you luck, and if I can help at all—and so far I haven't exactly managed to do that—just holler. I'll give you a ring tomorrow if I don't hear from you before then."

As soon as Nick and I hung up, I made myself some breakfast—a *real* breakfast. A bacon-and-eggs breakfast. After that, I cleared the table, washed the dishes, took out Belle's manuscript, and began to read. . . .

I started on page one. I mean, last night I was tired and pretty much in shock. So I probably wouldn't have recognized a clue if it had bitten me on my bottom.

This time around, however, before long, something *did* strike me as possibly being important, so I jotted down my thoughts.

Then, when I got to the final chapter, I read—and read twice more—this one portion:

> And for the first time, one small and, Gabe cautioned himself, very likely meaningless bit of information impacted on him. And he couldn't seem to dismiss it from his mind. Even in view of having learned of this particular occurrence from the very person who risked being placed under suspicion by bringing it to light.
>
> On the other hand, he countered, the disclosure could have been prompted by this individual's fear that someone else—perhaps even innocently—call it to the attention of the police. Rob Harwood's killer could simply have been exercising a form of damage control.

It all fit!
Suddenly I recalled Belle's having said when she hired

me that so far none of the clues to the mystery had been included in the manuscript itself. Yet here, in black and white, was what I was certain was the third clue! Apparently when it came to my unraveling the mystery, Belle had had a certain order in mind. And I could only speculate that by telling me there were no clues in the book, she felt I'd be less likely to look for any—until now, I mean. The fact is, though, it was this thick head of mine—and not her little white lie—that was responsible for my failure to spot the obvious until this moment. Well, Belle could rest easy now. It had all worked out according to her game plan.

At any rate, the incident that had aroused my suspicion appeared to mirror, in every way, the incident that Gabe had found so disturbing:

- The detective refers to "one small" and "very likely meaningless bit of information." And I, too, was troubled by a small bit of information—although I definitely didn't agree with the "meaningless."
- The matter had been brought to his attention by the individual whose disclosure of it could be construed as self-incriminating. This was also true of the episode I had in mind.
- Finally, according to both Gabe and his partner, what had transpired would never, by itself, have resulted in criminal charges. The same could be said of the circumstances I'm referring to.

Yes!

The more I thought about it, the more convinced I was that I'd found exactly what Belle had meant for me to find.

Chapter 39

By this time, I was 99.99% convinced as to which pseudonym in the manuscript would provide me with the actual given name of the individual who'd poisoned Rob Harwood—and Belle, as well. Unfortunately, however, it was one of the three I had yet to decipher. I thought of someone who might be able to give me a little help with this. But just then I wasn't up to calling anyone. I kept thinking about Belle.

She'd been so vibrant, so *alive* that it was difficult to conceive of her as gone. Nevertheless, I wasn't going to allow myself to sit here and get all weepy. The best thing I could do for Belle was what she'd clearly wanted me to do: identify the killer. Still, in spite of my resolve, I couldn't help but shed a few tears at her death. (Listen, I'm a woman who's been known to cry at cartoons.)

Anyway, a short time later, I phoned Mike—who else? He'd worked last night, so I was hoping he'd be home this afternoon. And he was.

A yawn, however, was mixed in with his, "Hello?"

"I woke you," I said, feeling guilty even though it was past two o'clock.

"Dez?"

"I'm really sorry. I should have figured you'd be catching up on some sleep now."

"Hey, it's okay. I had to get up anyway." (A lie, no doubt.) "There are a couple of things I need to take care of today," he added quickly. "But how are you feeling?" He didn't wait for a response. "Ellen and I spoke for a little while this morning before she went off to work, and she said that, physically, you seem to be doing fine.

Then she told me about Belle. That's just awful, Dez. Any idea who was responsible?"

"Actually, I'm pretty positive as to which *fictional* character is guilty. But I need your help in finding out that character's real name. I won't keep you long, I swear."

"I'll do what I can, only I'm afraid it might not be enough."

"Hey, you were the one who helped me work out the second clue. Remember Helen of Troy?"

"But—"

"No *buts*. Without Helen, I might have chucked this whole thing by now."

"You're giving me too much credit, Dez. But okay. All I can promise you, though, is that I'll do my best."

"Thanks, Mike. Now, just tell me what you think of when I say, 'Tess of . . .' "

"I guess I'm not fully awake yet, but I'm not exactly sure what you mean."

"Look, when I said, 'Helen' yesterday, you automatically came back with, 'of Troy'—right?"

"Oh, I get it. Okay, Tess . . . of . . . of the d'Urbervilles. Is this what you mean?"

"Exactly. I thought of that, too. But 'the d'Urbervilles' refers to a family, not a place—doesn't it?"

"I never read the book, so I really couldn't say."

"Uh, you can't think of any other Tess of . . . ?"

"I'm afraid not, Dez."

I told myself there was always a possibility I'd find this information on the Internet. Still, I wasn't quite able to keep the disappointment out of my voice. "Well, thanks very—"

"Hold it a sec. I have an old college buddy who's like a walking library. There's a good chance he's familiar with *Tess of the d'Urbervilles*. He might even have another suggestion. Would you like me to give him a call?"

"Would I? You, Mike, are a gem."

He chuckled. "Your niece has been brainwashing you, I see. Anyhow, I'll try reaching him now, and I'll get back to you as soon as I do."

*   *   *

The instant we hung up, I began once again to go over the occurrence that had brought me—and I'm certain—Sergeant Wilson to the same conclusion. It was an incident that had led me to ask myself a crucial question. . . .

Say you'd poisoned a drink at a party, and for a few minutes, this drink was left unattended. Wouldn't you keep your eyes fixed on that glass until it and your victim-to-be were reunited?

Certainly, I'd reasoned, the killer would want to ensure that no one drank from that lethal flute of champagne except the individual for whom it was meant. And if a waiter were to remove it, not only would this foil the perpetrator's no doubt carefully thought out murder scheme, but it could well have resulted in an unintentional death. I mean, it's not inconceivable that, once back in the kitchen, the waiter himself or another member of the catering staff might decide to sample that apparently untouched drink. So unless the murderer was a homicidal maniac, it's pretty much a given that he or she would have been in the immediate vicinity of the guest of honor's champagne flute, standing guard over it until the intended victim's return.

Well, only one person seemed to have been interested in the fate of that drink: the woman who threw this party to "celebrate" her cheating husband's sixtieth birthday. *She* was the one who'd prevented the waiter from carrying off the poisoned champagne.

Now, in going over the manuscript yesterday, I'd tried to avoid jumping to any conclusions. Was it possible that the *real* killer had been poised to say something to the waiter when Tess spoke up? I'll put it this way: The perpetrator would almost certainly have felt a sense of urgency in preventing the handling of that glass by anyone other than the chosen victim. So I found it tough to buy the idea that somebody could have beaten her to the punch.

But that isn't all. Two other things contributed to my conviction that I'd arrived at the right conclusion—the one Belle had intended for me to arrive at.

One: This incident between Tess and the waiter is referred to not once—but twice—in the manuscript. Evidently, Belle had wanted to ensure that I didn't simply pass over it. (Although until this last go-'round, I'd managed to do it anyway.) At any rate, the first mention is made very early on, when the narrator describes the party. And later, of course, Tess herself brings it to the attention of the detectives.

Two: That waiter business not only struck *me* as being suspicious, but, as I explained earlier, I had every reason to believe that this is what had troubled the senior detective on the case, as well.

And now, all that remained for me to do was to discover Tess's *real* first name.

Mike called about two hours after we'd spoken.

"My friend just got back to me. The only Tess he could come up with is *Tess of the d'Urbervilles*. And d'Urberville *is* the family name. But it's also the name of their estate. Does that help any?"

"Are you *kidding*? This wraps up the whole thing," I said. But I was far from happy to be saying it.

Well, I didn't have to try to decipher "d'Urbervilles." I could no longer fail to see in that word what I'd closed my eyes to the other day.

"The person who killed Rob killed me," the note had read.

Why? this voice inside of me screamed. *Oh, Belle, why?*

Epilogue

The week following Belle's death was fairly eventful.

Gary called on Friday to let me know Belle had left instructions with her attorney that she wished to be cremated. A memorial service was to take place in about a month, Gary said, and he'd keep me posted.

Then, Saturday afternoon, I spoke to Nick, who told me exactly what I didn't want to hear: Derek would be staying with him a little longer than expected. Tiffany had just phoned and informed him that she was extending her trip to L.A. another few days. Apparently, Toby was involved in some kind of business dealings out there, and they couldn't make it back until Wednesday night. Well, so much for Wednesday's dinner date with Nick. But we made tentative plans for that Thursday—the "tentative" a nod to Tiffany's always flexible schedule.

On Monday, at around two a.m., as I was desperately attempting to fall asleep, who should pop into my head now that it no longer mattered but Eleanor of Aquitaine. If I remembered correctly, her claim to fame was that she was the mother of King Richard the Lion-Hearted. Anyhow, before I could talk any sense into myself, I turned on the light, took a pen and pad from the nightstand, and to satisfy my curiosity wrote down "Aquitaine," from which I proceeded to extract Tina, Ina, Uta, and Anita. (Incidentally, later that same day, Simon of Galilee—which yielded Eli, Gale, and Lee— occurred to me at work.)

Tuesday, I heard from Herman Doyle, Belle's attorney. "I understand you were given three months to arrive at the solution to Ms. Simone's mystery, Ms. Shapiro. So you have until October fourteenth to present your findings to me. But if you should reach a conclusion prior to that date, you might want to call my office and have my secretary set up an earlier appointment."

I told Mr. Doyle that I was prepared to meet with him now, and he agreed to see me at nine o'clock the following morning.

On Wednesday, at nine on the dot, I walked into the law offices of Doyle, Doyle, and Martino. A dour-looking woman immediately ushered me into the inner sanctum of Herman Doyle, Esq.

Belle's attorney was a small, square little man with a cheerful face and dark hair slathered with so much gel that, from a distance, I could have sworn he was wearing a patent-leather cap. After graciously offering me coffee, which I gratefully accepted, he confided that he and Belle had had a long-term relationship (I'm sure he was referring to a *business* relationship) and that he was "extremely upset" by her death. Then he asked, per Belle's instructions, if I'd been able to unravel the second clue to her mystery.

My response was to hand him a typewritten sheet containing the given names of all the characters in the manuscript, along with the possible first names of their real-life counterparts. Herman read through everything carefully, then nodded. "And I believe that you also solved the murder—correct?"

"I'm afraid so." He was looking at me expectantly, but it wasn't easy to say the words. "It was committed by Belle herself," I finally managed, my voice a near-whisper.

"Yes," the attorney acknowledged sadly. Following this, he opened the top drawer of his desk and removed two items. "According to Ms. Simone's instructions, I am to give these to you on your successful completion of the project she'd assigned to you." With a slight flourish, he presented me with a cashier's check for $24,940. And a second later, he handed me a bulging, letter-size envelope, with my name handwritten on the front.

About twenty minutes and a harrowing cab ride later, when I was safely ensconced in my minuscule office, the door closed firmly behind me, I ripped open the envelope. Inside was a seven-page typewritten letter.

Hi, lady,

By the time you read this, I'll be gone, and you'll have just been the recipient of a well-earned check. But I don't want you to think too badly of me for murdering my husband. So I'd like to explain why I did what I did. (Consider this a slightly delayed deathbed confession.)

Let me start by assuring you that I loved the man when I married him and for many years afterward—even though, before very long, I began to suspect that Lee (his real name) was cheating on me. I wasn't certain, you understand—not at first—but I'm now convinced that this was because I chose not to be. You see, when I was a struggling young, single mother, Lee made a home for me and my child. What's more, in spite of his numerous affairs, from the day I met him until the night he died, Lee treated me like a queen. I believed then, and I still do, that in his own way—such as it was—he loved me. I used to tell myself his womanizing was like a sickness. I actually think I could have forgiven Lee anything—except what finally drove me to kill him.

The end of his life had its beginning one chilly spring morning twenty years ago. I was planning on going shopping, and I thought I'd wear this white cardigan sweater of mine. Then I recalled that Eve—my daughter—had borrowed that sweater months earlier and forgotten to return it. I decided to borrow it back. Well, at the time, Eve was away at Yale, so I went into her bedroom to retrieve it.

The cardigan wasn't in any of her sweater drawers, so I checked the closet. And there, on the highest shelf, was a pile of clothing with the cardigan on top. I needed to stand on tiptoe to reach anything, and when I tugged at the cardigan, almost the entire pile came tumbling down with it. I started to gather up the clothes when I noticed a small, white cardboard box that had apparently been concealed among the T-shirts and sweaters. I fully intended to return it to the shelf, along with everything else (my cardigan excepted), but, well, I was curious. I removed the lid of the box. Inside was a wine-colored leather book with the words, MY DIARY, stamped on the cover in gold letters.

I realized only too well that reading this would be a betrayal of my daughter's trust. But as I was about to put the cover back on the box, I wavered. Sitting down on the floor now, I took out the diary and opened it to the flyleaf. The date written on that page indicated that Eve's private thoughts had been recorded here when she was eighteen and a senior in high school—only one year earlier. The year that, for the first time in her life, my little girl had shown signs of being seriously troubled.

Prior to this, Eve had always been so outgoing. Then, suddenly, there was a change in her. It's difficult to explain. She *seemed* cheerful enough, but now it was as if she were making an effort. And she'd begun picking at her food, too. When I spoke to her about how little she'd been eating lately, she claimed she'd gotten a little chunky, so she was trying to watch her weight. Which was ridiculous. If anything, Eve could have used a few extra pounds. Then, one night, I woke up, and I thought I heard her crying. I got out of bed and listened at her door. But the crying had stopped— if it had ever occurred at all. Very likely, I'd dreamed those tears of hers, I decided. Aside from her eating habits, Eve *did* seem to be behaving normally.

I finally became aware that something was very wrong here on the morning she came down to breakfast with her usual bright smile—and red eyes.

As soon as Lee left for work, I told my child that I'd heard her sobbing one night, long after she'd gone to bed. "Don't say I imagined it, either—just take a look in the mirror at those red eyes of yours," I challenged. And following this, I pleaded with her. "I want to help you, Eve. First, though, you have to tell me what's been making you so unhappy, so that I'm able to." She maintained that I was mistaken. What did she have to cry about, anyway? she put to me. And if her eyes were red, it was because she was up until all hours, studying for her final exams.

Now, I'd hoped that once she started at Yale, whatever it was that was making her so miserable would either evaporate or be resolved. And when she came home for Thanksgiving and walked into the house with that dazzling smile of hers, for a brief moment, I let myself believe that she was back to her old self. But then I saw the puffy eyes and, later, all the food she'd left on her plate. Still, she insisted that everything was just fine. Have I mentioned that since Eve was five years old, she had been telling everyone she was going to be an actress? Well, except for those few telltale signs, she'd been doing an exemplary job of playacting these past seven or eight months. And I was at the point where I was beside myself, wondering what to do.

Sitting on the floor of Eve's bedroom that day, I began to think this little leather book could be a gift from heaven, my one chance to help my only child. And I *had* to read it. But once I did, my life was never the same.

* * *

Most of what Eve had noted in the diary was
typical of teen musings. I'd just finished an account of a spat between Eve and her best friend,
Teresa, over which of them some boy at school
named Brian had been winking at. Then I turned
the page. And I came to the entry that chilled
my blood.

Eve had written that on the evening of this particular Friday in February, she'd just come home
from dinner at Teresa's house (apparently, it
hadn't been much of a spat). I was at the theater
with a friend. And Lee, having clinched a lucrative
business deal that afternoon, was in the living
room, engaged in a bit of celebratory imbibing. He
invited my daughter, who wasn't used to liquor,
to join him in a cocktail. Well, she did, and the
drink went to her head. Before she realized what
was happening, she was stretched out on the sofa
next to her stepfather, with all her clothes lying
in a heap on the floor. Eve went into a little more
detail, but I prefer not getting any more specific
than that.

She ran into the bathroom then and threw up.
When she came out, she was almost hysterical.
Lee kept apologizing and blaming the liquor for
what had occurred. He begged Eve to forgive him
for what even he himself characterized as his "unforgivable" behavior. (*Unforgivable behavior?* I
call it rape!) If she'd swear not to tell anyone what
happened, he promised to buy her a fur coat, a
car—whatever she wanted. Eve told him she
wouldn't accept a thing from him ever again, but
that he needn't worry. She'd never say a word,
because she was afraid it could get back to me.
The last thing in the world she wanted to do, she
said to that bastard, was to hurt her mother.

I closed the diary at this point. Then I put my
head in my arms and sobbed.

A while later, when I was a bit calmer—but not

much—something struck me. Around that time, Lee and I had been talking about buying Eve a car for graduation. But one Saturday in February (it might very well have been the day after the rape), he had the doorman buzz the apartment and ask the two of us to come downstairs. When we got to the lobby, the doorman pointed outside. And there, in front of the building, was Lee behind the wheel of a red Mustang convertible. It was an early graduation present, he said. Well, Eve thanked us both—what choice did she have? But I remember thinking that she didn't look nearly as thrilled as I'd have expected she would.

As for me, I was pretty surprised to see him in that car. But later, when we were alone, Lee claimed that the reason he'd bought the Mustang now was that he was able to get it for a very special price (which probably wasn't true), and that this included all sorts of extras. The special price, Desiree? $24,940. (Sound familiar?) I trust you appreciate the irony in the fact that the amount Lee paid in an attempt to buy Eve's silence has been matched by the amount I paid to reveal something of the true nature of this man—even if it's never brought to light.

At any rate, after reading what I did in my daughter's diary, I engaged in a great deal of mental self-flagellation. If I'd had even half a brain, I told myself, I would have been aware that Lee had more than a fatherly interest in Eve. In fact, just knowing of his reputation with women, I should have picked up and left him long before—if not for my own sake, then for my daughter's. But, of course, I couldn't change what had occurred. I could only do whatever it took to ensure that it never happened to my child—or anyone else's child—ever again. And this is when I made up my mind to murder my husband.

I thought for a long time about how I would go about it. I couldn't see myself using a gun or a knife. Ugh! Much too messy for my delicate sensibilities. Poison really seemed to be the only logical choice. Then, after racking my brain for days, trying to decide on the when and where, I finally thought of throwing him a sixtieth birthday party—although the occasion was four interminable months away. Still, what better time and place to kill him than when he was in his own home, surrounded by family and "friends"—a number of whom, I'm certain, secretly loathed him?

You can't imagine the torture I went through, Desiree, waiting for that blessed evening to arrive. But when it did, everything went off seamlessly. Lee was dead. And for the first time since reading my daughter's diary, I was actually at peace.

Sadly, life wasn't as kind to my sweet, beautiful daughter. Although, outwardly, she appeared to be a poised and carefree young woman (she was an actress, remember?), Eve was never really the same after that horrendous experience with her stepfather. She went from one unhappy affair to another. And while she did get some theater work, her career never really took off, either. She had supporting roles in a few off-off-Broadway shows and toured with a small theatrical company for a while. But she left the company to marry an unemployed actor she'd met in a bar, who wound up drinking himself to death. And fairly close on the heels of that sad little episode, she acquired husband number two. This one was a drug addict who OD'd just prior to their first anniversary.

I finally persuaded her to go to an analyst friend of mine. But after only four sessions with him, she quit. I called and asked him what he'd learned. At first, he wouldn't say a word. But I practically nagged him to death, and he eventually told me that Eve appeared to be punishing herself for something. Naturally, he didn't tell me what it was. Very possibly, he didn't know.

Well, later that year she began seeing someone

who, from what she said about him, appeared to be a very decent person. But I never did get to meet him, because within three months, they went their separate ways. Before long, though, Eve discovered she was pregnant. And seven months later, she gave birth to a precious little girl, whom she named Elyse. I wanted them to move in with me, but Eve insisted she was doing fine. And for the first time in many years, things did seem to be going well for her. She had a good job as the manager of a rather tony dress shop, and she had an adorable child she doted on. Then, a month after my granddaughter's third birthday, that little angel and her nanny were crossing the street when they were struck by a drunk driver. Wanda—the nanny—died instantly. Elyse lingered for two days. And Eve killed herself three weeks later.

Now, I'd always felt that committing murder, while it isn't regarded as a particularly nice thing to do, can, in some instances, be justified. And for many years, I considered myself *totally* justified in poisoning Lee.

Soon after my daughter's death, however, it occurred to me that it was quite possible she suspected that I was the one who'd murdered her stepfather. And further, that she somehow convinced herself she was to blame for this by getting drunk and "allowing" Lee to rape her. You see, while Eve never did tell me about the rape, I've always had a feeling that *she* knew that *I* knew. She did ask me once if I had any idea who'd poisoned Lee; I said that I hadn't a clue. And when I put this same question to her, she shook her head. "I don't, either," she told me. Well, I'm no longer certain that *either* of us answered that question truthfully.

You can appreciate what this means, can't you? It could very well have been my act of vengeance—and not the rape itself—that was responsible for the sort of life my poor Eve led prior to the birth of her child. The words of the analyst I'd sent her to still reverberate in my mind: she seemed to be "punishing herself for something."

So if I had it to do all over again, would I lace Lee's champagne with that cyanide? I'd sooner tear out my heart!

But to go on . . .

From the beginning, it was never my intention to turn myself in to the police. I would do what had to be done when the time came. At first, I couldn't bring myself to leave my darling Eve. But with Eve gone now—Eve and my precious granddaughter—suddenly, I didn't feel like sticking around any longer. Particularly once I realized that in killing my husband, I might very well have ruined my daughter's life.

Initially, my plan was to write a confession and then swallow a handful of pills. But somehow, the confession began to evolve into a murder mystery. (I suppose this was because, in spite of everything, I wasn't as ready to make my exit as I'd thought.) I had already completed a couple of chapters when my secretary left to get married.

Enter Gary.

To my own amazement, my last months on this earth have, quite frequently, actually been fun, thanks to that young man. Not only has he been my secretary, he's been a dear friend. And besides, he's *such* good company. Gary and I would joke around. We'd work puzzles together. We'd play word games. I imagine that's how I came up with the idea of making a game out of my book. I thought it might be interesting to have a professional investigator attempt to solve the mystery of who'd poisoned my husband. Which, as you're well aware, is where you came in. At any rate, mapping out that little whodunit of mine became quite a challenge, one that, fortunately, consumed a good part of my time.

Don't misunderstand me, Desiree. It isn't that I no longer mourned my two girls. Not a single day has passed that I didn't cry for them at least a half dozen times. But having Gary here has helped me forget my pain for a bit, and I'm very grateful to him. (Incidentally, I've seen to it that this brownstone that has been his home these last eight months will remain his home.)

At any rate, I had already chosen today—Eve's birthday—as the day I'd be packing it all in. Gary's gone to a movie with Kyle (otherwise, I'd planned to send him on a very time-consuming errand). And very soon, I'll be mixing myself a nice cocktail—the same tasty little drink I'd mixed for my dear, departed husband all those years ago. But before I do, I thought I should fill you in on a few things concerning my manuscript.

First of all, while the bare bones of the mystery are pretty faithful to the facts, I did take some liberties in order to make the plot more interesting. For example, Nora (my sister) and Lee never had an affair. I never had a maid named Francesca (and neither did Nora). And, of course, the conversations between the two police officers had to be improvised, as well as their dialogue when questioning the witnesses, since I was privy to only one of those interrogations.

No doubt there were also other deviations from reality that I can't recall just now. But only one of them is actually critical. It concerns the incident where Tess (yours truly) prevents the waiter from removing the poisoned champagne. Well, this never happened. No waiter attempted to take away that glass. It was a fabrication designed solely to enable you—in conjunction with the first two clues, of course—to solve the murder. It is, you see, the "missing" third clue to the mystery.

Oh, one more thing. That very flattering description I gave of myself? While it probably sounds conceited, I really *was* quite a glorious-looking creature in those days. Besides, I'll no longer be available should someone take exception to it.

I guess that's about it. Thank you, Desiree, for helping to make these last few weeks so stimulating.

Belle

I put down the letter. My eyes were beginning to sting, so I tried to convince myself that, along with the tragedies in Belle's life, there'd been good things, too. But just then, all that came to mind was her daughter's rape and eventual suicide. Her granddaughter's fatal accident. And the rage inside her that had driven Belle to murder. Well, somehow I didn't feel that a bundle of money and a Manhattan penthouse (or a pricey brownstone) balanced the scales. Not even when you added a successful career to the mix.

And I reached for a Kleenex.

A short while later, I thought about what I intended to do with my check. One thing I knew for sure: Mike and Ellen would be going on a second honeymoon to some lovely island paradise—or wherever else they chose. I mean, without Mike's help, I might never have gotten to the bottom of things. And I'd be doing something special for Jackie, too. That lunch at La Vie didn't really count. After all, it was her request for the exact wording of clue number one that had enabled me to decipher it. Also, I planned on donating a portion of the money to a charity, in memory of Belle. As for the new car I'd thought about buying, I probably wouldn't have enough left over for anything too great—especially after taxes. Besides, that ancient Chevy of mine still had some life left in her. So maybe for now I'd concentrate on fixing up my apartment a little. Listen, my sofa would be a Salvation Army reject. No doubt about it. Ditto the two club chairs. And as for that end table with the glued-on leg . . .

It was on Wednesday night at eleven thirty that I got a phone call from Nick containing what could well be life-altering information. "I hope I didn't wake you," he said. I thought he sounded a little strange.

"Of course not."

"I had to talk to you, Dez. I just couldn't wait until morning."

"Is something wrong, Nick?"

"Yes and no. The fact is, I'm not too sure. Tiffany was just here to pick up Derek. And you know those extra few days she left him with me? Well, that was so she and Toby could drive to Las Vegas and get married."

"Oh, my," I said. Simply because I couldn't think of anything else to say.

"The thing is, Toby is relocating to L.A., so Derek will be living all the way across the country for most of the year. I expect that he'll fly back here for either Christmas or Thanksgiving—maybe both. And it's possible he'll even be spending his summers with me. Plus, I can always leave Emil in charge of the shop and just take off for L.A. for a few days. Tiffany promised she'd make it as easy as possible for me to see my son."

"And I'm quite sure she will," I said encouragingly.

"Actually, I am, too." Then, after a moment: "You know, Dez, I figured they might be headed for the altar— you and I even talked about that—and the idea kind of appealed to me, too. For reasons that I admit weren't entirely altruistic. But I had every expectation they'd be making their home here, in New York." He sighed resignedly. "Well, Tiffany and I will just have to work things out. Anyhow, I had to call and let you know. After all, this could affect our relationship, too—yours and mine, I mean. Maybe the next time you see Derek, he won't be so opposed to my having a woman other than his mother in my life—the same way he seems to have adjusted to Tiffany's having another man in hers. Anyhow—" Suddenly, Nick interrupted himself. "Hey, I almost forgot. How are you making out with your mystery?"

"It's a long story. I'll tell you all about it when I see you tomorrow."

*   *   *

We said good night then, and for a few minutes I just sat there, trying to absorb Nick's news. It occurred to me that with Derek physically removed from the scene for a good part of the year, Nick and I might actually have a chance to make a go of things. At least, that's what I hoped. So keep your fingers crossed for me. Please?

Desiree's Home-fried Potatoes

2 medium potatoes
½ onion, chopped
¾ green pepper, chopped
4 tbs.—or more—sweet butter
Salt and freshly ground pepper
Olive oil

Peel potatoes and slice very thin, immersing slices in a pot of cold water as you work. Melt four tablespoons of butter in a large skillet. Put in onion and green pepper. Drain potatoes, blot with paper towels, and add to skillet. Season with salt and pepper, and fry over medium heat, adding additional butter when necessary, and turning potatoes gently as they cook. (Try not to break them, although some will probably break in spite of your best efforts.) When potatoes begin to brown, sprinkle with a *small* amount of olive oil for flavor (a little olive oil goes a long way). Turn down heat and cover.

After about five minutes, remove cover and turn up heat. Cook until potatoes are brown and crisp, then blot with paper towels and serve.

Serves 2–3.